Gun Before Butter

Gun Before Butter

NICOLAS FREELING

All the characters and events portrayed in this work are fictitious.

GUN BEFORE BUTTER

A Felony & Mayhem mystery

PRINTING HISTORY
First UK edition (Victor Gollancz): 1963
First U.S. edition (as *A Question of Loyalty*) (Harper & Row): 1963
Felony & Mayhem edition: 2007

The icon above says you're holding a copy of a book in the Felony & Mayhem "Foreign" category. These books may be offered in translation or may originally have been written in English, but always they will feature an intricately observed, richly atmospheric setting in a part of the world that is neither England nor the U.S.A. If you enjoy this book, you may well like other "Foreign" titles from Felony & Mayhem Press, including:

Soviet Sources, by Robert Cullen
Cover Story, by Robert Cullen
Love in Amsterdam, by Nicolas Freeling
Because of the Cats, by Nicolas Freeling
Death of a Dissident, by Stuart Kaminsky
Black Knight in Red Square, by Stuart Kaminsky
Season of the Monsoon, by Paul Mann
The Ganja Coast, by Paul Mann
Yellowthread Street, by William Marshall
Belshazzar's Daughter, by Barbara Nadel

For more about these books and other Felony & Mayhem titles, or to place an order, please visit our website at

www.FelonyAndMayhem.com

or contact us at

Felony and Mayhem Press
156 Waverly Place
New York, NY 10014

Gun Before Butter

PART I

THE ROZENGRACHT is a street in Amsterdam. 'Gracht' means a canal between houses; the houses are there still, but the canal has been filled in as a concession to traffic. Now, alas, it is a broad and boring main road out from the center of the city, with trams and cars. Halfway along it rises the graceful building of the Westerkerk, which is one of the loveliest in Europe.

All the streets of the Rozengracht district have flower names, and the district itself was called "*le jardin*" by Napoleon. A joke, because this is the cockney district, where the true Amsterdammers live, who are poor because they are too crafty to work, but live through cunning, and having the quickest wits and the sharpest tongues in Holland. The joke is pointed because the streets of the "garden"— Palm, Laurel, Lily, and Rose—are old, crowded, and slummy.

The Dutch have corrupted the French word, and the "*jardin*" is called in Amsterdam the Jordaan. The district is much changed, but the Amsterdammer still believes that those who live there do no work and never have their hair cut, and amusing things still happen there. There is still a shadow, if only a small one, of the days when the law did not run here. Even crime in the Jordaan has a comic flavor.

Van der Valk, an inspector in the Amsterdam Police, working in the Central Recherche bureau, strolled along the Rozengracht, and lifted his eyes to the Wester Tower, with pleasure as always. He lowered them again, saw a potato lying on the pavement, and gave it a tremendous kick, happily.

What was so nice about this lousy town, he thought, you realized only after being out of it. A weekend, say, in the fresh air, so-called. You came back and thought: "Bah! filthy place this is." Public urinals everywhere, except where you needed them, of course, everything thick with dust, banana skins slung about by our charming children, and a frightful smell of cabbage. And as for the canals—this morning the Nassaukade had stunk like an overripe Camembert. Not surprising—he had reached the Singel—"Look at that; like soup." Full probably of rusty old prams; our delightful Amsterdammers, nearly as undisciplined as Parisians and quite as dirty, thank God. He disliked Dutch cleanliness. Who wanted clean water anyway? They got on without it in Venice. Hm; the Jordaaners used to get drunk and dive in, in the old days. Be a brave man who did that now.

It would be nice if we had some statues to liven these streets up. On second thought, perhaps not; the Dutch were no good at making statues. When they attempted a monument, the result was that horrible great concrete phallus in front of Krasnapolsky. Anyway, if there were statues they would be permanently plastered in pigeon shit.

To his nose there came a sickly waft of frying-fat from a croquette bar. What a town; nothing but stinks. Nice all the same after all that damned fresh air.

A small greasy rain started to mix with all the smells. There, he had suspected it; his left hip had felt rheumatic all morning. Well, it was a good excuse to take some medicine; gin is the best medicine for rheumatism. Must look after our kidneys, he told his reflection in a window, and disappeared gratefully into a pub.

It was an amusing job, but to him it had been a bore. A street fight by the Noordermarkt had been cleared up by agents from the local Jordaan bureau. It was twenty minutes after it was all over before the van driver discovered that three or four hundred pounds' worth of fur coats had been lifted out of the back of the van. A lorry had hit his back bumper—that was indeed how the caboodle had begun—and the impact had sprung the locked doors open. Somebody had lifted the fur coats—a somebody who had more sense than to join in the small fight and big talk that followed the dusty metallic kiss. And had lifted them very calm and neat; nobody had noticed a thing; they had all of course been too busy waving their arms and adding their opinions. The van driver, who had a split lip and a damaged ear, was fit to be tied. So was the insurance company; their lip was tight, so far, and only their pocket damaged. But Van der Valk, after listening with disillusion to monstrous lies, was not fit to be tied; he was only bored.

Shouldn't be that hard, he reflected. How would gin taste—a new fantasy—if you put sugar in it *and* added tonic? (It tasted revolting.) Transport was the key. The coats had been stuffed into someone's car or delivery bike. Hell, seven fur coats; you didn't just walk along with them negligently over your arm. Not on the Noordermarkt you didn't; not in the middle of May. Or they might have been stuffed hastily into someone's dustbin, right there on the corner. He wasn't interested; a clown's affair. Except for insurers—a type of person he despised for making money from the fear and greed of others—who cared about some rich bitch's lousy pussy?

Now this Italian business that had happened last night— that was people, and to him more interesting.

Interesting although it presented no particular problem; it was open as daylight. Three Italians—we're full of Italians here, these days—had been walking across the Leidseplein in the company of a Dutch girl. Outside the Hirsch building some corner-boys, six of them at least, had expressed their feelings at seeing Italians escort a Dutch girl, and had done so in loud, vulgar terms. Italian indignation. Corner-boy aggression. Clash of temperament and knuckles. One of the Italian boys had lost his head and pulled a knife. Well, one corner-boy had got a badly gashed thigh and had bled all over the Leidseplein. The police had pounded up on big boots and the whole lot were now sitting in the cooler. Except the girl. Nobody had found an excuse to hold the girl, though she had slapped a corner-boy spinning into a flowershop window.

Van der Valk was interested in these human frailties, but his interest became much greater when he heard the name of the girl. Agent Westdijk had written it down in his little book; disturbance of public order and tranquility. Van der Valk was standing drinking coffee, doing nothing much, and that languidly, when the name was spoken.

"Lucienne Englebert," said Agent Westdijk laboriously. "What's that for a name? Belgian? She spoke Dutch all right. Not a Dutch name, though."

Van der Valk was acid. "You mean she can't be Dutch, because she hasn't a name like Keeke, or some other farmyard sound?"

Mr. Westdijk had kept quiet prudently; Van der Valk was a senior inspector and very much his superior officer. Still, he was known to every policeman in Amsterdam as a queer character. Rude words of this sort about Dutch provincialism and isolationism had roused suspicion and distrust in his fellow workers. And these "indiscretions"—an apparent contempt for careful Calvinist Dutch conformities—had injured his career by blocking his promotion; oh yes.

And yet the Procureur-Général—and when he talks he is listened to—had once said, even if tartly, that it was no bad thing to have one policeman with imagination. After that Van der Valk noticed an inclination growing in his superiors to gloss over his nonconformism a bit, even to license his enormities. In revenge he got treated, faintly, as a buffoon. It might be admitted that occasionally he was clever. But he knew he would never be more than a chief inspector of police.

He got thrown the queer jobs. Anybody with a funny name or a funny business. Or who talked other languages—had he not said that Dutch was a language for farm-girls to call the chickens in? In fact his superiors had given up detesting him. Now they merely disapproved of him. He set a bad example to junior *rechercheurs*, to be sure, but there were things he was good at. He was in consequence perhaps the only policeman in Holland who could get away with drinking on duty and laughing out loud, and not wearing gray suits and speckled ties.

Had it been understood at last that he did not care a damn? Did he even get a sort of grudging respect?

Aliens. Cranks. Artists. Anything the others found difficult to understand. He was useful after all. A chap who read poetry, spoke French and even some Spanish, must be useful. As for Italians, he was given them as a matter of course. Together with Lucienne Englebert. He did not have to ask for her. He did not have to mention that he had seen her before in other circumstances. When, years after, he came to summarize the whole affair—there were months, even years, between the different episodes—and he wanted a connecting link, he could have written *The Different Circumstances in Which I Saw Lucienne Englebert*. But that is no title for a book. Had he been more literary in his tastes, he might have called it *The Romance*. Because from first to last it was a romantic story. He found himself, too, behaving in a romantic, absurd way while it lasted. That was very foolish of him, and was not at all like a good policeman. They are not romantic; it must be added in fairness to him that he made an effort to understand the romance. His own private name for the affair, even, was romantic. He called it "The Diamond Cutters." He saw each character as a diamond that cuts others into facets, and is itself cut, and throws out light, and sparks, and strange fires.

The first time he'd seen Lucienne had been six months before this moment. Soberly, he had been driving along outside Utrecht. There was a notorious fork ahead, and he thought, vaguely, that the gray DS passed him going much too fast. When the Volkswagen van, with its moronic butcher's boy, came out, paused, and then dithered, and then dynamited the gray Citroën full in its shark nose, he had time to tell himself as he braked that he was not surprised.

The girl was cut across the hairline and bleeding slowly, semiconscious—but not badly hurt, he thought. The butcher's boy was sausage, simply. The man, crumpled under the steering wheel of the Citroën like an old sack—was there anything Van der Valk could do there? He doubted it. Severe chest injuries. Pulse bad, color bad, breathing very bad. Reflex-to-light poor. Not to be moved. But while waiting for the ambulance, and the fast wagon of the state police, Van der Valk did his best. The man's wallet told him a name: Arnolf Englebert. And he knew it, as he should have seen that he knew the face, which had looked at him many times from the sleeves of gramophone records. A conductor. Very good with Mahler. Will I ever enjoy those records again? Fine style, rather like Walter.

Unexpectedly, the eyes opened and managed a blurry focus. Gradually they tried a little movement. Throat muscles still functioning. Larynx, pharynx, even lips. Even the brain still does something.

"I've crashed," said the lips in German, thin and small, but clear. The tone was unsurprised, unindignant.

"Yes."

"And I'm dying."

"Yes."

"You'd better forgive me my sins." No irony in the voice.

"We'll do our best. On their way by now."

"My daughter?"

"She's all right. Just a bit cut, that's all."

"Ah. Doesn't matter. We all die. Doesn't hurt."

"I'm a policeman. Can I take any message, do anything for you?"

The eyes thought.

"No. But thank you." There was a flicker of humor suddenly. "Be absolute for death," the voice told him, in English. The words were familiar somehow; where had he heard them? But the voice said nothing more; the man had slipped into a quiet thought of memory and contrition, perhaps.

"Waste of time," said the state policeman, leaning across the bonnet of his little Porsche and staring with a professional trade-union eye at Van der Valk. "Can't cut him out of there without killing him."

"Finished," said the ambulance man. "Ribs caved in, all sorts of abdominal injuries too. Ruptured spleen, liver too, maybe. Hopeless."

And indeed he died, still in quiet thought, a quarter of an hour later.

They brought the girl to the Academic Hospital in Utrecht. Only shock, bruises, and slight concussion. The cut needed three stitches.

When he got home Van der Valk looked up the reference, though it took him some time to find it. *Measure for Measure.*

"'Either death or life shall thereby be the sweeter.' Very sensible," he told his wife, coming in with herrings in oatmeal.

"Isn't there a translation of Shakespeare?" Arlette's English was good, but not very literary; Shakespeare defeated her.

"There's supposed to be a good one in Russian."

"You are a lot of help."

"French one's not up to much. Better stick to Racine."

Arlette was up in arms for her France at once: "I'm damn sure it's better than the Dutch."

"That doesn't say much. The Dutch only read *The Merchant of Venice,* and that is to learn about Venetian business methods—might be handy. Sad disappointment for them."

He had been busy then, too busy to find out what had happened to Lucienne Englebert. Now he would find out, maybe. He would pay her a little call. Agent Westdijk had the address, written neatly down in his blasted little book.

A big building near the Roelof Hartplein: a heavy, lumpy building of the sort that disfigures all Amsterdam-South. A big, rather somber flat. And a very hostile reception.

"Who are you? Oh, police, of course. I suppose I can't stop you coming in, but don't think I'll ask you to sit down."

Lucienne Englebert was about nineteen. Tall bony blonde; haughty go-to-hell features; classical, fierce, and now electric with fury. He decided he had to do something to try and disarm this paratrooper, this moon-maiden; she might stick a knife in him.

"Your father spoke to me just before he died. I was there by accident. He told me to be absolute for death."

She softened, a scrap. "It was a saying of his. But that's nothing to do with you."

"I helped fish you out of there."

"Then I suppose I owe you thanks. Hell, you'd better sit down then."

"Was he absolute for death?"

"Yes. He liked driving too fast. He didn't want to die lying down. As Kleiber did. He really wanted to die working. Erich did too."

"Is it better, then, to die on a road, outside Utrecht?"

"Better than what?"

"Than in a hotel room in Zürich."

"You know that?"

"I read it."

"He was my father's best friend."

"When I could, I used to go to his concerts. Your father's too."

"As a child, he was my great hero."

Better. He had not sat down; he wandered about. He had melted the hostility; could he now establish some sort of rapport? Give her a bit of confidence? On the gramophone turntable he saw a Piaf record; he picked it up.

"I like her, too. Don't know this one."

"*C'est formidable.*"

"You know the one about the accordionist? Where she shouts 'Stop' at the end?"

"Stop the music. Yes. But that is an old one... Do you drink?" She added the afterthought abruptly, as though she were a little ashamed of having been rude.

"Yes. But unhappily I have to talk a bit of business too."

"I suppose you can't help it," she said, reflectively.

He offered her a cigarette, which she took, holding it in her mouth like a man. The grand piano still stood in the center of the room, with a photograph of her father at work. Underneath was written "*Freischutz—Wien.*" Obviously she had been fond of the father; a good point.

"*Freischutz, Figaro* and *Fidelio.*"

"Yes," with affection. "Erich's big three. You are a less narrow-minded person than I thought," naïvely.

She was pouring a glass of white wine, which she did with grace; a good hostess, when she wanted to be. And she moved with a dignity and freedom that he found sympathetic. The wine was German, and not at all sweet, and that he found sympathetic too.

"Good," with sincerity. "You know, you could have avoided this trouble. It's a fleabite, but now it's an annoyance. These things get magnified. They go down on paper and acquire unnatural importance."

"I was insulted," said Lucienne sharply, "and the boys, who have manners, being Italian, resented it. Is that a crime?"

"Ah, insulted," said Van der Valk comfortably. "You are touchy, mademoiselle; it's not necessary. They were just trailing a coat for the Italians to step on."

"They used filthy language."

"I can understand that you aren't accustomed to them, as I am, say. If you knew them better you'd see that these urchins live their whole life with a need to insult, to get their own back, as they think. They simply know no better than to resent anyone with more manners and education than they have. But it's childish to take them seriously. That's what they want—to provoke just that reaction. But their being childish is no real excuse for your being so too. However—it's these three boys. You were with them; why is no affair of mine. But now they are in some trouble—one is, anyway. I haven't even seen them yet. But there was some play with a knife."

"That silly Nino," with a comic maternal expression. "He's only a boy."

"But exactly. Playing with scissors or with knives endangers tiny children's lives. The Officer will make a fuss over that knife, and the judge may well be inclined to take him seriously. The other two will just get fined a couple of pounds for brawling, but they'll be told, as well, that if there's any more trouble their permits to stay here will be canceled. That's simpler, see, than a suspended sentence or anything. The implication is—don't go out in public with Dutch girls; it's not approved of."

Her eyes spat. "What is not approved of, I am careful to do. And those who do not approve, *je les emmerde*."

He laughed. "Ah, how I agree, and how often I have said the same. The trouble lies in being in a foreign country; one has to show more tact than at home. And particularly in Holland. We're sensitive; things that wouldn't be noticed in France or Germany cause a scandal here. We are small-minded and insular; you ought to know that. This is irrelevant to you, of course; nobody will say anything to you. The judge may look a little disapprovingly over his glasses."

"Because I'm Dutch."

"Nuisance, isn't it? Often feel it myself."

"But I'm in Holland: I'm at home. Nobody can dictate to me who I go out with."

"Nobody's trying to," said Van der Valk peacefully. "I'm

suggesting, gently, that if you are less edgy your companions will find it easier to be tactful. You are obviously intelligent; you will see that."

She was silent; he studied his surroundings. Several expensive pieces. Englebert had been brilliant; more, he had been well known and an admired musician. A thought too dramatic, perhaps, a scrap too theatrical. But good. He had made lots of money, but easy come, easy go. Great chaser of women, with his handsome, flamboyant looks—how would that have affected the daughter? Would she ever realize, perhaps, that all that womanizing might have been the thing that lent Englebert's music a tiny touch of the spurious, a hint of insincerity?

In elaborate crocodile and python mounts were many photographs of women; silver, leather, crystal everywhere. A rich, sportive, rather vulgar atmosphere.

"Is one of those women your mother?"

"No. They are all mistresses," quite casually. "After a short interval of official mourning, I'm going to throw the lot out. They mean nothing to me and I don't care to look at them."

Mm, all these women and no wife. Whose daughter was she? Who looked after the flat anyway? Who was responsible for her now that her father was dead? Had she a mother still? He wanted to know. She would think him an ignorant nosy-parker; he didn't care. His job was to satisfy his policeman's instincts, and something about this girl bothered them; this one was not born on her knees.

"Where's your mother?" he asked, point-blank, but in a neutral voice; he disliked the bullying, disapproving intonations used by cheap policemen.

She was unperturbed. "In South America. In Mexico perhaps. Or in California—she has a valid United States visa, I believe. I am not myself interested where she might be."

"Ah. Like that."

"Like that," she agreed gravely.

"Who does the housekeeping for you here?"

"A daily woman my father employed, who was much devoted to him."

"And who pays the bills?"

"The bank manager. A pompous bore."

He felt some sympathy for this bank manager. "And what bank is that?"

"I don't even know its stupid name. On the Rokin."

His mouth twitched with amusement; there was no difficulty in understanding this. She would be a headache to Papa's assigns and executors. Some notary, no doubt, who would be inclined to give the young lady well-meant advice. Perhaps he had been so kind as to ask her to dinner; he'd bet the poor fellow passed a tiring evening.

"Good. It was only that I wanted to know a little bit about you, so that I can decide how to handle the boys. I'll see about digging them out of their concrete palace; it shouldn't prove complicated."

She looked at him, still a little sullenly. "I don't want you to do me any favors."

"Who said anything about a favor? I'm only trying to keep myself a human being. If I went about doing everybody favors, I'd soon be out of a job." This kind of tone would go down better with her than any kind words, he could see. She was still at the age when one thinks all politeness no more than hypocrisy. He got up to go. On the long wall hung a portrait of her as a child. Good portrait, he thought, good picture, not that he knew much about pictures, but he was learning. He looked from it to her; she shrugged. She had been a striking child. She would be a striking woman, any day now.

Below the portrait were bookshelves. A policeman has no scruples about this kind of curiosity, and he never passed bookshelves without scrutiny; they always told much about their owner. There were technical and professional books in rows;

Englebert had been a serious artist. More rows, but of pocket-books, plastic-bound French and German and English thrillers. Few serious books, though, outside music. No history, biography, literature, or philosophy. He was not surprised. Musicians were often startlingly narrow-minded and uninformed. This girl was probably totally uneducated. Knowing five languages, and illiterate in all of them. Ah well, what could he do about that?

"Good wine," he said appreciatively. "And thanks for the company."

"Don't mention it," she said indifferently.

Back in his office he had the boys sent for. This was trivial. It could probably be cleared up in half an hour's work, and he would promptly forget about it; these occurrences were common coin. He would not have bothered with going to see her had he not known her name. But now that he was interested in her, he had become interested in these three Italian boys as well. What, after all, had they done, to take up the day of an inspector of police? It was a job for a simple rechercheur to tidy up. Anywhere else, an affair like this would be practically disregarded. A good talking to and a suspended sentence. Even here, it was only the Dutch distrust that made it difficult. The double distrust. Of foreigners as a whole inside Holland—we have too many people of our own for comfort in the little space we have available—and the automatic distrust of anything imaginative, unusual, unconventional. He sighed; life was a pest, to be sure. It was a slack day, that was the trouble. The fur coats had been discovered stuffed into a baker's delivery tricycle; charming. Poor fellow; an instant's temptation and now he would get hammered. All the fault of—who? Not the truck driver, not the van man. Not really, even, of the owners. That poor baker's roundsman, on his rotten little wage, was another who would be finding life difficult this morning.

The three boys sat in a row in front of him now; they had nice manners, these Italian boys. They refused his French cigarettes—found them too strong, they explained politely. Feeling sympathetic, he found a battered packet of Golden Fictions, which won them over. There would be no further difficulty with them; they were already much subdued by their night in jail.

Now, which, at a glance, was Lucienne's boy? Not the little Trocchio, whom they called Nino. This was the one who had pulled the knife. Even subdued he was talkative, abominably so. Short, stocky boy with wavy hair. A waiter. Pleasant, unintelligent face, rather pasty. Undoubtedly did elaborate exercises to develop his muscles, knew all the song hits, and would never stop talking.

The second boy was more likely. Waiter too, but not a real one; supporting himself with it through some study. Athletic, handsome boy; sleepy movements but a quick, nervous face. Tall; smooth blue-black hair that needed cutting; distinguished pallor—very good-looking; must be him. Van der Valk decided to start there, and spread out the passports that lay on his desk.

"Valmontone, Dario, born third April thirty-nine, in Milano."

"Correct." Quiet voice; his French, soft and southern, better-sounding than Van der Valk's hard Lillois.

"Your father, I see, is an electrical engineer. You're here to study something?"

"Interpreter's diploma. I have French and German, but not English yet."

Excellent—this was the one. But he was wrong. Directly he mentioned Lucienne, tactfully, the third boy, the fair one, intervened.

"*Non*—her friend—*je le suis.*"

Hesitant French; quiet voice; shy manner. Shorter and broader than the city boy, but not like a peasant; more a mountain build. Studious, well-brought-up behavior. Fair hair cut very short. Born in Trieste, apprenticed to a Vermouth company near Bolzano, here temporarily to work in a distillery.

"Ah. You're here to pick up some more tricks of—what d'you call it? Alcohol engineering?"

The boy agreed; he had a pleasant smile, with gold on two teeth.

"Different ways of putting—how to say—herbs, and flowers, in wine, or eau-de-vie. Different sorts, to make aperitif, like quinquina, or digestif, like anis. Is complex, delicate."

Amusing, the boy had a pleasant didactic way of talking, as though he thought everybody should be interested in everything. Quite right too; he himself was interested, at once.

"And here, what d'you learn?"

"We work much with flowers—Alpines, you know? —*la gentiane* and so, but here it is all fruit. Not so interesting we think, but I must travel to learn. Other countries, other tastes. We try at home to make more exports; they finding our drinks too *secco*, too *medicinale* in flavor. So I come here to learn some things. I speak some Austrian, so speaking little Dutch, not very much."

Fascinating.

Good heavens, the little Nino was an aggressive child; kept interrupting. Trigger-happy, of course; just the type that carried knives about with no good reason and was fatally inclined to show off by producing them. He would need a smack; too bumptious altogether. The Officer of Justice would sober him down.

The other two were plainly inoffensive quiet boys who would give no trouble. And plainly had given no trouble. Had merely tried to act like gentlemen while with Lucienne. When you are with a lady, and you have courage, you do not run away from a shower of uncouth louts who call obscenities after you. He would take pains to ensure that the said louts got held well under the cold tap.

"And tell me: how did you come to meet Miss Englebert?"

"I am most interested in music," said the studious face primly. "I go often to Concert-building, and was *abonné* for the concerts this spring. Signor Englebert was very polite—he speaked to me in Italian, and his daughter has been by him and he has introduced me. When he is unhappily dead, I am writing her a letter of *condoléances* and she is answering."

"I see."

He made out a *procès-verbal*, explaining that this only applied to the fracas with the knife. Consequently Trocchio would be detained; the others were free to go. They would have to make an appearance before the "police court" judge, where they might have their heads washed a little. Broad grin at this from Dario, the Milanese city boy—not quite the first time he's seen a street-fight, thought Van der Valk. Serious, deploring face from the studious Franco, dejection from the deflated little Nino.

He wondered whether they would promptly have a celebration party, with Lucienne. Be sure they would.

A few days afterward he again found himself with a spare hour. Wasn't it always the same? One minute, you could not call your soul your own; the next, you were kicking your heels over paperwork. Van der Valk loathed paperwork; he made an excuse to stroll over to the Rokin. He proposed, out of idle and vulgar curiosity, to do something immoral, which all policemen do occasionally. He was going to use his official position to satisfy a personal wish for information. If somebody had asked just why he was interested in—really curious about—Lucienne Englebert, he would have been hard put to find an answer. But it should be a simple matter to find out which bank handled the Englebert affairs.

"Is it an official inquiry?" asked the director, with disapproval disguised as faint politeness. One had, considered Van der Valk, as a businessman to admit the existence of policemen, but there seemed always to linger a faint odor of corruption after they left, in one's nice clean office.

"Not a bit," he said easily. "Quite unofficial, paternal interest."

"And in what way is my client involved with you gentlemen?" smoothly. The director was not quite satisfied by the paternal interest.

"No way. She was tangentially connected with an incident. We are interested officially only in learning whether she has a stable life and is provided for, in view of the recent death of her father."

That went down all right, on consideration.

"In such circumstances I am not bound to disclose anything. However, in view of what you tell me—she is, at the moment, reasonably provided for. As to personal circumstances, you might do better to ask the notary. If your interest extends so far," he added, a little dryly.

"Just so. Who is it?"

The director hesitated—not that it mattered—just that one never really wants to give the police any information, "Mr. van 't Hart in the Frans van Mierisstraat."

"Obliged to you," politely.

The director inclined his head slightly, like royalty being given a totally unwanted present.

Although it was another week before circumstances brought him anywhere near the Frans van Mieris, when they did Van der Valk made the necessary time. Though his interest was challenged by many other things more important, it was still unexhausted. He was a little surprised at this tenacity; it was a tiny bit unprofessional.

The Frans van Mieris is a dreary street, rather typical of the district. Quiet, ponderous buildings, full of velvet curtains and too much over-polished furniture, and yet only two minutes away from the almost Neapolitan uproar of the Albert Cuijp. It is a street quite suitable for a notary, being largely given over to dentists, obscure manufacturers' agents, and philatelists. It is not smart enough for procurers, abortionists, or fashionable photographers.

Van der Valk enjoyed this gloomy dignity, as though the street were drunk and wore a wig. There were dusty trees, two or three aimless dogs, and a businessman accelerating a dusty Mercedes away from the curb in harassed haste, and looking guilty, as though sneaking out of a hotel-by-the-hour.

However, Mr. van 't Hart was a youngish, baldish man. Not drunk, and no wig.

"He was no businessman, of course. And little Lucienne. Engaging child; bit of a problem. And as you mention, no mother."

"You aren't surprised, then, to see me?"

"Never surprised at anything, Mister Uh. But I hope there's nothing—menacing?—in your interest."

"Interest is incidental to quite another matter. It occurred to me that circumstances might arise in which this girl caused us anxiety."

Pale greenish gray eyes considered him legally. "But such circumstances have not arisen?"

"By no means."

The lawyer sighed a little. "Well, I can be frank with you, I suppose. There is not much I can do to control—even to advise—a willful girl of nineteen, who was her father's pride, but who has been, I fear, sadly spoiled. I have urged her to take steps to earn her own living. The estate will run to providing for her for some time, even to training her for some useful post, but it will not support her indefinitely. There was no insurance. And that's all there is to be said. I have given her what advice

I can—or rather, what she will consent to accept, which is very little. Further, her future is in her hands."

He had thought as much. And what good did knowing do him?

It was over a year later—May had drifted on to October; a poor summer had become unexpectedly a wonderful autumn. Everybody leaned out of their windows to enjoy the delicious impact of warm sun on the cool clean air. Van der Valk had been on the ferry over the Ij, away to hell and gone in Amsterdam-North; dirty work among the smeary backyards of factories. He could not have enough of the sun that sparkled on the sluggish water of the inner harbors. He stopped by the Central Station, tempted, like a child, to ride back again on the ferry; it was so wonderful on the water.

Like a child, too, he stopped to look at the boat leaving for Marken, and to stare at the crowd of sun-glassed tousled tourists flocking into a waterbus. When he saw Lucienne, sitting alone on the terrace next to the landing stage, behind an empty cof-feecup, it was not so much curiosity that brought him toward her—it was a good excuse to stay sitting in the sunlight.

She looked fine. Framed against the gray and gold after-noon, she had a Sisley look with her blond hair and gray frock. She did not recognize him, but she was changed too. For the better, he thought; she looked thinner and better proportioned, her fine eyes bigger. Her hair was different, she wore no jewelry, and no make-up (an improvement, in his opinion). She too was admiring the sun over the dancing harbor, but lackluster, som-ber. Still, she accepted a cigarette, and a tint of warmth came around her wide mouth.

"First in a week. Good."

"You've been giving up smoking?"

"No, I've been economizing. I buy one packet, for weekends. I'm poor now, you see."

"And do you mind that very much?"

"Of course I mind. Not so much being poor; one gets accustomed to that. But having no money makes one a slave—that I mind. My life is nothing but a succession of hypocrisies, because I haven't got more than enough to exist. I don't hanker for things—but I hanker for five thousand a year and to be a free woman." She rested her chin in a strong hand and looked at him gravely. "Can you understand that, or are you like all these peasants, who could have millions and still be slaves?"

"Yes, I can understand."

"I don't intend to go on that way, though."

The words gave him a curious feeling of kinship with her. There was a certain physical resemblance between them; she could—just, perhaps—have been his baby sister. And at her age, he had thought the same way; hadn't he just.

"You work now, to earn your living?"

"Yes. There's a man who sells pianos—Mr. Markiewics on the Sarphatistraat. He knew Father; he's a nice old man. So I work for him, selling records, sheet music—I know it all even if I've never been trained. Sweet easy little mazurkas for lumping schoolgirls. But I prefer it, at least, to being a typist serf in some lousy insurance company. And I can live on it, just. This frock cost me twenty-one fifty francs from Vroom. I don't mind that, though I'd give a lot for a decent lipstick. Rather than wear a cheap one I go without. What real expense has a girl? Stockings? Behind the counter I never wear any. Hairdresser? I get it done by one of the Italian boys for love. What's left? Rent, food, and shoe repairs. I can just about manage that."

He laughed. "But surely your father left some money."

It was her turn to laugh. "Ah, there was a big row over that. I wormed it out of them, I sold everything in the flat, and I blew the lot. I went all around Europe for six months, free as air. I had a hell of a good time, and I did all the things I never would have done. That—that was my education, call it."

"Yes. You come back with all your wealth stored up."

"Back to this. Weekends a packet of cigarettes, a bottle of wine, and a lump of Brie: I just manage that. Oh, I can live. But how does it end?"

"*Je n'en connais pas la fin.*"

"How true. It's like something out of a song; it isn't life. I still get free tickets for concerts. I sell them in the shop. What use have I for concerts?"

He left her with a feeling of having watched a blood horse pulling a brewer's wagon. And a little inclined to shrug his shoulders at his feeling of sympathy for her.

An unfamiliar voice spoke quietly in his ear. "Mister van der Valk?" it said, gentle and courteous. He held the telephone, thinking, That is a civilized voice, which is a rarity, and said "Yes?"

"I have been given your name, and since I find I need a police officer I take the liberty of calling you."

"Can you tell me the nature of your problem?"

"I should prefer not to, on the telephone. Is it possible to ask for a quarter of an hour of your time?"

Van der Valk was interested in this civilized voice. "Is it urgent?"

"I think I could call it so."

"Your name and address, if you would, please."

"Markiewics. Sarphatistraat seven hundred. A music shop."

Well well. "I will be with you in a quarter of an hour."

Mr. Markiewics was a gray full moon of a face, with a fine forehead, beautifully made gold spectacles, teeth to match, and a gray Toscanini mustache. His office was fuller of music than his shop, where two housewives were listening to Cavalleria Rusticana with looks of moronic concentration, and a sad Freddy of a man was looking at a clarinet he had taken to pieces, with apparent astonishment at the result. Lucienne sat in the office too, staring out of the window with her chin in her hand, just as she had stared out over the water the last time he had seen her.

Mr. Markiewics sat down with a weary sigh, and gave him a slim greenish cigar with a very good smell. He took his glasses off and closed his eyes.

"I have been forced into a course of action that I deplore. A customer of mine has been to see me. He claims—conclusively, I may add—that he has been short-changed, twice, by an employee of mine. He noticed it, the first time, and, as a check, paid again with a large note on this occasion. I have received other similar complaints. I made them good and was considering what action to take when this man left me without alternative. Either I charged the girl, he told me, or he would lay formal complaint at the police bureau. My dealings with my customers are the cornerstone of my life. I cannot deny this, or gloss it over. Ah, Lucienne. Why did you not steal from me?"

"I would not steal from you."

"My poor girl. What you have done is worse."

Van der Valk said nothing; he enjoyed his cigar.

"I asked her what I should do. Finally she gave me your name."

Van der Valk looked at her, expressionlessly. "I don't imagine you gave my name thinking that would make things easier for you, but because you thought I would understand. Huh?" He did not wait for an answer. "Maybe I do and maybe I don't, but it alters nothing. A charge is a thing written on paper, and my ideas don't enter into it. Paper understands nothing. A *procès-verbal* is a formal action like pressing an electric switch. It's the first stage in the judicial machinery, which I cannot stop, alter, or influence once it is begun. I explain this to make it clear that I'm not prepared to make any judgments here. I know nothing of all this. If I am instructed to make a charge I make one; it has to be backed up by definite facts. Am I clear?"

"I will do no such thing," said Markiewics with decision. "I refuse to prosecute the daughter of an old friend, who is moreover my employee and as such under my care. This occurrence is my responsibility. I should not have asked you to come."

"You have nothing to regret," said Van der Valk. "I'm only here as a person. As a policeman, I'm not even alive; I haven't had my switch pressed."

"Does that mean you can leave this house and forget all you have heard, or have I misunderstood?"

"It does and you haven't."

"If I may say so, with no disrespect to you or to your profession, you would be doing me a kindness."

"No," said the girl suddenly. She leaned forward toward the old man. "You gave your word to the customer. You told him that I would be charged by the police. If he won't charge me, you must." She turned on Van der Valk. "You know that's right."

"I know nothing. Don't appeal to me."

"Lucienne," said the old man. "You are continuing to behave foolishly. Please do not meddle with my conscience, nor with this gentleman's."

"I know perfectly well what I have to do," with more calm. "I'm quite ready to be arrested."

"Don't let's have any heroics, please," said Van der Valk over his shoulder. "This decision isn't yours. Shut up, sit down, and keep quiet."

The old man smiled for the first time. "It is pleasant to have two nice people in my office," he said. It was a little unexpected. "I will not argue with you, Lucienne; your instinct is after all a good one. You have done wrong; you should certainly be free to choose your punishment. But think; do not give way to emotion.

An officer of police represents the apparatus of justice. You cannot trifle with that."

There was a short silence. The girl stood up and walked to the door. "I am waiting for you," she said, in the tone of someone telling a page to open a hotel door. Mr. Markiewics looked from one to the other with intelligent eyes and said nothing. Van der Valk did not laugh, or shrug, but got up too and walked with heavy footsteps. Outside in the shop, the sad man was still gazing with absorption at the clarinet, which he twiddled between thin, hairy hands that stuck out of rather dirty shirt cuffs.

In the car he turned to Lucienne, with a polite, bored voice. "I'd better drive you home first. You can change your clothes. Wear trousers and a warm sweater; this may take a day or so."

"I'm all right as I am."

"You'll still go home first. Take handkerchiefs and a toothbrush. If there are one or two personal things, nobody will shout at you."

In his office he went quietly through the professional movements. He asked his questions in brief dry words, and wrote in a neat staccato longhand, a cigarette lying peacefully between the fingers of his left hand. From her mouth the smoke went up from another cigarette, in an untrembling vertical ribbon. When he was finished he put his Bic down and let a grin grow on his face.

"Minimum fuss; you did that well. Now you'd better realize what will happen. I get this typed and then I read it to you. You approve it and sign it. That is the end of the unpleasant part. Writing these things is disgusting; to listen to them is even worse. After that there's nothing to do; you wait for the wheels to turn, which is sometimes quite quick and sometimes painfully slow. You have to go to the Palais to make the acquaintance of the Officer of Justice, and a day or two later you get popped up in the local court, before the judge. For a thing like this you stay in custody and you are likely to get a few days' detention, depending on what sort of impression you make. None of this is really disagreeable, but you'll notice an obscure sensation of being in a world where nobody is quite human. It's disconcerting till you get accustomed to it."

"Have you really got accustomed to it?" asked Lucienne coolly.

"No, mademoiselle, I have not, but this is my job, and about any job there are things one dislikes, so don't imagine I complain about it. That's the lot. You were right to behave the way you did, but you'll probably come to regret it. You now have a police record. Don't say I didn't warn you."

After doors and locks had clicked in front of the arrested party, he sat back and yawned, his hands clasped behind his head. He was tired; odd, he had done nothing to make him tired, he thought. It would be easy to get emotional about that girl. He opened a drawer and brought out a little bottle of eau de cologne; it was one of his habits that upset colleagues, but the clean Napoleonic smell conquered the judicial atmosphere as well as these momentary fatigues. He slowly rubbed the dinginess off his face and as an afterthought took a small sip, licked his lips with enjoyment, and started typing.

Lucienne got rather more heavily strafed than her performance deserved; she cannot have made a very good impression on the Officer of Justice. Rebellion must be suppressed. He saw only a cold and hostile face. As for the police-tribunal judge, he had little opportunity of seeing more. A young lady in need of a lesson, and he gave her the sentence the Officer asked for. He might have thought he was contributing to the better bringing up of his own daughter, who was much the same age and secretly giving him a lot of worry.

Since Lucienne admitted everything, the papers prepared

by Van der Valk were the only evidence. She had nothing to say. Mr. Markiewics had written a little letter, which was not produced. Mr. van 't Hart in the Frans van Mierisstraat did his best, but had been discouraged by feeling that Lucienne disliked him and was ungrateful to him. She had not listened to his good advice; therefore she was ungrateful. It did not occur to him that she was indifferent—it must be dislike.

Still, he produced an expensive advocate, who uttered excuses in a voice of perfunctory passion, like a prostitute saying "darling." The judge listened politely and shrugged. Lucienne had no father or mother; quite. But was she not an intelligent and well-brought up young lady who should certainly know better? Had she not been befriended and well advised by all? Had she not been given a position of trust, which she had promptly abused? No, no, he felt it his duty; fourteen days.

Why did Van der Valk feel himself involved? He had had so many pass through his hands in the same direction. Was it because her father had died in a gray Citroën DS outside Utrecht? Because he had helped to fish a limp girl's body out of the wreck? Because he himself, at twenty, had also denied bourgeois notions of respectability? (He had been lucky; in wartime one had been able to sublimate these feelings by galloping about with a loaded gun.) Or simply because she looked like him?

What did it matter why? He loathed sentences that began with "Because."

He saw her again, shortly after she was freed. She was walking along the Wetering Schans; he was bicycling, rather crossly; there was no car, and it was an unpleasant day. A dull wet chill, real November weather. An inflamed red sun hung uselessly, low over the rooftops, giving the gables a livid, sinister aspect.

He had a slight reluctance to accost her—not quite the

usual policeman's indifference as to whether anyone wants to see him or not. But she grinned when she saw him, and he got off his bike with a relief he could not have explained. He surely wasn't losing his detachment over this tiresome girl?

"Let's go somewhere and have a drink."

"Do policemen drink with people who have records?"

"Don't know about the others. Make a point of it myself. One can't talk leaning over a bloody bicycle in the street. Let's go to the Vinicole; 's not far."

She hesitated.

"Policemen never come there; too expensive."

"Very well then." She showed no embarrassment, made no nervous little jokes. She was childish, for twenty, but she had self-possession, he thought.

In the bar he gave her the slow hard look that is not rude, though in anyone but a policeman it is rude. She was nicely dressed; stockings today, city shoes, lipstick, earrings.

"Pernod?"

"Definitely."

"Lipstick, I see. You putting out more flags?"

She grinned too. "It became necessary. Being in prison is contemptible, isn't it?"

"I did try and warn you."

"You did and I'm grateful."

"I like your suit very much."

"Yes, Castillo. You understand that jargon?"

"Enough to know it means a lot of money."

She drank her Pernod with enjoyment. "Means a greatly heightened morale. I had saved some mad money—last of what my father left. The bank was kind enough to let me have it," with ferocious emphasis. "I have laid it out extremely carefully, on very classic clothes that don't date. How I hate banks." She looked out on the Leidsestraat with indifferent eyes. "Let them all burst."

"What?"

"*Laat ze maar creperen. Qu'ils crèvent, tous.* You stupid or something?"

"I've got the message. Me too?"

"Yes, you too."

He grinned. "That idea is a well-known reaction to being in prison."

She shrugged. "Maybe. I thought of it before that. Anyway, I'm not staying here. I'm going to Brussels. In Belgium or France a girl can do any job, and does. Without being stared at as though you were crazy. I can get a job as a service girl in a garage. I'm good with autos. I don't care what I do, but I refuse to be a secretary, or a hostess, or the other stupid things that are thought respectable for a girl here. They're all degrading; polite prostitution, the lot of them. Nobody understands. Look at you; face of polite disbelief. I suppose you won't even believe that I'm a virgin. Now that I've been in jail, I am good for nothing but to be a call girl, I suppose.

"I don't care. I intend to be my own mistress; I refuse to kiss anybody's stupid arse. Yes, you heard; I'm sick of being a lady. I wish I was a Jewess, I'd go and build roads in Israel. They know how to respect women."

"And does nobody here, then?" Yes, it was very childish, but he could quite see the point. That was the trouble with him; he could always see everyone else's point.

"No, nobody. Thanks for the drink all the same. What do they expect of me here now? I've been in jail, so I'm a fallen woman."

He watched her sashay along the pavement. Not really very pretty, but with her own beauty; very good to look at, those long handsome bones in the elegant suit. He imagined her in overalls; there she would look good too, leaning over to polish a windshield; he laughed. No, seriously, she would look good: aristocratic and independent, contemptuous of big shiny cars. She had a good idea. He agreed with it, and thought she would likely be a success. She would get good tips, and certainly have a better, healthier life than the sallow little typists.

He laughed again at the thought that any fat businessman who ventured to pat Lucienne's hard, boy's bottom would probably get his face slashed open, and a mouthful of argot thrown in.

In two years he saw nothing of Lucienne, though occasionally he thought about her, in a "What's become of Waring?" sort of way. He had too many other things to think of. Boring details, of sordid incidents, too often. The routine existence of an officer of police in a large city, contrary to expectation, is not often interesting to the amateur. The reader of crime fiction tends to get blasé over his dead bodies. In reality they are generally miserable and squalid.

What about his dead bodies during this time? He got the wretched wife of a *souteneur*, who informed the police of his activities and then killed herself from fear of reprisals by his associates, who were as nasty as he was. It is unsympathetic. It is not always easy, either, to remember that all human beings have to die, and that these corpses are human too. What does it matter how you die or where?

Few exciting things happened to him during these two years. Sometimes there was morphine smuggling, or a blackmail, or some white slavery—he got one of those but it turned out dull and nasty. What he did get, often, was girls who died of septic abortions, or smooth young men with Rembrandts to sell, or presidents of farmers' loan banks (pillars of rectitude, churchwardens) who suddenly absconded with pensioners' savings. Or sitters on committees, who said afterward that they had been led away by the desire for willing typists.

He certainly got nothing that reached the front page, which is often a good way of catching one's superiors' eyes.

It needs luck. I have been a lucky policeman in my time, he told himself, but I catch nobody's eye in this (last year's suit, Peek and Cloppenburg, much cleaned but had stood up well to wear).

When he came upon the white Mercedes car, consequently, he was pleased, almost excited, for the unworthy reason that he smelled a headline in it. "Just let them try to drag me away from this one," he thought. "This one is made for me." All those first days he congratulated himself. "Just what we ordered; mysterious, rich, photogenic; public can't make head or tail of it. Neither can I, at present, but it'll probably turn out no worse than usual."

It even arrived at a good time, with nothing much going on—the mad dog story had worn a bit stale. It caught everyone's imagination; a plummy job. It made Van der Valk laugh, often but sourly, in later years.

It began with a policeman walking along the Apollolaan. He merits notice, because if it hadn't been for him nobody would have noticed the auto, and it would have been stolen, and then Van der Valk would have been flummoxed, maybe. He remained grateful to that policeman.

He was strolling gently, without anything to do, killing time until his tour should be ended. His jacket was faded; the black was looking whitish along the seams, and his breeches were as slippery in the seat as wet soap. His cap looked squashed, and his revolver holster sat comfortably, pushed round in the small of his back. He was enjoying his stroll; he would dearly have liked to put his hands in his pockets. It is not important, but he had seven years of service, and under a recent regulation had been promoted automatically to the rank of chief agent. He had never done anything to deserve this promotion, but though he did not know it, he was about to start.

When he saw the white Mercedes he stopped for a leisurely stare. It was the latest model, 220 SE, the coupé, with the fuel injection motor; it is a very beautiful piece of machinery. However, he had seen them before. It was more the color that caught his eye. In Holland, one does not have white cars. The Germans, or the French, often have white cars, but as everyone in Holland well knows, all Germans are vulgar and all Frenchmen frivolous. A tiny car can be bright red perhaps, or yellow, or even an orange terracotta—you have a cheap car and you can be forgiven for knowing no better. But a big car—an executive car—must be black or gray, or at a pinch dark blue, though that is frowned on. Anything else is definitely not respectable.

There was another reason for staring, and it was while examining this, revolving it, like chewing gum, while staring, that the policeman decided upon action.

The Apollolaan is a broad, quiet street, lined with quiet rich houses. In the middle is a wide belt of grass, with trees and benches. It presents no parking problems. Had the car been a Volkswagen, or a Citroën, or even a little Ford, nobody would have bothered that it was very carelessly parked indeed, skewways, a good three feet from the pavement, and with its front wheels cocked arrogantly out into the roadway. But because it was a white Mercedes coupé, and an offense to Dutch morals by its very existence (for the Dutch, like the English, see something indecent about open cars), the policeman decided to do something about it. It is possible too that his morals were not much offended, but that he wished to relieve the monotony of his life.

He looked at the houses. The car lay midway between two, a big one and a little one. The little one lay back from the pavement, behind a pleasant little garden that was badly overgrown. Dripping bushes encroached on the pathway; a rambler rose needed pruning, and a big syringa tree would steal all the light from the windows next spring. These windows were all curtained, too. Odd, at ten in the morning. He looked for a nameplate; there wasn't one. But the house was cared for—the brass of the bell-push was polished. He pushed it twice; nothing happened at all.

Disappointed, he turned to the big house, a large square block sitting right up against the pavement. This was much better. Well-cared-for brick, a chastely clipped tiny hedge of box, window frames glistening with fresh white paint. On a large brass plate the name of a well-known surgeon, professor at a big teaching hospital. He was rather nervous about ringing here; it was a bit overwhelming in its atmosphere of wealth, comfort, and intense respectability.

The maid, a sturdy-calved wench with incongruous spectacles, stared at him, at the car, back at him. In a broad accent she knew nothing, understood nothing, would call Mevrouw. Mevrouw came, not very pleased; she surveyed his breeches with distaste; he stuck to it.

"Now, what is this about a car?"

"Has Mijnheer perhaps a Mercedes?"

"Yes, but what, may I ask…"

…has that to do with you; quite. He was flustered. "Er—what kind?"

"How do I know what kind. A big one."

"White?"

"Certainly not. Black."

"But there's a white one outside the door."

Mevrouw was very sorry, but she hadn't the faintest idea, and would, if she stayed any longer, be late for a fitting. She was a corseted personage, and her bosom, which was large, caused her frequently to sigh deeply. The policeman consoled himself with the thought that it would soon be time to go off duty. And back in the bureau, to show his superiors that he was not altogether asleep, he mentioned the matter.

"Brig, there's an auto in the Apollolaan, parked all over the road. Big white Mercedes."

The brigadier was not greatly impressed. "Some doctor in a hurry."

"That's what I thought. Doctor lives there sure enough, but don't know nothing about it."

"Well, what's the number?" The brigadier wrote it on the report; there wasn't much else that day, and he could just fill the page nicely.

The report was read by the brigadier on the next tour of duty, and an agent on a bike was sent to look. It was still there. Further, it was unlocked and the keys were in it. Now, that was odd. If it hadn't been so ostentatious a car it would certainly have been stolen. At seven that evening, in default of anything more exciting to do, it was decided to do something, and a plain-clothes *rechercheur*, very polite, knocked at Doctor Buys' glittering front door.

"Yes, I saw it. Know nothing about it. Doesn't belong round here as far as I know."

"Doctor, do you know your neighbor next door?"

"By sight. Has something to do with films, I believe."

"And what kind of car has he?"

"Lincoln sedan," said the surgeon with fluent enjoyment. "Dark green. Leopard upholstery, rather nice." There was a subdued relish in his voice; he would have liked it himself. But he told himself that he would never be really happy sitting on a leopard. And his dear colleagues at the Wilhelmina Gasthuis would have acid comments. Think of the time he had the white-walled tires fitted.

"And on the other side?"

"The little house? Old Jonkheer something—what is his name, Snouck, Snoek, no, not that either. But he's gone, I believe; haven't seen him for months. I do believe I've seen someone, subdued personage, flitting about, looked like an estate agent or something of the kind."

The plain-clothes man got no answer from the closed door, and little help across the street. Some gossip; nothing helpful.

A little puzzled, he went and phoned in. The adjutant was not altogether happy about the tale.

"Can't leave it lying around there, valuable thing like that, with keys in and all. No such car reported stolen anywhere, either. And nobody in the house, you say, but last night there was someone?"

"Well, I found a man who let his dog out, who says that at eight there was light, and he thinks that someone lives there; seen light often when he's been out with the dog."

The adjutant scratched irritably. "Like to find out who it belonged to...I don't much like it, sounds fishy. I think we'd better give *recherche* a buzz and see what they think."

Van der Valk's telephone rang just at a time when he was hoping something would happen.

"Van der Valk." Hm, Beethovenstraat bureau; what was putting them in an uproar? He listened, gradually getting interested. "Who've you got there?...I've nobody at the moment...I'll come myself. Yes, now."

There was little traffic; in ten minutes he was reading the reports and listening to the tale. He decided he wanted to see for himself. While telling the telephone service where he was he looked at the plain-clothes boy.

"What's your name? New, aren't you?"

"Vogel, Inspector."

"You come with me; we'll give it the buzz. Probably storm in a teacup, you know."

"Ever worked with him?" said the adjutant to the brigadier as the door shut. He wrinkled his nose at the clouds of incense from Van der Valk's French cigarettes.

"No, thank God. Lunatic."

"Can't think how he gets away with it."

"Clever, though. Very educated."

"I suppose so. Not my idea of how to go about a job."

The car still stood there; Mr. Vogel had been alarmed that

it might have vanished while his back was turned. Or worse still, just as he turned up with an important personage like an inspector, a highly respectable and aggrieved owner would appear, and complain about jacks-in-office... But it was still there, thank heaven.

It had a hurried, distracted look, thought Van der Valk. Almost a contemptuous look. Why did someone throw a car like that upon the street as though it were an old rag? Leaving it there for twenty-four hours with the keys still in. Either one was very rich, and very lordly, so that one just did not care—were there any people like that left?—or one was in an emotional state that was pitched pretty high. He gazed with interest at the neglected garden. That wasn't very usual either. Like the car; it didn't look Dutch. He was going to enjoy himself.

"We'll go round the back. I think I want in; this house interests me." The back was not very promising; no handy open windows, and the doors looked forbiddingly solid; a good kick would only hurt one's foot, here. He prowled. Everything in order, nothing broken or disturbed-looking. It certainly hadn't been entered by breaking.

"Now, how am I to get in? Let me look...give me your torch a minute. Yes, kitchen...catch on this window here is sticking up a bit, looks as though perhaps it might not be quite home. I wonder if we jiggled at it a bit...might come loose." The blade of his knife clicked open; he pried busily.

"Can't get any proper purchase but it is coming a bit... need something stronger. Look in the boot of my auto...yes, better now, I can get more leverage... I'm buggering the woodwork... there she comes."

"We're making a hell of a noise," said Mr. Vogel anxiously.

"So we are. Naughty of us." Van der Valk got his knee up, swung himself in, and arrived with a bump. "Bloody fine burglar I make. Key's in the door; wait and I'll open it."

They advanced as far as the living room. Silence met them everywhere. The house was clean, tidy, and did not smell musty. Van der Valk opened the living-room door and turned the light on; he stayed where he was, his arm still out. Over his shoulder Vogel peered, breathing heavily through an open mouth.

The sensation of fear, of excitement, of shock at seeing a dead body where none should be—though one may have seen many more. The professional quickening, the trained instinctive shift into a top gear of observation and heightened sensitivity. The satisfaction that one was right; it will be an interesting business. Van der Valk had these professional sensations. But he felt as well the sharp pull of reality. Here is a man, who until a while ago was an alert, breathing human being, with his own vivid eyes and ears and nose, with his public life and his private life and his own inner, secret life. And he lies now like a sack. About to be poked and prodded, photographed, stripped and pawed over. To be served up hot, finally, for the breakfasts of five million bourgeois. Rolling round, now, with rocks and stones and trees. No motion now nor force.

"Steady on," said Van der Valk. "We've strolled in here like farmers; we've got to walk a bit lighter."

He looked at the curtains and plugged in more lights, gingerly. The man lay half on a chair and half on the floor, face down, head hanging, limp as a thread of cotton. Van der Valk prowled forward softly, walking round the chair and back again like a cat. The texture of the big vein in the neck was greasy and horrible, like a pig hanging in the butcher's refrigerator. He was not limp at all; he was stiff and creaky under limp clothes. Van der Valk withdrew to the doorway, still like a cat, sniffing curiously at the dead atmosphere.

"All right, son, you fly back to the bureau and get those stuffed characters moving. This'll wake them up. I want the full emergency service—doctor, ambulance, and the wrecking crew. Photos, prints, stick-and-string boys; this is one for the products of modern technology." It was not easy to tell from his voice whether he was such a great admirer of modern technology. "And I want a uniformed man here at once, to stand at the gate and keep people out. No filthy fingers on that car either."

Mr. Vogel was excited; he looked excited. Van der Valk looked about as excited as a tram conductor taking a pound note for a fourpenny one. Sad. Funny bloke, thought Mr. Vogel—not the first to think so.

"Press won't be long, once the neighbors see the boys roll up. They'll just love this. Don't stand there, boy, get a move on."

He didn't want to sit, or walk about; he stood, with his hands in his pockets. He didn't want to smoke either; he felt about hopefully and found two peppermints in a remnant of silver paper. He didn't have long for peace; that lad would be back soon. He wanted to make the most of what he had. He sucked at his peppermint.

Chap's been dead a good time; last night, probably. Car's his, presumably. Can't see what killed him, hanging upside down like that. Small caliber pistol, maybe? Died pretty sudden. If there were any interesting smells they're gone now; pity. Anything in the room at all that won't be captured in a few minutes now by the flashbulbs, the snapping teeth? No. Too late; pity. All gone stale. Blood dried, champagne gone flat, fire out, perfume evaporated, party over. Nothing's upset, nothing's rumpled. No sign of anything like an argument, let alone a fight. There's been two people and one got dead and the other walked off. And there's a car outside. Why is there a car outside?

When Mr. Vogel got back, rather breathless for fear he would miss something—it was his first homicide, and he had been trying hard to remember everything he had learned in training school—he was deflated by finding the inspector still standing where he had left him, chewing—worse, sucking—a peppermint. Van der Valk disgusted him even more by sending him to the nearest automat for another roll of peppermints. Had he known that he would be sent to buy sweeties, like a six-year-old for Mum, he would not have hurried so.

The room was interesting, thought Van der Valk; there were features of it that immediately asked questions. There had been plenty of money spent, and an effort made to make it comfortable and livable. But it didn't look in the least like a home. A rich man had lived there, but what had he done there?

There was an open hearth—a rich man's fancy, in Holland. It was of large rough stones, mortared together. And there was a broad oak chimney piece; the rustic look. Big antique poker and tongs of wrought iron. Half-burned logs, plenty of wood ash. At one side of this was a Zaanse clock, the old-Dutch pattern with a figured brass face and weights on chains. It was all supposed to look like a country house. An old map, framed. Thick candles in pewter holders. Two solid oak chairs. A set of Tarot cards in frames over the chimney piece. The hearthrug was a polar-bear skin.

It was a large, long room, and had been split by one of those cabinet-bookshelves with glass on both sides. The end toward the door had been thought out as a complete contrast; there the furniture was modern and expensive. Long, low and broad; chairs and a studio couch in oyster leather. Lamps with drum grassweave shades, a coffee table long enough, he thought sourly, to stand a coffin on. There was a Japanese tray with Scotch and Lillet, and a bottle of Perrier. On the long wall hung a rather splashy-looking picture. Looked like a Breitner—could it possibly be a real one? He wished he knew. A champagne bottle lay in an ice bucket, and there were two Baccarat glasses. Very few books. No sign of a job. No sign of a wife—or of any woman, come to that.

Noisily, cars arrived outside. Photographer came bursting in, damn his eyes.

"Hallo, what we got here? Love nest?"

"Maybe. Haven't been upstairs yet."

"Woman shot him?"

"I'm waiting for the doc to tell."

Flash flash went that inhuman startling light; blackened bulbs fell soundlessly on the carpet. I wonder if that can be a real Breitner, thought Van der Valk. He had a quick look upstairs, but there were no more dead bodies.

The doctor had no false feelings and very few compunctions.

"Got your snaps, Cartier-Bresson? Lend a hand then; take hold of him and heave him over. Stiff enough; set him up like a deckchair—so. Now let's have a look—wow!" In the man's chest, sent in upward between the ribs with either horrid luck or horrid efficiency, was a spring-blade pocket-knife. It is not nearly as easy as it looks to knife people.

"Pooh," said the photographer, disappointed. "No love nest. Woman didn't do that."

Van der Valk did not answer.

"Take one of that picture for me." ... "Nothing upstairs?" "No. All clean and tidy. How are the powder-puff boys doing?" "Plenty of them. Woman—cleaner, I suppose; potato-peeling fingers. Man's—probably his. No dark strangers yet." ... "All right to take him away, Inspector?"

"Neat," said the doctor with admiration. "Bit too much blood for our delicate tastes, but neat. Very lucky shot maybe, but a damn good one. Left ventricle, from below. Done from close up, so." He demonstrated with relish on the photographer; his fingernails were broad, strong, and beautifully clean; his expert hand made even a nail file formidable. "Died of that without any doubt. Report tomorrow."

"Make a collection there of anything in his pockets before you take him."

The technical crew worked fast. They measured distances, heights, angles; figures were jotted down in a monotone mumble. There was nothing much for them to go on; it was all much too neat, too tidy, too new. No handy stains or smears, nothing dropped or broken or left behind. Somebody, perhaps a man and perhaps—could it be?—a woman, had sat and drunk a glass of champagne at leisure, knifed his companion, and quietly walked out, leaving no signs. Unless one counted the car—was that a deliberate sign?

"Here," he said to young Vogel, who might as well make himself useful, "arrange for the car—have they finished with it?"

"Yes, Inspector."

"Well, get it towed back, for the technical boys to have a good go at tomorrow. Understand?"

"Sure, Inspector. The press are asking for you."

"All right, I'll deal with them."

He looked around the room. They were finished. Nobody had bothered to tidy; flashbulbs still on the carpet, furniture disheveled; everything covered as though with a plastery dust, showing unsuspected marks and smears. Room looked as though it had been bombed; just so had he seen rooms, abandoned and sad, also powdered with dust everywhere, after the sirens had finished whining. The ambulance had disappeared with its body; the doctor was long gone. He shivered; it was cold.

When they saw him the reporters perked up; they had been growing restless. There was a cackle of vulgar jokes and childish remarks. Van der Valk was known; he was generally amusing.

"Inspector, tell; there's a good boy. Let's have the dirt."

"I haven't much for you, boys. You can invent all you want."

"Who's the geezer?"

"We don't have any notion at all. He seems to have lived here."

"Incompetent, these police. Come on, Van der Valk, you can do better than that."

"You can have photos. Got the car?"

"We got the car," happily.

"Good. There's a man and he's been stabbed. That's all. To-morrow we may know who he was and what he was doing."

"Did he know who killed him? Man or woman? Any struggle, any robbery? Don't be so sticky."

"No robbery; could be either; he knew whoever it was; no struggle. And that, until tomorrow, is all."

There were moans of frustration.

"Come now," grinning, "you've got a nice splash of color. When you get facts you'll all be disappointed. Facts are dull. Readers don't want them anyway; they want conjecture, gossip, and, if possible, sex. That's all you crowd are fit for anyway."

"No sex?"

"No. Nor gossip."

"Surely there's some dirt. Hasn't there been an orgy?"

"Pity about that. No orgy."

"What about the champagne?"

"You can have the champagne. If you can turn one half-empty bottle of Mumm into an orgy, you deserve the readers you get. Tomorrow in the office, children."

There they went. Police baffled by identity of mystery corpse. Whose was the second glass? He could write the tripe for them. Vogel came in again, helpfully. Van der Valk swallowed his irritation.

"Anything I can do, Inspector?"

"Yes. Go home now and think it all over quietly. When you're quite calm, write down anything that struck you. Anything you've seen, that you understand or don't understand. No theories, just facts. Material objects. That's valuable, and you give it to me in the morning."

The boy looked dubious; he wasn't sure he ought to take this seriously.

"You know the classic definition of poetry?"

"No," completely foxed.

"Emotion recollected in tranquility. You've had your emotion; now go and recollect it."

Mr. Vogel went off rather dissatisfied with his first homicide. Had he known what his brigadier in the Beethovenstraat had said earlier that evening he would certainly have agreed.

Van der Valk was just as dissatisfied. He knew nothing at all, but at least now he was alone; he sighed with relief. How he hated the chatterers, the tramplers, with no respect, no imagination, no faith. Which were worse, the police or the press? He lit a cigarette at last with deep pleasure, shrugged it all off, and plodded back up the stairs again.

It was a small house, but the rooms were large. Built a hundred years ago for a rich man who had not wanted a large town house. There were only three bedrooms, and one was small, really, but they each had a dressing room and a bathroom. The old fireplaces were still there, but central heating had been installed and everything had been modernized. There was an attic floor—servants' rooms; empty, unfurnished. The large front room had a double bed, and it was made up, but showed no sign of occupancy. The second was a single bedroom. Here the man had slept apparently, but there was no more sign of life than downstairs. It was meager; nothing but bare necessities. All very neat. In the dressing room, four suits, plain and good quality. Three pairs of town shoes; leather slippers, a raincoat, a dark overcoat, a silk dressing gown. Underclothes, shirts, woolens—all following the same pattern. Everything good, expensive, and well cared for. Anonymous ties and socks, a plain beige camel-hair scarf; a cashmere pullover. Sober town clothes, businessman's clothes. All bought or made here in Amsterdam. No country clothes at all; no golf trousers or scruffy jackets, no heavy sweaters. Nothing to be untidy or comfortable in, nothing old and loved.

The bedroom worried him still more. Why were there no possessions? Where were the things with which every man surrounds himself? Ugly and silly things, broken or friendly things? There was a shelf of pocket thrillers, an ivory hairbrush. There were no photographs, but there was one picture. Old-fashioned, quiet, academic. Well painted, rather pleasant. A beechwood, with a sunny glade and a clump of harebells. A sentimental, gentle, friendly picture.

In the bathroom was an English cutthroat razor, and expensive soap. Rochas aftershave, and a pair of nail scissors. Maddening. Why was it all so bloody cautious and slippery? The third room had a fitted carpet, and curtains, but was otherwise unfurnished. Not the slightest hint of a woman, anywhere. He looked in the big linen cupboard on the landing. Adequate sheets and blankets and towels, but certainly not royal. Here too everything nearly new. He went downstairs shaking his head.

The kitchen was no better. Certainly one man had lived here, if you could call it living, but equally certainly he had lived by himself. The refrigerator held small quantities of simple, frugal food; the cellar held the unlit central-heating plant. There were three or four more bottles of champagne. There was hardly any china or glass. A few everyday kitchen things of metal or plastic, a cupboard of cleaning equipment and material. The house was everywhere clean and tidy. But no individual character anywhere; it might have been a stage setting. Completely frustrated, Van der Valk tramped back to the living room. No bureau, no papers in any drawers. Hardly any books. The only thing that looked as though it had belonged to a real person was that Breitner.

It was a winter scene; a canal, with bare trees and a little bridge. Houses behind and a shop on the corner. It was a picture he would have liked himself.

Elsewhere on the ground floor there was only a paneled hall, a little dining room, and a sort of morning room, a study, perhaps, or a library, that might have been a woman's room when the house was built. It was a very pretty little house, comfortable and charming, with generous, fine proportions. None of these rooms were furnished, but in the hall hung other pictures of Amsterdam. Two little oils, the Westerkerk and the Singel flower market; tourist stuff. And three little watercolors—looked like silverpoint drawings, aquarelled. He was no expert, but they were pretty. The Schreiers Toren, and the Montelbaan, and the Waag, with harbor backgrounds. An Amsterdam lover—it was all Van der Valk knew about him.

He found paper and wood, and logs in the cellar. Hell, he was going to light the fire. With the room a bit gay and warm and looking more normal, he might arrange his thoughts better.

Indeed, he might as well be comfortable. He took a cigar, and some Scotch, and added Perrier water, and at the first lovely sip he felt better. He looked at the chair where the dead man had lain with something like friendship. I'll get to know you better, he told himself. He slid into speculation, very profitless.

Did he drive the car? If the visitor—sinister word—drove it, why leave it? And why like that? Why draw attention?

Does champagne mean a celebration? For you or me, perhaps. For a rich man, quite likely not. Was it a personal meeting? A business meeting?

Women do not carry spring-blade knives, do they? Do they? If there had been a woman, she was a very neat one. He thought of Arlette, who was decidedly untidy.

I am being very stupid to get worked up about these fiddling things. The line of thought was a dead end. What kind of man was this? Why had he such a neat, bare house, but a Breitner on the wall? If I knew that, I would be better off than sitting breaking my nose on was-the-knife-wiped.

Had the man deserved killing, a little?

How stupid can I get? We can go on around the mulberry bush all night.

Van der Valk glanced at the little pile of belongings, depressed. He wished questions would start answering themselves. Those things were as impersonal as the house—might have come out of absolutely anyone's pockets. But he had to start somewhere. He had told himself that it was a job for in-a-little-while. He couldn't put it off any longer.

Two handkerchiefs, one clean, one nearly clean. No initial. A little silver penknife, a leather notecase, a purse with small change. No initials anywhere. No checkbook, no cards, no letters, no papers. "Is he playing a game with me?" muttered Van der Valk crossly. "What sort of hide-and-seek is this?"

Plain gold Eterna watch on black leather strap. Wedding ring. Straw cigar case. Key ring. Spectacles. No notebook or diary. Not even a driving license. Hell, there must be a driving license. In the car? Van der Valk was tired, but he had passed beyond irritation at last. This might be sordid and stupid, like most of them, but he was beginning to think not. This was not just a tiresome man. This strange orderliness and passion for anonymity, this surely deliberate lack of anything personal—he was beginning to be fascinated, even to feel a sympathy with this man. Didn't it mean someone interesting, varied, many-faceted?

Like a diamond, he thought. They have the same mysterious qualities as people. Hearts of fire, which do not always show. Each strange and individual. But the more facets, the more lights—colors, heat and cold, sudden life and furious fire. Like people, they held, concealed—and suddenly showed. There was some English metaphor about rough diamonds.

People were cut and polished by the lives they led, the people they met—the other diamonds. And in some, flaws appeared. Few were of gem quality. But every diamond is beautiful; strange and fascinating. And very occasionally there will be a really fine stone. Brilliant cut. Something that repaid knowing, handling, studying, loving. Diamonds, he knew, were a passion. Pleased with his fantasy he stumped home to bed.

He was early in his office next morning; there was a lot to do. A report, first, to make out and bring in to the boss. Because the boss himself would have to make his own report to the chief, the Hoofd-Commissaris, who controls the whole apparatus of recherche, with all its different services and branches. The boss—Commissaris in charge of *Justitiele Dienst*—a sort of Dutch Maigret, would, in theory, control this investigation; all murder cases. In practice he would be too busy—anyway, that was the story. The truth was that Commissaris Samson did not at all resemble Commissaire Maigret. He was an oldish man, within a year of his pension, and he liked peace. He had no wish to appear in the papers, nor to use unnecessary energy. He cared neither for praise nor promotion—his race was run.

He left everything to his inspectors—if one of them was saddled with a murder on top of all his other work, why, that was just too bad. Arlette did not care for that, but Van der Valk found it a fair price to pay for full liberty of action. Old Samson let you do exactly as you pleased, and if you happened to get in the cart, on the wrong side of the burgomaster or the Officer of Justice, he stood up for you. Bullishly, unmoved by cutting words or nasty letters. And when little chits came in—perhaps because you had upset the personal friends of important functionaries—he did not flap. He scrawled on them, in his antique Gothic writing. Under where it said *"Onderzoek en bericht"*—investigate and report—he put "Am looking into it—Samson" and promptly forgot about them.

And as for the Hoofd-Commissaris—he was known as His Highness, and was a figure of terror to young inspectors—he was a pure civil servant, only concerned with smooth functioning and correct grammar on forms. He did little beyond persecuting his subordinates about electric light, oil, and paperclips. Old Samson, very square, gray and white with tiny eyes, like an old badger, with a mumbling voice coming round a cheap nasty cigar, knew how to handle him.

Van der Valk wrote up his report—luckily, the old man liked them brief—and examined the catch. Clothes. Contents of pockets. A pile of glossy, glaringly lit photos. Medical report. Careful sketch plan, with all measurements, everything to scale, from Technical Devices. There would be a report on the car this morning too.

Was that all? What about this identity business? He reached for his telephone.

"Knol, get on to the camera crew. Tell someone to go down to the mortuary with the clothes I have here, and rig up a nice identity photo—yes, my subject from last night. A nice live one."

He got up and went into the rechercheurs' room. "Doing anything?"

The detective—Rustenburg, big easygoing lad, quiet but bright—put down the report he was studying. "Why no, Inspector, I sort of reckoned you'd be on at me. Big doings in Apollolaan, but we don't know who the geezer is. I guess right?"

Van der Valk grinned. "You did. Find out about the house, who it belongs to, and if there's a tenant; that should do it. I want to find out more about him—not just his name, that's child's play. Must be papers with the auto—check them. Ring me when you've got anything to go on."

Mr. Samson was not perturbed about the dead man, nor his name.

"What you doing about it?"

"Photo, and we'll put a notice out for information. No press publicity, I thought. I've a man on the house title, and I'll see about getting hold of the cleaning woman. She'll probably turn up by herself when she goes to the house—or reads the paper even."

"Uh. All right, my boy, go to it."

"You don't want to come down to have a look, sir?" Only tact; formality.

"Good God, no. That's what you're there for. Just if it turns out political, let me know. If he seems to be a Russian spy or something." He put a cigar in his mouth, and turned a page on his sheaf of typed documents; Van der Valk bolted.

"Beethovenstraat just rang. They've got the cleaner; they're sending her up here."

Mevrouw Bijster was only too willing to help; he could hardly get a word in edgewise. But she was not much use.

"I looked after the house, you see, mister, only three days a week, but between you and me, see, it wasn't much work, I could take it easy, mister, get me, but that's just what I want, now my old man's on nights I have the time but I still have to do my shopping and get his dinner, so when the agency give me this I..."

"What was his name?"

"Mister Stam was all I ever heard, mister, he didn't talk much, though always very polite, perfectly friendly and money in advance even, and if I wanted a floor polish or a new broom I only had to ask and he never questioned, though knowing me of course he could be sure I wouldn't waste money but go to the Hema and get the same what I use at home and you can't get better not paying double..."

"Did he get letters?"

"Well, some maybe, a few anyway, really hardly any now I think, I've maybe seen three all the time I've been but there were the days I wasn't there so I can't really tell..."

"How long has he lived there?"

"Not much longer anyway than I've been coming and that's not much above two months now I come to think of it, because my boy Wim was in the Army..."

"So, let me understand. He lived there maybe three months?"

"Yes, not more because he bought all new stuff..."

"He lived there all that time? He was always there?"

"No, no, always coming and going..."

"He had regular days for coming?"

"Not to say regular, he'd often come on a Thursday but he'd be gone again Friday, or he might come Saturday and stay two days."

"Never more than two days?"

"No, never, and sometimes weeks he never came at all."

"Did he have guests? Friends? Business? People for drinks?"

"Never saw a soul the whole time I've been there."

"Never any woman? Nobody who stayed the night?"

"I never saw no sign, not that I meddle with what's not my business, but he didn't seem like that."

"Nobody even for a drink? Think carefully."

"Well, I won't say there couldn't have been anybody seeing as I wasn't there every day, but they'd have had to clean up after themself and that would have to be very good for me not to see not to mention I have my own ways with the dusters and such, but I never saw nobody and that's God's truth..."

"All right, Mrs. Uh; you can run along and many thanks."

"What am I to do? Do I go and clean up as usual?"

"You'd better find another place, my dear. We can't afford to pay your wages. Job's finished as far as you're concerned."

She hadn't really thought of that and went off a little dashed.

Mm, thought Van der Valk. Why was the double bed kept made up? But she would know all right—those sharp eyes wouldn't have missed a sheet changed.

That kind of woman was reliable on that type of subject. If anyone had slept in that bed she would know. Mm, the love-nest theory was looking sick. But if he only came there a day or two a week, and never brought anybody else to the house, what did he want the house at all for? Everything about this man was decidedly eccentric.

The telephone burred; Rustenburg. His calm voice sounded apologetic.

"It's straightforward enough, Inspector, but it doesn't help much. House belongs to some old baron, with about three names; I've got them written down. He's over seventy; lived in the house till about a year ago, then went to live in France for his health.

Bronchial trouble. He's in Menton, and means to stay there now. I've this from the notary: he looks after the estate, pays taxes, and so on. House stood empty; 'bout four months ago this chap turns up with a personal introduction from the baron, wishing to rent the house. Notary made a simple agreement, on a yearly basis. Knows nothing about the man. Name is Meinard Stam. Never made a fuss, behaved like a gentleman, paid everything a year in advance. Notary only saw him the once."

"Where is he supposed to have come from? Didn't the notary ask for any references?"

"Came from abroad; met the baron in Menton. He came with a personal letter, so the notary didn't think it necessary to ask any further. There's a bank account—I've been there too. Manager knows nothing either. Turned up about three months ago with a large cash balance. No investments, no papers. Cash, loads of it. Several payments by check since then to shops, and further regular sums paid in, always in cash. Like a horse dealer, the bank said—they thought he had something to do with racehorses; it seems they have some tradition in that business of always using cash for payments. Never asked for a loan or anything, always simple and regular—bank never queried him. Why would they on that basis?"

"What's the current balance?"

"About three hundred thousand."

Well. He wished he'd that much.

"We'll try Menton," without conviction. "You may as well get back here."

Somebody would know him, somewhere; he would have a notice circulated. Not the press; Van der Valk had no wish to be bothered with three hundred false trails a day.

He had the photograph now. Full face, half, and profile, a good job. The face told nothing. A man of maybe forty-five, neither thin nor fat. Firm, healthy. Calm, unemotional face that had learned to keep secrets. Intelligent, yes, and decisive.

Looked a nice chap. Remarkably unremarkable face, nothing distinctive.

Despite himself, he was rather enjoying this. He liked the man. Meinard Stam: pale, colorless name. The dead eyes, with a careful glint of artificial light in them, seemed to have a grin. And yet this careful, respectable man had been knifed. Murdered. Van der Valk turned to the last page of the doctor's report.

"Subject to further examination and tests, the subject was in good health. The hands are slightly calloused; that, and the degree of sun/weather tan, indicate a degree of outdoor life. There are no visible scars or signs of any injury. The indications of the wound (position/angle) make suicide very unlikely. I would rule it out."

Roos was a most careful doctor, with twenty years' experience of police work; he could be dogmatic because, before he spoke, he would be very sure.

What sort of outdoor life did a rich man live? Yachtsman, perhaps. He would have this photo, and the notice asking for information, gazetted in every police bureau in Holland.

Now, what about the car? Let's go and see Brokke.

The head of Technical Devices was a thin, small man, only just big enough to be a policeman. He was going bald too. But he was no fool. A Limburger. Van der Valk liked him. The people from "below the rivers" are quicker, more imaginative and impulsive than the Dutch of Holland; Brokke was a good example.

"Your report's as good as ready; my boy's just typing it. Nothing much. Auto is nearly new, hardly any dust or marks." Everything of Mr. Stam's seemed to be nearly new. Yet he had had three hundred thousand pop in the bank. Where had all that money come from? "Your subject's prints, and a few old ones; oily—some garage man. Papers give the auto as bought in Venlo, big Mercedes agency; I know it well. They should be able to give you a line on him. The tires have been on untarred roads somewhere along there; we found soil—quite characteristic. Couldn't mistake it—I was born with it on my boots. One thing—did your man smoke cigarettes?"

"Only cigars found."

"We found the butts of two Gauloises in the driver's ashtray."

It was a small point won. His notice had been sent off; he put a note on the telex to pay attention to the whole Venlo district, and to have the garage questioned. The cigarettes didn't help much. He smoked them himself. Few Dutch people smoke French tobacco, but more, maybe, down there in Limburg, between the German and the Belgian borders.

Venlo—probably be another dead end, he told himself. He would find that the man had simply walked into a garage, bought a car, paid cash—it seemed to be his specialty—and driven out. They would never have seen him before. Now they would never see him again.

It was laughable, but he was right on every single point. The garage remembered it perfectly. It had only been a couple of weeks ago; the white coupé had had to be specially ordered from Stuttgart. And waggish Mr. Stam had paid on the nail—in Netherlands banknotes.

He could not discover one single item of information in Amsterdam, though he trotted about all day. All available staff were sent to talk to bartenders, shopkeepers, prostitutes, gangsters. Where did he get those huge cash sums from? Must be a fiddle somewhere. Van der Valk talked to all his colleagues, to the experts on fraud, on vice, on smuggling. On hunches he tried diamond merchants, and picture dealers. Total blank. He sat sullenly, wrapped in smoke and meditation, and gave himself up to yoga practices, wondering whether he would suddenly get an inspiration.

So convinced had he been that Limburg would prove nothing but another blind that he was agreeably surprised when he got a signal later that afternoon. A short twelve words on the telex.

"Venlo bureau reports subject Stam known and seen recently in Tienray. Investigating."

Van der Valk reached for the telephone. "Get me State Police Venlo... Allo... With Van der Valk, Central Recherche Amsterdam... Yes, that's my man right enough... Where the hell is Tienray?...lived?...cottage?...they're sure?... He's absolutely definite, is he?...very well, I'll be coming...yes, tonight— when d'you think, next week?"

He thought for a second, speared the phone again as though it were a fish. "Arlette, listen. I'm on something... I'm going to Venlo, so don't wait up. Be back tomorrow... Yes, hard, even if not good. Big one... All right, see you."

He jumped almost with passion into the little police car, and brutalized it, enjoying the loud clockwork noise a Volkswagen makes when pushed hard in low gear. He headed for the main road south. When passing Utrecht he remembered—he eased up a little—that just here he had seen Arnolf Englebert chewed up by a DS Citroën. "Wonder what happened to Lucienne," he thought vaguely. "Haven't seen her in a while, but of course she said she was going to Belgium. What was I doing that time here?" Yes, the man who ran away with the funds from the Lijnbaansgracht, and turned up next day drinking coffee on a terrace in Eindhoven, where, apparently, he thought he would be invisible.

The watch-commandant in Venlo was a tanned, handsome man, with almost a musical-comedy look about his sparkling clean uniform—a hussar out of *Die Lustige Witwe* rather than the Netherlands State Police. Suitable to Venlo, a gay carnival town. His wiry dark hair was en brosse; his broad tough hands lay quiet on his desk. Van der Valk, although tall and solid, felt that he must look pale and nervous by comparison.

"Tienray," said the watch-commandant in his soft southern

accent, "is a dorp, about twenty kilometers off, not far from the main road up to Nijmegen. A bit farther west is a whole region of woods. The local *veldwachter*"—funny, he still used the old word for a country gendarme—"knows your man, it seems; saw him often. It appears that he had a cottage there in the woods and came regularly for weekends. Went fishing a lot. The Maas is not far off, of course. The *veldwachter* is a good chap. Describes him as a quiet, friendly man, always alone. Nothing known against him and even less about him. I don't see what you came tearing down here for." These Amsterdammers, his tone said, thinking everybody outside their precious town is an illiterate, perched in a hut in the middle of a howling desert.

Van der Valk grinned soothingly. "Easy on. I know already that nobody will know anything about my man, because that's the sort of geezer he was. But the cottage interests me. He lived and was killed in a house in Amsterdam, and would you believe it, there isn't a single piece of paper in that house. We don't know a damn thing; he might be Alfred Krupp. A mask—a carnival mask. This might help me to penetrate that."

Wakening interest sharpened the other's look. "I'm at your service. I can get you a technical squad."

"Thanks, but I see no need to rout out your boys. I was thinking of talking to the *veldwachter*, and then seeing what I can find in this cottage."

The state policeman unbent. "Sure thing. But anything you want, you've only to let us know."

"Just a detailed map of the district, if you would."

The *veldwachter*, a quiet, beefy personage with a huge nose, was quite sure about his identification.

"I knew him by the same name: Mr. Stam. I've had papers for him occasionally; fishing license or whatnot. If I biked over that way I'd find him, mostly Saturdays or Sundays. Haven't been there hardly these last couple months, but I seen him pass in the village once or twice.

"What sort of chap he was? You want a personal answer because as a policeman I never run foul of him. Always polite and quiet. And friendly. We got on well because I like this conntryside, wouldn't be anywhere else, not if they paid me. And so did he; liked the woods, the Maas. Mad on fishing he was, went every weekend. Don't fish myself; birds are my hobby. Many's the chat we've had about birds. But fish—he'd be off whatever the weather. He had a motorbike; go different places according to his fancy, I suppose.

"He wasn't no gangster, Inspector, I reckon. 'Course I'm a hick, but I saw him as a decent chap. Hear him talk about a wild orchid or even a clump of foxglove—he felt them. Mushrooms, herbs, any sort of a plant. Did a bit of shooting. Had a hunting license, but mostly just for fun, you know—a jay, a rabbit. I know you're on duty, Inspector, but maybe you'd not say no to a drop of gin. I've got a good one.

"He'd give me a woodcock times he'd bagged a couple. And he knew how to stalk—there's wild pig in them woods and you'll know there ain't no more cunning animal.

"Where was he from? Spoke like a southerner right enough, but educated, not like me. I took him for a businessman, Maastrichtway maybe—wasn't my business. Came here to get away from it p'r'aps. Don't blame him. We may be backward, but we live long and healthy. He thought that way, I guess."

"Where is his place? Was it his? Did he build it?"

"Ah. One thing at a time. 'S about two, two 'n' half kilometers from here, right in the woods. Used to be a shooting lodge; them woods is owned by an old baron, whose family had an estate round here. Now we've got the forestry commission and all—but the woodwatcher'll tell you about all that; he's a local chap, knew the baron. I've only been here ten years. Mr. Stam rented that lodge, though, these ten years and more."

Van der Valk sipped his gin, which had black currants in it and was good. So that was how the baron came into it—there wouldn't be two barons. Why didn't the notary know, though, if he had handled the baron's estate and rents?

"What about his supplies? He buy stuff in the village?"

"Naw. He brought whatever he wanted with him. Wasn't much. Fruit he'd pick, and stuff for salads. I've got hens; times he'd ask me for a few eggs. Meat he could shoot, and fish I reckon he could catch. He brought stuff in the auto.

"But I don't know about that white auto; that must be new. He had a Mercedes all right, but an old one, an' it were black. A white one like you showed me in that photo, that doesn't look like him. He wasn't one for show, though you could see he'd plenty of money. I'm sorry to hear he's dead, myself, but I knew him straight off when that young state police boy came round with that photo of yours. Queer business. Still, that's your business, Inspector, an' none of mine.

"Visitors?—have some more gin, glad you like it, picked the currants myself—never had any that I ever saw. Mark, there ain't no reason why I should, special at night, 'less I happened to be that way on the bike, but that path don't lead no place particular. If you want to go through the woods there's a shorter an' a better road—that's just more or less a track. They use it for hauling timber.

"Woodwatcher might know—he's more or less the nearest, but still about a kilometer off. They got on right well too. Shared the same interests, you might say; mushrooms and such. He could have had visitors—wasn't bound to tell us about them, huh?

"Yes, sure I'll point you the way. You bear left along here. First right after the shop, and 'bout three hundred meters farther there's a fork; bear left again there, that's the track. Auto'll go along it all right—bit bumpy maybe. You'll see a big beech marked with white paint; bit old, but you'll see it in your lights. There's a path in there on the right. Lodge is about hundred meters into the wood. You going to break in there, Inspector? I'd have to keep an eye on the place then, for form's sake, we'll say."

"No. I've got a bunch of keys. One of them will fit."

He found the track—a grass-grown rut, hardly more, made by tractors that had hauled wood. Yes, there was the beech tree, though the paint was very old. He could get the Volkswagen on to the path easily; the big Mercedes would have been difficult. He got out with his torch. The dry autumn weather had hardened the ground, but there were faint tracks. He worked with care up to the clearing, but there was nothing definite. It was all grassand moss-grown, and he was no Indian.

The shooting lodge was a simple affair, a solid little one-story house of wood and stone. It looked innocent there in the clearing among beech trees, not at all the witch's house. The door was stronger on its own than a whole modern house. Wanderers might come here in summer; Mr. Stam had been careful. A Chubb bolt; yes, he had the key to that. He admired the men who had built this—perhaps for the baron's grandfather, in the time of the Emperor? The oiled bolt slid easily inside a solid oak balk. He flicked his torch on with a fierce expectancy. This would be something different from that stage-set out in Amsterdam. He was not disappointed.

The shooting lodge had consisted originally of only one large room, with a couple of pantries where servants could prepare a meal. It was only a shelter in the woods, ten kilometers perhaps from the baron's house, where he could change his clothes and rest, eat and plan the afternoon's hunting. Nobody had ever slept there—an occasional huntsman or forester maybe. It was still practically unchanged, and the groom or the forester would have felt quite at home. There were a heavy wooden table and three big high-backed chairs, the baron's crest stamped on the leather back rests. A huge sideboard-dresser with many shelves and deep cupboards below, corner cupboards with carved arms above them, and a long wooden settle, where gentlemen had had their boots pulled off with loud grunts of satisfaction a century before.

All unchanged. Even the big brass lamps were the same. Only the old pot-belly stove, with wreaths of cast-iron ornament, had been replaced by a modern one, square enameled, the French type that will burn any wood trash, heat your room, and cook your dinner. On the smooth, beautifully even flagstones now lay faded Persian rugs. It was a good room. The walls were paneled, roughly but efficiently, in oak, and the ceiling was beamed. It would be warm and there would be no drafts, thought Van der Valk. The house was built by craftsmen; it would withstand a tank.

He stood gently rubbing his forefinger along his nose, wondering whether he should get a technical crew from Venlo after all. He decided not, and immediately felt a weight slip off him. Not only relieved, but gay and amused. Here, where Black Michael and young Rupert of Hentzau had admired dead boars, drunk too much claret, boasted about their horses, their stalking prowess and their shooting eyes, and planned the abduction of village beauties, Stam had lived, gently pottering about, for ten years. And that was now a matter between them. A quiet, private matter. No chalk or string here please, no flashbulbs or ignorant wisecracks, no prints or big boots. He was under the spell of the place; he already felt that he understood more about Meinard Stam.

For the Ruritanian atmosphere was intensely romantic. Hares had lolloped about under the beech trees; powder-blue and sulphur butterflies had flitted in the dappled sunlight. There was a Napoleonic smell of horse sweat and leather and burned powder.

He shook the lamp to feel the oil level, struck a match, and waited for the flicker to clear and settle. The beauty of the quiet yellow light, making a Rembrandt of his shadow on the paneling, made him very happy. He lit the stove, as he had in Amsterdam. "Doors shut, candles lit, and read the *Iliad* in three days."

Here there were books, plenty of them. *Care and Mainte-*

nance of Type 220, Edible Fungi, Ferns and Grasses, Home Carpentry, Freshwater Fish, Habits of the Hare, How to Cook Game Birds, Along the Maas, Diseases of Trees. Botany and natural history, confirming what the *veldwachter* had said. But on the next shelf were paperbacks, in French and Dutch and German. Fiction. He was lucky; many of them he had read, some he even owned. These told him more about Stam's tastes and character.

Law books, a medical encyclopedia, many nineteenth-century editions from sixpenny stalls, foxed old copies of Balzac and Flaubert and Chateaubriand. A row of war adventure stories; escaping and spying, guerrilla warfare, sabotage and betrayal.

Could Mr. Stam be an old National Socialist, some ex-SS man? But these were mostly written from the Allied viewpoint. Dostoevski in German and Turgenev in French. Hm.

There were plenty of cigar butts—no Gauloises. He went into the little pantry to see if there was any coffee. Old copper cooking pots, a couple of plates and soup bowls—all clean and tidy. He found a kettle, and a jar of coffeebeans.

The other pantry was now the bedroom. A neat wooden bed, blankets but no sheets—of course, laundry would be a problem and he had kept it to the minimum. Here there was a big old clothespress, which had once held loden capes and elaborate fur-collared shooting jackets and soft low Wellington boots. It still did. There hung, certainly, one of Mr. Stam's neat anonymous suits, but the other clothes were those a rich man chooses for the country. Old and stained and much worn, and good for a lifetime. Leather and suede jackets and beautifully cut jodhpurs. Flannel shirts, thick socks, a thoroughly saddle-soaped, flexible pair of high boots. A Norfolk shooting jacket, all flaps and pockets, that might have belonged to King George the Fifth of England. All these things, he noticed, were German, and the label on the suit still said, "Metzger, Hofgartenstrasse, Düsseldorf." Van der Valk liked all this very much. There should be more treasure in the big press in the living room.

Now, that was a lovely piece of furniture. The heavy doors fitted so well that one could not have worked a razor blade between lock and frame. He found the key on his ring. A deep drawer, sectioned, was full of oddments: needles and thread, cartridges, handy cleaner, oil and polish, pull-through. On clips above were a handmade English shotgun—that would cost a fortune now—and an even older Mannlicher rifle. He took them out to examine them with admiring hand and eye. By the lock of the shotgun there was fine silver engraving, worn down and scratched; below was deeply stamped, with fine arrogance, "London." On the butt plate, in fine print, the legend "Maitland, Duke Street, St. James. 1924."

The rifle had a little curly rococo silver shield let into the wonderfully shaped butt. The worn old grain of a wood hard as ebony—what could it be?—followed the curve naturally; he caressed it with instinctive love. In old Gothic German on the shield, only barely legible now, he read, "Manfred von Freiling, Imperial German Navy, Oktober 14, 1911." The workmanship of the rifle was fantastic; it would shoot through a hair at three hundred meters. In a leather case on a strap was a modern Leitz telescopic sight.

In the other half of the cupboard he found an ancient parabellum pistol, with its screw-on butt separate. Ugly, wicked old thing; even now, tamed in its chamois holster, it looked as bloodthirsty as a Viking. And an old canvas rod case, its green tapes faded to khaki. He knew nothing whatever about fishing; he drew the rod out gingerly. It was shiny, new-looking—the joints were bright and unscratched. Mr. Stam certainly kept his gear in good condition; thing looked hardly used.

In the drawer on this side was an old faded leather flybook with soft woolly leaves; the silken lures were bright as birds of paradise. A cigarbox held weights and leads, nylon casts, several odd metal objects that he guessed were tempters of some kind—for pike maybe? An elaborate reel was as carefully packed and greased as the day it left the factory. It all looked very new—a contrast to the much-used binoculars, the thumbed bird books, the guns polished by years of skilled lover's handling. Maybe he had recently treated himself to new gear; that fishing stuff must be fragile.

There were still the corner cupboards. One only held brooms and mops, a little store of household items, and a galvanized tub with a lid, for heating water on the stove. But the other had shelves, and on the shelves he found what he had been looking for.

A farmer's pruning knife. A Longines Flagship watch on a worn heavy leather strap. The keys to the shed at the back; several other keys; he pocketed these. A passport with several stamps—German, Austrian, French. This gave Stam's age as forty-seven, his place of birth as Maastricht, his profession that of army officer—retired. A notebook, full of figures and initials—500—T.S. 850—J.R. Meant nothing to him, but he might find the answer with a bit more patience. A wallet with German currency. A storm lighter. On other shelves were an electric torch and various tools. Twists of string and wire, packets of screws. The notebook was all that could be called a possible clue to Mr. Stam's business, and it was by no means helpful. Still, it must be his business, whatever that was. Why else were those other diaries there on the lower shelf, each in its place in order of years? They were not personal diaries; each one represented a year's business, he was sure of it. They were just small and thin enough to go in an inside pocket; they had leather bindings and durable India paper, a page to every day. Often there were entries such as any man may write as reminders: "Antifreeze, peanut butter, tarred twine." And again a week or so after: "Chisel, cleaners, elastoplast." Nobody would keep those so carefully were there not much more. And more there was. That looked like a traveler's itinerary: T., B., and again Ber, Val, Bre. Could they be people's names? And what were these rows of figures with weekly totals? One set seemed to go in hundreds, the other in thousands, even tens of thousands. And these code letters again: "Sa—Has./Rio." He thought of Mr. Samson's words: "If he turns out to be a Russian spy or anything, let me know."

Where did all his money come from? What did he do in Amsterdam—and here? Was it only bird watching? This was surely not territory for a spy. But what about the missing weekdays? Düsseldorf might be more fruitful terrain. Not the secret submarine kind of spy. Perhaps—it was more likely—the new-antibiotic kind, the jet-set kind? It did not really accord with what he had guessed of Stam's character. But there was a funny smell about all this. He had been knifed, after all, and he lived a very peculiar life. Perhaps a smell—what the French called a "Rue des Saussaies" smell?

He took the keys over to the table to get a better light. Those would be the padlock to the shed. Those were spares, and that flat thing was like the key to an office filing cabinet, the tall narrow steel kind. Yes—but there was no such thing here. Or in Amsterdam. He bit his lip, thinking. And that—that was the key to a safe deposit box, or he had never seen one. Still chewing his lip, he looked with careful, narrow eyes around the room, at the ceiling, at the floor.

Let's look at the shed. It was not very exciting. A bin of logs for the stove, cans of oil and paraffin, a big BMW motorbike. That was what he took on his fishing trips—but why not take the car, all the same? An ax, a saw, a few gardening tools. This had once been the stable for the horses; that woodbin might once have held their corn.

The other side of the pantry door was a lavatory; old earth closet, he guessed, replaced by one of these chemical caravan things. Flags led from the back door to an old well, deep and still. The water was very cold, and had a clean, pure taste. There was nothing for him here. However, the shed did provide hospitality; a metal rack against the wall held three or four dozen bottles of good wine. He chose one as a trophy, and carried it back inside. Its owner would never enjoy it now. Van der Valk had seen a corkscrew somewhere, in the oddments drawer. It would help him to get to know Mr. Stam a little better. He settled down to his research. He had plenty of time; it was only ten. It was warm and still, the wine was good, the mind was receptive. He worked for two hours, and went pleasantly to sleep on Stam's bed.

He was up, though, at dawn, and prowled the clearing carefully around the house. He loaded all the guns, and the fishing rod, into his car, and called on the *veldwachter*, where he accepted the offer of a cup of tea.

"I've locked up, but it might be a good idea to keep a bit of an eye open around there. Especially toward any strangers about the place. You might tell the woodwatcher, mm?"

He drove hard, back toward Amsterdam. He intended to come back in this direction, but he would need authorization now, from higher up, before the next stage.

❀ ❀ ❀

"Sounds fishy, right enough," said Mr. Samson. "Now, don't let's have too much of your literature, Van der Valk. I agree with you up to a point. For me, I'm not against it. You're quite right that character is the important thing—God, how I hate these whippersnapper walking law books, and I hate all jurists. But you know what His Excellency will say. And I'm not going to argue your case for you. Put in a full written report. Man might not have been Russian, but sounds as though he might have been for the Germans. Not an old SS man? Keep the press away from all this. We don't want *Der Spiegel* knocking on our doorstep; they're on one of their antiministry ramps again these last weeks."

Van der Valk had to be very careful. If there was a "Rue des Saussaies" feel about all this, and anything confirmed it further, it would all get taken away from him. He didn't want that. His Highness would have to telephone the *chefs-de-cabinet* of half a dozen ministries, and there would be a lot of cautious palaver and how's-your-father, to establish whether anything was known in higher circles about Mr. Stam.

One of the most important stages in a policeman's training is his ability to write reports. At the school for police officers a great deal of time and trouble are devoted to this. And if the apprentice-sorcerer is not naturally good at putting things on paper, he will never make an officer. Van der Valk was very good at this. His skill had got him through his exams, had won him the diplomas without which no modern policeman got promoted. He loathed paperwork. But he did have the talent for reducing a rambling, incoherent tale to concise prose, innocent of adverbs.

Reports, by sacred tradition, are written in a dignified officialese, stiff and wearisome. It is intended to be dispassionate. Bureaucracy has a horror of human beings, and since policemen deal in human beings it is difficult not to enclose the living subject in a strangling corsetry of phrase. In these reports, dry sand is thrown upon the most ardent happening.

Van der Valk loathed this Third Republic language; he sighed and began writing. This would take him all day. Had he known about it, he would have agreed with Talleyrand that to be truly civilized one should have lived before the Revolution. He would have written an eighteenth-century prose. Without his knowing it, the style of his reports was sufficiently Voltairean to be readable.

He hoped he had disposed of Stam as a sinister political figure—he didn't really believe in the idea. He hoped by God the fellow didn't turn out to be a spy. First stage over; he started to suck his Bic. The second was quite as difficult. Having fought for Stam, he now had to fight for himself. These reports, halfway through a tedious, expensive investigation, were what made an inspector into a commissaire. His case must not be allowed to peter out, to be shelved, or, worst of all, to be put into other hands. The policeman must be an advocate; he must be convincing enough to persuade his superiors into a course they may not greatly approve. Van der Valk did his best not to let Stam sink into the quicksand of bureaucracy.

He got his document typed by the evening. It was immensely proper. No spelling mistakes, no crosseyed syntax, and exquisite in format, splendidly spaced and paragraphed. And good and brief. Tired, he went home to his wife and ate chicory *au gratin*. This is a good dish; when not quite cooked it is wound in ham, covered in cream sauce, sprinkled with cheese and breadcrumbs, and finished under the grill. He was fond of it. He ate three, and drank some Alsace wine Arlette had found; not very nice, but went well with this.

Next morning Mr. Samson—without having read a word of it—laid the beautiful document on the desk of the Hoofd-Commissaris, who read every word twice, and then went to see the Procureur-Général. Later that afternoon he rang for Mr. Samson.

"Samson, this report, that Apollolaan affair. Your young man, Van der Valk—it alters my view of things. I have sometimes had not altogether—hm, full, shall I say?—confidence in him, as you know, hm. But I will say, yes—he can write a good report. He is promising, hm? Indiscreet is my criticism, or has been, but he has ability, yes...even if at times too much imagination, hm."

Samson nodded stolidly and said nothing. One always had to give His Highness plenty of time to come to the point; like Philip the Second of Spain, he had to wrestle with his conscience.

"The Procureur-Général has been in touch with several ministries, hm. This political question—there are no positive indications. But he feels that we might be well advised to turn it over to the State Recherche—get in touch, in fact, with his colleague there in Maastricht. He's quite against any contact with or hint to the Germans...no evidence, hm?" There was another long pause.

"Now, Samson, I'm not altogether absolutely keen; you follow me, hm? The State Recherche people—very fussy as you know— treading on our ground. *Esprit de corps*, Samson, you know. And I was impressed by young Thing's report. I have suggested a compromise, hm, which the Procureur approves of. May be a good solution. Hm? Shall we say...you instruct your young man, yes, to have a little talk with the State Recherche folk; keep them informed, in the picture as it were. But I should like him to continue to pursue the affair. The Apollolaan belongs to us, Samson, hm? But if further investigation shows this, uh, political character, the dossier must be turned over to the Procureur-Général's office in Maastricht, hm...with no further ado," he added, suddenly sharp. "Am I clear, Samson, hm?"

"Yes."

"Very well. In the special circumstances, authorize him to go to Düsseldorf. No exaggerated expenses. The city of Amsterdam can't afford to roast Venlo's chestnuts, ha ha, hm? Hm?" Pleased with his phrase he unbent. "Very well, very well. Understood, then, Samson, you instruct your young man in what I think advisable. Good report, cogent argument, yes."

While all this guarded, cautious nonsense was going on— it would have fascinated him—Van der Valk was talking with an acquaintance. Charles van Deyssel was a picture dealer on the Singel. Van der Valk had once come to him to ask about two Rembrandts that were suspected fakes. They were fake; Charles had shown why, in language that had amused him. They had taken a liking to one another. Charles too had been amused at the simple, quite humble way the other had asked him "to teach me something about pictures."

"Morning, Charles. You got ten minutes for me, I hope?"

"Morning, you sly bastard. Come to pick my brains again; I see it in your hypocrite's eye."

"Yes, of course. Mark, it might interest you too."

"Have you found me some nice pornographic etchings at last, then? There's a Belgian who specializes in them. Like Vertès, most amusing. How's Arlette? You know, I have a very good theory, that good food greatly improves the mental processes. You're an excellent example. If you weren't married to Arlette, one of the four women in Holland that know how to cook, you would be much more stupid." Charles always talked like this. He was not at all an old queen, but he had a love for the sweeping gesture and the rolling phrase. What he most liked was conversation; next to that, food. He had been to Van der Valk's house, and was greatly attached to Arlette.

"Very true," innocently. He scrabbled in his briefcase for the photos. "Tell me, Charles, could this be a real Breitner?"

The dealer studied it; he went and got a magnifying glass.

"Could be. Even if not, it's rather a nice little picture. I'd like to see it. If it's not known—and I don't know it—and it's real, I'd like to know where it came from. I'll have to look it up first. Who owns it? The thing to do is to find its history."

"That's just the point. Man's dead. I'm hoping that if I find out something about the picture, it'll maybe tell me more about him."

"Well, can I see it?"

"I can arrange that."

Charles was excited when he saw the picture. He gazed around the room with fascination.

"Lovely thing, lovely. Most extraordinary; what's it doing here? Man seems to have liked pictures of Amsterdam, but how the devil does he get hold of this? Those watercolors and the others—they're just kitsch—oh, not bad of their type. I sell lots worse; he had an eye for what was real. But nothing like that. That's not only real, it has all Breitner's intense feeling for the city. Look at it, absolute essence, lives and breathes the air of Amsterdam in the eighties. I couldn't perhaps go into court, but I'll stake my hat it's real. Not known; I've looked it up. Do you know, I think I could hook the Rijksmuseum with that; they wouldn't sneeze at a good Breitner."

"What would be its value?"

"Can't say at all. If it's not known, its history is dubious, which lessens the value. But if it were to be accepted as genuine by the museum—mark you, they'd be fearfully slow and cautious—then the value would become considerable. He's not all that prolific and he's quite sought after these days. Should be quite easy to prove. One knows all about him; he only died in about nineteen twenty-five. Look at it, really very lovely. Delightfully romantic—funny really, your man must have been rather a romantic personage."

"Yes," said Van der Valk slowly, "I rather think he was."

If Mr. Stam turned out to have been any sort of criminal, the ministry of justice would distrain on his property to pay the police expenses. This Breitner was a valuable object; now that Charles was willing to buy it, he would go to any trouble to find out where it had come from.

His next call was on the notary. He had had the report from Menton—wash-out. The baron could not remember how many years he had known Stam. When Stam had entered the army as a very young officer, the baron had been his commanding officer. But the old gentleman had not been near Venlo for years and could tell nothing about Stam's life. He described him as a gentleman, and had always treated with him "as between gentlemen." Which meant asking no questions. He had met him again after the war, probably shooting there in Tienray; he had still gone sometimes in the autumn. As for the house in Amsterdam, Stam had called on him here in Menton. The baron had been delighted to find a tenant he knew and liked. He had never given the matter a second's thought since. No, he knew nothing about Stam's origins, and his tone rather implied that the police were no gentlemen to ask.

He had come to France for his health and for repose, not to be pestered by a rabble of constabulary. The old gentleman was vague and, though polite, peppery. All Van der Valk could do now was stir the notary up a bit.

"Did you not know that Stam was the tenant of the shooting lodge there in Tienray?"

"How would I know?" tartly. He felt a little caught out perhaps.

"There is a large country house, which is now used as a sanatorium. Then there is the forest, over which Monsieur the Baron retains the shooting rights, though it is cut for timber. Then there are two or three cottages and lodges, and a farm, which goes with the sanatorium. All these things bring in a peppercorn rent, which is collected quarterly by a firm of agents in Nijmegen and forwarded in a lump to me. When the sum is correct, as it always is, less a small commission, of course, I take no further interest in the matter. I don't know the name of the director of the sanatorium either," he added spitefully.

Van der Valk nodded. It would be hopeless down there too. The man had been a fixture, and known for years as "a friend of Monsieur the Baron's"—he would never learn how he had come by that distinction.

Back in the office, drinking coffee, the intercom burred at him.

"Yes, Commissaris? Be right with you."

Mr. Samson was sitting reading a magazine; his poker face got as near a grin as it ever did when he saw Van der Valk.

"It appears that you aren't quite as stupid as you look and like to act. Anyway, His Excellency is pleased with you. On this occasion, you represented the honor of the department. Any criticism of you was one of him. 'You follow me, hm?'" he mimicked.

The old man, thought Van der Valk, would never have

talked like this in earlier years. Discipline, authority. His pension was safe now; he just didn't care any longer. The voice rumble-bellied on, the eyes weren't even looking. "There was a suggestion that the whole thing get turned over to Rijksrecherche. Been pleased to, myself. You're no good to me running round the countryside. However, the arrangement is this. You're to go to Maastricht, and see the holy gentlemen from the Procureur-Général's holy office—and just you be careful, hear me? None of your funny jokes with that crowd. You inform them whatever you like. You remain in charge of the file, for just as long as it remains personal, get it? A breath of anything political, and you get out, you hear? Turn the whole file over to them and come straight back here. Bloody fellow belonged down there as far as I can see; don't know why he had to be so stupid as to come and get himself killed in my territory." He turned a page of his magazine, and appeared absorbed in "The new model Wehrmacht—at work and play."

"You can go to Düsseldorf. What you find there will decide the business one way or the other—if this conjecture of yours has anything in it. Got it? All right, boy, you did a good job on that report, apparently—I didn't read it. You're off His Highness's shit list; now stay that way. In another six months I won't be here to fight your battles for you; I'll be fishing."

Fishing. It gave him an idea. He went and fetched the rod case. Mr. Samson was sufficiently interested to put down his scandal sheet.

"That's fresh-water gear—I don't know much about it. I fish in the sea. Good rod. Cost a bit; wish mine were as good."

"Am I mistaken, or is all this brand new?"

"Sure it's brand new; see that at a glance. Where was it he went—along the Maas? Not with this rod he didn't, anyway."

"I suppose he just bought new stuff."

"Funny-coincidence department."

"Don't ask me. I wondered too."

The old man grunted, stared a moment, and went back to the misdeeds of minor German public servants.

Just before he went home he got two messages. One said: "Inspector van der Valk has an appointment with Rijksrechercheur Sluis in Maastricht at ten A.M. Tuesday nineteenth inst." The other had come on the telex and read: "Following request for all possible information on photo circulated Customs Post Valkenswaard can identify but have no definite facts will you advise ends." That was down south of Eindhoven somewhere—Stam seemed to have been a great frontier wanderer. If, of course, it was him at all. Probably some officious functionary with a long tale about nothing at all. He arranged all his papers neatly in his briefcase and went home.

There was bouillabaisse for supper, Arlette's economical one of cod and conger eel, but she had a good hand with the sauce; it was one of her best dishes. He ate tremendously, and afterward he put *Fidelio* on the gramophone.

"I do so love this," said Arlette when it got to the sinister rumtytum of Pizarro's entrance. He sat happily, thinking that if this terrible man in Maastricht was a nuisance tomorrow he would abolish him by breathing great fumes of garlic all over him.

"Good morning, Monsieur the Inspector."

"Good morning, Monsieur the Rijksrechercheur," with equal polite formality. These people made themselves extremely ridiculous; it was as bad as a Deputed Representative of the Land of Schleswig-Holstein. But that was the only way to handle these types. Be as stiff as they were.

These types—these gentlemen—of the Security Service belong neither to the state police nor to the city police. They are only answerable to the five Procureur-Générals of Holland. They have the artificially low-sounding rank of State Detective, which sounds rather like Adolf Eichmann. Belonging to this high judicial authority, a small and select body, they are officers, whatever their rank sounds like. In training, pay, and police protocol, they hold the rank of inspector.

They are, in fact, the political police. They interest themselves in rabble rousers and provocateurs who manipulate trade unions, disseminators of subversive literature, Ukrainian partisans, and Spanish Republicans——in short, they are the Sûreté, the branch that sits like a spider in the Rue des Saussaies in Paris. This sounds very impressive, but they spend a great deal of time persecuting the innocent members of Japanese trade delegations. They are a necessary nuisance, but Van der Valk did not greatly care for them.

They have, of course, a characteristic attitude. They tend to regard everybody as not-quite-all-they-might-be in loyalty and patriotism. They have a characteristic technique too; they apologize with profuse politeness for an inoffensive question about trivia, and the next second they pose the most complex and far-reaching query on the most personal subject, without even noticing. "Now tell me, Mister Uh, do you practice your religion?"

They give an impression—perhaps without meaning to—that all other humans are superficial and frivolous, and appear—without caring—both patronizing and nit-picking. Their forte is to give everybody the impression that they are deep in the counsels of the Minister of Justice, the European Economic Community, NATO, and the Synod of the Reformed Church. Van der Valk found this regrettable but risible.

This one was a tall, thin man with neat, dark wavy hair. He had a worried, scrupulous expression, like an intellectual playwright being investigated for un-Americanism. His face was deeply lined; he had a habit of pushing his horn rims up and down on his forehead. He might have been forty-five. He wore a good bluish-greenish suit with a faint brown line; his tie exactly matched it. He had very clean, long, carefully manicured hands. Van der Valk could not have noticed all this at once; he assembled it gradually while they were talking. At first glance he only thought the fellow looked nice, intelligent, competent, as narrow-minded as any farmer could be, and as self-important as an advertising agent.

They shook hands gravely.

"Sluis, Veiligheldsdienst."

"Van der Valk."

"Coffee, Inspector?"

"Gladly."

"Not a bad morning."

"Foggier our way than here."

"That'll be the North Sea, I suppose."

"I suppose. These cigarettes any good to you?"

"No, no, thanks all the same; prefer my own." An expensive gas lighter popped its pretty little flame up under Van der Valk's nose.

"No trouble driving down?"

"None at all. Thank you, miss, one lump."

"Well, I suppose we'd better get to business. I'm told you've uncovered something in our line."

"That's by no means certain," firmly. "Briefly, the Procureur in Amsterdam instructs me to put you gentlemen in the picture. The ministry has no file on this man. I'm handling it on the basis that it is a personal affair. If it turns out to have any political motive, I am ready to turn the file over to you."

"I'm not clear what there is pointing to anything political."

"First point is that the man carried large sums of money and possessed more. No business, commerce, or activity found to explain that. Why does anyone carry ten thousand in cash to buy cigarettes with?

"Second point is a secret and obscure life. Had a house in Amsterdam; scarcely lived in it. Had a country cottage in Limburg that might have belonged to a totally different person. In a place that is very isolated, very secluded.

"Third point, he was in Amsterdam a day, at most two, a week. He spent the weekends in his cottage. Where was he the other three days? Only indication I have is Germany. I haven't checked that yet."

Plainly, such things should not be allowed—would never be allowed if Mr. Sluis could help it.

"Final point, the man was knifed, very neatly and quietly. No prints, no indication at all, but a big flashy car was left outside on the street as though deliberately to attract our notice. Keys on the dash—just chucked there for us to wonder why."

"Yes…yes. And what do you want us to do that you can't do yourself?"

Van der Valk answered smoothly. Tactful he had been told to be, even if he found pleasure in kicking this character in the teeth. "His passport states that he was born in Maastricht. I'm not interested in that. I'm pursuing my own thoughts and conclusions. Plainly, a different approach, a second line of inquiry, might give other or better results." He let it hang in the air.

Mr. Sluis put out his cigarette carefully. "Yes, I have had instructions. A bit unusual perhaps, this working in double harness as it were. However, naturally we are happy to cooperate. I take it you have a dossier for me?"

"All relevant papers have been photostated and you have my full report."

"Good. And we count on you, then, to keep us informed of any progress made on your side."

Van der Valk went off with the feeling that he had been scrutinized a lot more closely than Stam was likely to be. That damned disapproving look—fellow is probably busy right now compiling a memorandum on my un-American tendencies. Good luck to him—that'll make nice reading for a rainy afternoon on the Prinsengracht.

He drove north to Venlo; it was on his way. He could have crossed the border as easily from Maastricht, but he wanted to follow whatever path Mr. Stam had been accustomed to follow. He called at the shop where the fishing equipment had been bought. Here he got a talkative and enthusiastic man, only too willing to help.

"Certainly very curious, Inspector. All this equipment that you've shown me was certainly bought from us, but I feel sure that the reason I don't recall it is that it was bought quite a time ago—something like three years, possibly. It's hard to say. We have no records of cash transactions, but there are two points that make it easier to say. You see, it is very good gear, an excellent make, but a little obsolete in pattern. As you know, a maker, any maker, thinks up improvements and incorporates them. This part of a joint, now—here—for three years now this maker has been using nylon here. And here—the pattern has changed. And because it is an expensive model, and we don't stock many at a time, it's not likely that we sold this rod less than three years ago. You'll of course find plenty like this in use still; indeed it is a very good one."

"And would you say it had had three years' wear?"

"No, I would not. It looks handled, but not as though it had been much used. Look at this over here now—same model, a little cheaper, more simplified, and only two years old, but used constantly. Left for repair by a regular customer. See here?—and here?—and there? That's quite characteristic of what we call fishing wear."

"Very odd."

Certainly it was odd, the man agreed. The more so because he was a fisherman himself and, if he might so claim, knew every fisherman along the Maas. And had never heard of Mr. Stam.

"We are quite a little confraternity, you see. We hold meetings and discussions. We exchange information—about new equipment. Some firm produces a landing net, say, or a gaff, of a new pattern—we'll try it out and compare impressions. Then—there's so much else—the habits of the fish, the state of the water and the banks, the types of bait we find best along a certain stretch. I can hardly believe, Inspector, that there's a fisherman along the Maas that we wouldn't know. We are very sociable."

"Maybe he went fishing in Belgium," cheerfully.

"Maybe," agreed the shopman dryly, "but if he did, his equipment shows no sign of it."

Van der Valk ate lunch in a snack bar and wondered whether after all he ought to check with Valkenswaard before going to Germany. He thought not. Everything pointed to Germany. This question of borders—it had looked as though Mr. Stam might be engaged in smuggling. Indeed, he had thought of that right at the start. But he didn't think much of the notion. A report from Venlo had told him that Stam had crossed the frontier station here, known as the Keulse Barrier, every week for some years, perfectly openly. And that had made it the more unlikely to his mind that Stam was a smuggler. What did people smuggle anyway between Holland and Germany? It would need to be something rare to have made him that much money.

Drugs? The vice squad in Amsterdam had pooh-poohed this. And he was not taken with the idea himself. He went straight from the frontier to his cottage, where he sat smoking opium? It made no sense. Now, admittedly, there was this fishing business. Could there be some illegal traffic along the Maas? But if the frontier people had observed him crossing weekly for years, it would have occurred to them too. They would have checked on any peculiar happenings. They had their informers, their whisperers. Smugglers generally got known by things going wrong with the distribution network, the sale and resale of whatever it was.

The frontier guards were indifferent, as he had guessed.

"Sure we know him. Not a white car, no—black one. Had a weekend place in Holland. Nothing wrong with him, was there?"

The customs too—it only confirmed what he thought.

"You know how it works, Inspector; we have a purge every so often on watches or cameras. We don't bother now about coffee or blankets unless they get really insolent about it. How many German housewives come now and do their weekend shopping in Venlo because it's that much cheaper?" with a shrug. "As for real smuggling, morphine or gold, we don't try and control that here—this is the Keulse Barrier: main road into the Rhineland, maybe five thousand cars a day. If we get a signal from the vice squad in Amsterdam or Rotterdam—then we'd pull a car off and search it. But you don't just search odd ones here and there. You could wrap an ounce of morphine in plastic and scotch-tape it to the undercarriage of any car—any at all. Are we to catch that with our little X-ray eye? You know as well as I do, Inspector—smugglers aren't caught that way. They're sold out by someone who hasn't had a fair share of the cut."

Exactly. Down here nobody noticed a man who crossed the border every week. Plenty crossed every day. How many lived on one side and worked on the other? One hardly noticed who was Dutch and who was German. Here on the border even the two languages had got so mixed one couldn't tell them apart.

No no, this smuggling business was not of any use—his idea was different. All this to and fro over the border—he thought it was a distraction, a deliberate confusion. He had formed a theory about Stam, which he now proposed to go and test. Shrugging, he drove on into Germany.

Crossing the Oberkassler bridge an hour later, planing down into the gaudy, dismal heart of Düsseldorf, he was more convinced than ever. The city somehow suited the notion he had formed. He rather liked Düsseldorf. It had a second flavor, like Amer Picon. The artificial bounce, the sad glitter, the noisy allure and dead desert stillness—it was somehow suitable.

Van der Valk was not one for a long wearisome search; he had had too many in his day. He would have sent someone else had it been, to his mind, a question of a real hunt. He wasn't going to the Polizei Praesidium or the Chamber of Commerce; he wasn't going to hawk his photos round poste-restante counters or hotel reception desks. He wasn't even going to the tailor's shop in the Hofgartenstrasse. He had one fixed object in mind, and if that didn't work he was flummoxed.

He had thought long and keenly about Stam's character. What he would do, and how he would go about it. Wherever Stam went in Düsseldorf, he had decided, it would be somewhere anonymous, where he would never be noticed. Maybe he lived and did business here—but first, Van der Valk felt sure, he established an alias.

How did one do that? The trouble with going anywhere regularly is that people see, and remember. There are always people. Porters, cleaners, concierges, clerks, always somewhere. Was there a place where one could go that was impersonal, automatic, where one would never be noticed? It has to be, he told himself. He turned from the Breitestrasse into the Graf Adolf and up to the Wilhelm Platz, where he parked by the post office and crossed the road to the Central Station. And ten minutes later he was out again, brimming with triumph, carrying a suitcase.

Mr. Stam had not used any cheap hotel or backstreet lodging house. He had simply used the public lavatory next to the rows of left-luggage lockers, which are so like filing cabinets. It was the key that had helped Van der Valk think of that. What on earth could Stam want with a filing cabinet, when he could keep his business in a row of diaries on a shelf? How he had puzzled over that key. So many notions, all rejected, and then he had gambled on a notion he had gotten from a paperback story on Stam's shelf. And by God it had been the right one.

The suitcase held nothing but a complete change of clothes. A dark, anonymous suit—so similar to the ones hanging in that room in Amsterdam. Shirt, tie, shoes, scarf, short driving coat. Mr. Stam had gone into the Hauptbahnhof in Düsseldorf every week for years, gone politely to wash his hands and reappeared in ten minutes a different man. But not a German, as Van der Valk had thought. A Belgian.

In a little leather briefcase lay his complete spare personality. A Belgian driving license, a Belgian passport, a crocodile wallet with money and papers, a silver cigarette case, and a new ring of keys, to unlock his new self. And a new hat, to go on top. The new self was called Gérard de Winter. He lived in Erneghem, was forty-four years old, had been born in Amsterdam—so?—and was by profession a hotelier. Van der Valk, sitting in his Volkswagen in a dreary corner of a dreary square, with clanging trams bumping past him, looking at the broad behind of a big Mercedes bus that was painted a dirty yellow and had post-horns painted on that, felt enjoyment warming him with a rosy glow. Stam was not only interesting; he was a comedian. How long had he been keeping this up? "What are we to call you now? Which is your real name? Is either of them, indeed, your real name? For all we know you can be Vasco da Gama, born in Lisbon, forty-six years old, profession sea captain." He went out happily to get his facts tidied up. Works out quite nicely, he thought. Mr. Sluis can occupy himself with Stam. I'll try and make the acquaintance of Gérard de Winter.

The garage—there might be two, there would be two—was not more than a few minutes walk, he reckoned. A Dutch gentleman would leave a black Mercedes to be cleaned and serviced. Half an hour later—yes. A Belgian gentleman with a black Peugeot had soberly driven off.

Beautifully easy—once one knew how.

PART II

EVERYTHING WAS PECULIAR THAT YEAR, thought Van der Valk. Not least the weather. That year the autumn stayed dry and warm almost up to December. Sometimes a violent wind shook the dead leaves into the ruffled water of the canal, where they drifted about, sullen and penitential. Other times it was so still that the reflections of the tall houses stood unwavering in the water—as Breitner painted them. Sometimes there were sharp little frosts. And sometimes the sun shone, warm and comforting, so that Van der Valk leaned out of the window in his shirt sleeves, smoking and ruminating. And there was no rain.

In Spain and Italy there was. One heard nothing but horror stories, of flash floods of eleven centimeters of rain in an hour and a half, floods that tore down from the high ground in fearful torrents, crumbling villages like so many soaked biscuits, flinging trees and cars playfully across fields. The papers were full of ridiculous photographs of policemen, gallant in soaked boots, struggling along with fat, rather indecent women slung over their shoulders like bedraggled hens.

But in northern Europe—and in Holland, land of rain—there was no rain. You would have thought people might have been grateful for once. Instead, quite as usual, complaints were loud. Farmers muttered; the Rijn skippers cursed. The water level of the Rijn was the lowest in ten years and traffic had stopped altogether.

All these silly-season oddities did not bother Van der Valk. To him it was reasonable that the weather should be odd. Life was odd; he didn't understand a damn thing. He thought he had understood Stam; he couldn't understand de Winter. The Rijn skippers waited for the Advent rain to raise and inflate their beloved river. He waited for a rain of enlightenment.

It had looked easy for a while. Had he been too cocky after his cheap success in Düsseldorf? Overconfident perhaps? Was he now being punished because he had been boastful and had thought himself clever? Now he sat in thick darkness, and nobody cared a brass farthing. The Hoofd-Commissaris was content, as old Samson had been content, to write off the death in the Apollolaan with a shrug. What did it matter how a criminal died? He should have been content himself. He wasn't; it gnawed at him.

At first it had all been congratulations. He had broken the mystery. No more worry, no politics. Rijksrecherche could go on back to bed—they were delighted, he suspected; they hadn't been able to find any more out about Stam than he had. Now he could begin, Mr. Samson said, with his own work. Who was the man carrying false papers, shot dead while running away, by an Amsterdam agent who had caught him red-handed breaking into a warehouse on the Reynier Vinkeleskade? Van der Valk could not care less—his heart was in Belgium. But nobody higher up was interested now. The man had been a swindler and had died the death of a swindler, knifed for double-crossing, no doubt, by some other double-crosser. Why worry further?

It didn't explain to Van der Valk why a white Mercedes coupé had been left so carelessly on the street.

He had called at Valkenswaard on his way back from Düsseldorf. It was only seven in the evening, and not far out of his way. He had some notion now of what it was he would hear. Indeed, the name of Valkenswaard should have told him before. But he had only thought of a little place down in the south where the firm of Willem II made cigars, and he had had his head full of Germany; he had preferred to disregard this hint. But now he knew that Gérard de Winter was a Belgian, he was very interested in Valkenswaard. It is a quiet, tiny town on the Belgian border, deep in the south of Holland, in Brabant. Warfare is waged there, but nobody elsewhere in the world is interested in this warfare or informed about it, though occasionally pieces of gossip creep into the Dutch papers. To the people who live along this straggling border, from the Maas at Roermond to the sea at Bergen, the warfare is a very important part of existence.

The chief officer of the customs station was a tall, thin man, handsome in his neat uniform. He looked like the late Leslie Howard. He had slow gentle movements and a slow gentle voice.

"So you're Inspector van der Valk. Royaard is my name, very pleased to know you. Take a chair. Would you like coffee?"

"Thanks, I've been in Mofland—had all the coffee I can hold."

"Theirs is better than ours anyway. A beer? Belgian beer," with a twinkle—Van der Valk had never met anybody before who really twinkled.

"Grand." It was Stella Artois; very good.

It was a comfortable, warm office. On the long wall hung a huge map of the frontier and hinterland, marked with many little flags. There was something funny about those flags. He got up to look, and grinned. Each little flag was the "*Boter Controle*" coupon of the Netherlands State Dairy Industry—the royal arms in blue and silver that is stamped upon every packet of butter in Holland. The customs officer smiled.

"Our stock in trade. You know all about that?"

"Nothing beyond what I read in the papers."

"The papers," with contempt. Van der Valk warmed to him. "That's worth precisely nothing."

"Then I know nothing. I'm interested, though."

"I can tell you," said Royaard, filling a long straight pipe. "I know a great deal more than I would prefer. But I won't waste your time yet. I'm glad to see you. I put no details in that telex message because, frankly, I didn't know what to put. I've no facts; I've only suspicions and conjectures—no good to you," with an abrupt shake of the match. "But now you've come to see me, perhaps I can be of some use to you. And perhaps you can help me. The man who is dead, whose death you are looking into, is a man we know. Not well. Not as well as we would like."

"Butter smuggling?"

"Butter smuggling." He closed his fist round the stem of the pipe; smoke trickled obliquely from the corner of the long shaved lip. He opened a drawer, and brought out a tray of filing cards; he flicked through them, and handed one to Van der Valk.

"We'd better check that you agree with me. Would you say that that was your man?"

On the card was typed: "Fisherman—name unknown. Thought to be an organizer for tramps. No details available, but has been seen in all border districts talking to known contrabandists. Rides BMW motor, number 33-32 LX-67. Information about this man is sought. Attached photo taken August 4th outside café Marktzicht, V'swaard." The photo had been snapped in the street while the man was looking away; the profile was a little foreshortened. He wore a leather jacket that Van der Valk remembered having handled. A silk scarf masked much of his jaw. But the angle of the forehead, the jut of the nose, the set of the ear—no, this man Royaard was not stupid. He nodded.

"What are tramps?"

The customs officer smoked and thought.

"I'd better try to explain briefly. You know that enormous quantities of butter are smuggled from Holland into Belgium, owing to the great difference in the fixed retail price. It is one of the complex anomalies that the Euromarket has not yet abolished—gives the Belgians, and us, a good deal of trouble. Most of this traffic, classically, is or has been made by wide boys. They get old American cars, soup the motor up, reinforce the fenders, and load in anything up to a thousand pounds of butter. Then they crash the border at full speed. If they meet a barrier, they reckon to break it. If pursued they throw out these."

These—he tossed one on the desk—were wicked little caltrops; small steel balls set with four sharp spikes. However they lay, a spike pointed upward.

"They take a back road, they ride on full hammer, and if an officer signals them to stop, they've been known to run him down and let him lie." His voice had sharpened. "We've lost some good men with bad injuries. Now we've got tougher. We raid the villages—sometimes we can pinch them out before they start. We've our own fast cars and system of patrols. But it still wasn't enough. Now—now we've at last been allowed to carry arms. I had to plead for months, but finally we got them. We're carrying smoke grenades now, tear gas, and carbines." He smiled a little sourly. "Do you know that I was sent on a training course with the Paris riot police? I learned things there they don't teach to customs officers. Now we have mobile brigades—we're hurting the panzer boys. We've put a few in the hospital, a lot more in jail, and we've sent a lot of old Plymouths to the scrap merchant." He smiled, with a thin curve of hard mouth.

"We've not yet put them out of business altogether by any means, but we've so knocked their profit margin that it isn't easy pickings any more. Too much butter lost, too many cars lost. Beginning to be a shortage of drivers who know the back lanes and are willing to face us. So far so good.

"But it hasn't affected another sector of this traffic at all. If anything it has encouraged it. And we were able to control it better in the old days, just walking about the byways, than we can now in battle wagons. The tramps are not affected by carbines. We can meet force with force now, but we haven't the reserves of craft. The tramps are carrying more butter than ever they were.

"They're both simpler, and more sophisticated. They're mostly older men. Farm laborers, poachers, all men who live legitimately on the border. There are pubs where half the bar's in Belgium and the door's in Holland. Where the border is a real border—the sea, the Maas—there are no problems. But here— it's ludicrous. Politicians draw a line, but the border doesn't exist. A ditch, a hedge, a rabbit run. A farmer can start to plow a field in Belgium and turn his tractor round in Holland. What can we do? Sow minefields, put up barbed wire, with sand behind it that we rake every night? Like the Russians? We put flimsy bits of red and white wood across roads. My job is hopeless when it comes to a man who can walk quietly in the dark, not scared of a bramble bush or of getting his feet wet. And these old men are much harder to watch and much harder to anticipate than the panzer boys, who are mostly stupid oafs. Taking butter over is to them a better sport than anything they've ever heard of. They're happy with moderate money—because they wouldn't know how to spend it if they had more.

"Old Benny—lives within a stone's throw of me, seventy if a day. He might bike up to twenty kilometers either way and then whip over a hundred pounds of butter on his back. They drop it in a ditch and pick it up with a tractor hauling turnips, or a bread van, or a milk lorry. And if I catch him at dawn, he has a hare in one pocket and his dog in the other, and butter wouldn't melt in his mouth or under his armpit.

"Ten of these old rascals can shift a thousand kilos in a week. If it's raining, you wouldn't see them before you fell over them. No noise, no bang-bang, no expenses—and a fantastic profit.

"I've torn my hair over who the man could be that master-minded all this. Who arranged for the leaving and picking up? I've suspected our fisherman friend and it looks as though I was right. I couldn't do a thing to him. What has one got on a man who goes fishing?—even if he never does any fishing. I can't stop him from dropping off here to ask the way, there to ask what time it is, t'other place for a quiet beer in some country pub. In other words, I'm not able to stop him from making a clear profit of a good three thousand pop a week. I could put it in my pipe and smoke it. He knew the border himself like they did. Don't know why, but I've given it a lot of thought, and all I can think of is that he knows this country from wartime. Resistance movement, maybe.

"Well, if he got knifed last week in Amsterdam, I'm not sorry, I don't mind admitting. It'll save me a hell of a lot of trouble."

Van der Valk drank the last drop of his beer and wiped his mouth vulgarly on the back of his hand.

"You've fitted my jigsaw very nicely for me, Mr. Royaard, and I'm glad it's done you some good. No doubt this is your man—I can identify him positively, and the motorbike. He lived up in Limburg, and used to slip over to Germany all the time. I thought of smuggling, but I was looking at the German border—customs there weren't a bit interested. I'd wondered about the fishing and I'd wondered about the motorbike. But the Maas is long—he could have gone fishing in Luxembourg if he'd wanted. I had disentangled him a bit, but you've put it into place."

The eyes crinkled behind the pipe. "Glad to have done you a small service looking after my own interests, Inspector. He's dead and won't worry me any more."

He was back home by ten, and got soup and salad from Arlette. She grated carrots while he undid his shoes slowly, deep in her *Express*. He had got to the book reviews when she came in with the soup.

He never discussed police business with his wife, but he was rather proud of himself at having read the Düsseldorf trick so accurately, and sniggered with his mouth full of carrots. She might easily have something illuminating to say.

"Hey."

"*Ja?*" with a drawl, and her mouth full of bread and butter.

"What would you say was the recurrent theme—say, the obsessive element perhaps—in Simenon?"

She gave one of her rather dusty answers from behind her *Express*. "I should think—am I *twisteuse*, would you say?"

"What is twisteuse?"

"It's a new word—a black jersey frock I rather liked. Described as '*Aguicheuse, voyageuse, twisteuse.*' I wanted to know whether I am sufficiently *twisteuse*—it must be a question of the hips. Really, the Académie is supposed to look after the language. Old parasites, dressed up as Court Chamberlains and all carrying umbrellas. What would Cardinal Richelieu say if he saw these carpet-slipper heroes we have now? … What were you asking? Oh yes…I should say"—judiciously—"the biggest obsession is the pretty young servant girl in the country hotel."

Van der Valk looked blank.

"She has a little black frock and it sticks to her—she's a little bit too *twisteuse*—because she wears nothing underneath. Recurs in every damn book. There's a story there somewhere."

He had to laugh; it was quite true. "No, seriously. Wouldn't you say perhaps the man who runs away, who changes his identity, who finds another world for himself to live in? New name, new life. Think of Monsieur Monde, or Monsieur Bouvet…"

"Or Harry Brown," agreed Arlette, tearing herself away from Madame Express. "Yes, it's true. Why, have you found someone like that?"

"Yes, but he lived both identities together. Changed them over in midweek, in the Central Station in Düsseldorf. Rather remarkable."

"Interesting. Is it someone I'd want to hear about?"

"He was killed."

"Then no, no horror stories please."

"Is there any more soup?"

"I'll get you some... She smells of bed," irrelevantly.

"Madame Express does?" fascinated.

"No no—the servant girl. Most disgusting. Do I smell of bed?"

"Sometimes," grinning.

"How repulsive."

He could not stop laughing.

He shut up about his thoughts. Anyway, she refused to listen to anything with murders in it. But he wondered whether you became a smuggler as a possible consequence of having changed your identity? Or did you change your identity as part of your smuggler's technique? Or were the two ideas quite independent of one another—a possibility if not a likelihood.

Next morning, in the office, Mr. Samson's desk was full of flower catalogues. Van der Valk suspected the old man of having a calendar hidden away and crossing off days as they passed, till the great day.

"I found out about Mister Stam."

"You did? Good boy. I can't make head or tail of this thing, it's all in bloody Latin."

Van der Valk felt he could risk a joke. "Ring up the bureau on the Linnaeusstraat."

"Huh? Well, not a Russian then?"

"Not even German. He was in the butter business, on the Belgian border. Used to go fishing and never used his rod—remember, it puzzled us."

"Didn't puzzle me," infuriatingly. "Only I thought he'd be busy taking photos somewhere. New secret-model public lavatory or whatever. That's what we've got the damn Rijksrecherche boys with their toffee noses for."

"He used to pop over and line up the local poachers. They

walk over the fields on cloudy nights with butter on their backs. Seems these panzer autos we read about are old-fashioned. The customs are mechanized and chase them with smoke grenades and tear gas. They've even got carbines."

"Charming country we live in," deep in a gaudy picture of improbable gloxinias. "Can't make out why the Belgians don't make their own butter cheaper. Carbines indeed. Tom Mix joins the customs…can you prove all this?"

"Yes. The Valkenswaard people have a photo that ties it in."

"Well then, it's easy, isn't it? Chap knocked him off to cut in on the racket, or his own racket was cut in on or what the hell. What does it matter?

"His Excellency will be pleased. Black market, illegal speculation, evasion of excise, half the criminal code broken there. They'll confiscate all his money and they won't care a damn who killed him."

Carefully, Van der Valk produced his ace.

"You don't want to hear what I was doing in Düsseldorf?"

"Not much. I want a report and an expense account. Well, what were you doing then?"

"Stam isn't necessarily Stam at all—he's not even Dutch. In Düsseldorf he kept a set of spare clothes, papers, the lot. Which say he's Belgian and lives in Erneghem. That's a dorp, somewhere outside Ostend." That at least got the old man to put his gloxinias down.

"Which one's real?"

"I want to go to Belgium and find out."

"You want to go to Belgium to find out," heavily. "The Belgians can check his identity."

"They won't tell us why he was killed, though. If we knew why, we'd know who, seems to me."

"I'm not convinced that it's going to be all that important now."

"I'd like to tie the job up. I'm not at all convinced that it had anything to do with the smuggling. Anybody in that business wouldn't have left that auto outside the door like that."

"Look, my boy. I understand you want to see it through; not leave a sloppy job behind you. What I foresee is a considerable amount of trotting about in Belgium, and at the end finding out, after a lot of time and effort, what we know already. I'll mention it to the Hoofd-Commissaris, and if he thinks it necessary to pursue the matter further—very well, go to Belgium. I think he's more likely to agree with me, that, if anything, it's a job the customs people can sort out, and the Belgians can worry over it if they feel inclined. They can have our dossier. Whole thing's nothing but a nuisance and I want to get shut of it."

His Excellency, however, confounded all this by agreeing—for rather different reasons—with Van der Valk. Bloody busybody, thought Mr. Samson with secret malice, which did not show on his functionary's face.

"No no no, Samson, we can't rest on that, however much we'd like to. We'll have to make sure that the man had no other activities. And he may have had associates here—what was he doing in Amsterdam, hm? Drinking champagne, hm? Now, besides, this butter business, I happen to know—for your ears only, Commissaris—is an embarrassment to our government. If we see an opportunity of clearing it up, we mustn't let that slip to the Belgians, hm. Feather in our cap. Cement good relations with our neighbors—good policy, Samson, hm. Yes yes, I know what you'll say, nothing to do with our department. However, you can take that as my decision. Hm?"

"Certainly, Commissaris." The captain is welcome to think the admiral a fool, but he does not argue.

"As you wish, sir. I'll send Van der Valk to Brussels."

"He did well in Düsseldorf, hm. That's as I like things, Samson—no waste of time, no shilly-shallying or expense. Discreet, too, not telling the Germans. How'd he happen on this notion of the double identity?"

"I have no very clear idea, sir," quite unbothered. "But he's a good lad. Bright."

"Good, good, excellent. Glad to have my faith in him confirmed in this way."

His Highness did not believe in official commendation—if one cheapened praise, it only encouraged the staff to be lazy—but a little evidence of good humor, that costs little, hm?

Mr. Samson plodded back, and gave Van der Valk the instructions in a stimulating voice. Like flat soda water, Van der Valk thought, that has stood and gathered dust. Next day he was in Brussels.

That pleasant city presented its usual aspect – sharp commerce and considerable vulgarity, under a patina of medieval bourgeois grandeur. It is sometimes tiresome, he thought, to be in a town that proclaims so unashamedly, "Aren't we rich? You've no idea how nice that is." There were the usual posters of French gangster films. An elderly classical actor, encrusted in bloodshot ferocity and gritty stubble, surrounded by submachine guns, glared at a slut in a torn blouse a step or two below him on a very squalid staircase. Charming.

Van der Valk, who was fond of Brussels in small doses, stopped for a filter coffee on the Adolph Max before strolling back through foggy winter sunlight to his car. He progressed leisurely toward Ostend, not in any hurry. In Erneghem he had lunch and some of that nice lambic beer in "Ma Bicoque." Mr. de Winter, he learned, was hardly ever at home.

"Oh, he drops in every other week or so, but it's Madame who runs the place. A sharp one, that."

The hotel stood on the highway from Ostend to Bruges and Ghent: medium-sized, quite expensive, prosperous; a thriving business. A type of hotel one sees quite frequently—the old building left as a façade because it is "attractive," and modern additions tacked on in every which way. The attractive part was a dignified but ugly block of the eighteen-seventies—a bad time for architecture; Haussmanesque-grandiose. Ponderous but draft-free. The new part, which was frankly hideous, had been built on as an annex since the war and further extended in the last year or two; the new concrete looked cleaner than the old. On neither occasion had there been any effort at architectural merit, dignity, or homogeneity.

As with many hotels of this sort, it was now impossible to tell the front from the back. There was a huge parking lot; round the corner was a long terrace, with bushes in stone urns, a fat heavy balustrade, and chairs of plaited red plastic. He tried the first door and found a dark plushy dining room decorated with enormous rubber plants. After that a lounge, with chandeliers, a mirror, S-shaped loveseats, spindly circular coffee tables, chairs with lions and greenish brocade upholstery—Second Empire grandeur. Everything was gilded; the mirror had belonged to Nana.

He went through into the new part and found a bar, and beyond this the new hotel entrance, with an abominable plastic reception desk and a neon tube above it. This shed a nasty light on hundreds of tourist photographs, two scarlet telephones, and the porter. He was in a uniform, also dating from Napoleon the Third—a sort of frogged frockcoat, like a shady stockbroker. One of Nana's customers, decided Van der Valk. He had a bovine West Flanders look, which rather spoiled the hustling impression. Van der Valk bared his teeth at this porter, who returned the charming smile with rustic suspicion.

"Mr. de Winter please."

"What for? You a traveler?"

"No. I had no idea that was any of your business."

"Well, it's my job."

"Not your job to be rude to callers. Business personal."

"I only meant you couldn't know him well, or you'd know

he's never here except the beginning of the week, Mondays or Tuesdays. Not always then." He seemed to think he had a point.

Van der Valk did consider boxing the oaf's ears, but thought better of it. He understood the mentality of country-hotel porters, and covered a horrible picture of a bell tower with a ten-franc note. The porter smiled amiably.

"Near three weeks since we've seen him, sir." Reflection. "Thought it funny we didn't see him this week." More reflection. "What I reckon would be maybe best, yes, if you've personal business, would be to call Madame. She's upstairs in her flat, but I could ring her."

Van der Valk went into the bar, where he found a lethargic waiter. There was English beer, Hero tonic, rather dubious Scotch, export gin, and strange cognac, in a bottle with an artificially aged label and a fake coat of arms, all at prices he found distasteful. He ordered white wine and cassis, sat down in a discreet corner, and decided against lighting a cigar. He reckoned Madame would not keep him long. Did she know what had happened to Gérard de Winter?

Did she guess? Was she still wondering? Or hadn't she bothered at all?

It is never very easy to get hold of anyone who works in a hotel during the afternoon, because it is the only slack time of the day. They start early in the morning, and get steadily busier right to the end of the luncheon service, and only then does a delicious stillness descend. A hotel manager is up and about by eight. He will have breakfast and maybe glance at the morning paper around nine thirty. He will only have a break and his midday meal at two. Rather reasonably, he then likes to disappear till seven at night, since he will be busy again till nearly twelve. Woe to him who disturbs this afternoon rest.

Madame Solange de Winter, manager and co-director of the Hôtel de l'Univers, was no exception to this rule.

Van der Valk did not know this, or rather he had never

thought it out, or he would have realized. He was accustomed to people who worked and were available during the afternoons; the Spanish siesta habit of hotels had never occurred to him. He thought that Madame might be counting sheets or something; he had no idea that she was in bed.

She was off guard. She had had a good ration of gin and a fairly quiet day; the end of November is not a busy time. As usual, at two thirty she had undressed and gone to bed and was now nine-tenths asleep. There was a problem occupying her, but she was only sucking at it lazily, like a peppermint bull's-eye tucked away behind a wisdom tooth. Not quite knowing what was happening about Gerard was a worry. A small worry, but a worry.

Her bedroom was very comfortable; well heated, overfurnished, luxurious in an ostentatious way, and filled with every self-indulgence she had been able to think of. In a silky, wallowing bed, her delicious cocoon, she lay and replaced Gerard in her mind by daydreams of obscenities. Her Pekinese and her Alsatian were probably doing the same. When the telephone rang she was cross.

"Who is that?...what?...for Monsieur?...what does he look like?...mm...very well, I'll be down." That Bernard was a fool, a stupid dolt. Still, this might be an official; this might be the call she was expecting, had been told to expect. Here was the time to pull herself together and clear her head. She never had difficulty in clearing her head; she was a most competent woman. She was successful because she knew how to discipline as well as to indulge herself.

She got out of bed, irritable but firm in her decision. She never indulged her ill humor. However stupid the staff were, it didn't do to be abusive. They walked out, and not only was it hard to get new ones, not only did one have to train them, but it did the hotel no good if the guests constantly saw new faces. She was sensitive to expediency. She sometimes bullied, but only the old sad horses who were incapable of going, who didn't have anywhere to go. Like poor old Mademoiselle Brantome, the housekeeper, or that old wreck of a Léonie who worked fourteen hours a day in the stillroom, or *le vieux* Billy in the basement.

She felt a tiny seed of doubt and fear; she paced about smoking. Then she calmed herself resolutely, looked at herself in the glass, and massaged her body with love. It would not let her down. Gigi, the Pekinese, who had growled at the telephone, stared at her with globular, careful eyes. Charlemagne rested his chin on the rug, bored. Naked women were no treat to him.

She gargled with mouth wash, not wishing to smell stale, of bed or gin, and sprayed herself with fresh perfume. She did her bending exercises without thinking, six times; her waist was as narrow and supple as when she was nineteen. Her taste in underclothes was deplorable; she dragged on a black bra and violent parma-violet knickers, congratulating herself, as she always did, on her figure. She had never worn a corset in her life. Lucky, never to have had a child. I keep well, she thought, like a good wine with a sound cork.

She put on her working clothes: narrow black frock, rather pale stockings to show off her good legs. High-heeled patent-leather shoes, no jewelry at all but her diamond ring. Her hair was bouffant, youthful. She looked, as always, slim, graceful, active, and charming as she went downstairs.

Van der Valk watched her floating delicately toward him; he could admire her figure when she stopped to speak to the porter. She leaned over to pick up a couple of message forms; he had leisure to observe her through the archway. Her voice, when she arrived, was low and soft, but he could easily believe that it would sharpen in timbre for the occasion. He thought her rather a fine example of the Belgian *commerçante*; even if she got as fat as an oil-tanker her mouth would not alter; about as tender, he thought, and gentle as a football player's right boot. Her eyes were a pale, pretty aquamarine. She would be good-looking if it were not for her nose—it was puggy, *chienne.*

"I am Madame de Winter. My husband is not here at present; can I be of service to you?"

"My name is Van der Valk." He bowed. "I am an inspector of police of the city of Amsterdam."

"Really. You speak good French."

"Your husband is called Gerard de Winter, and owns this hotel, I believe."

"Quite correct. You sound official. What are you drinking, by the way?" She had been right. A moment to get a good grip on herself. "Joseph...another white wine for this gentleman, and a fresh cassis, and—yes, I'll have a white Cinzano."

"No, this isn't official. In the sense that it is not judicial. Informal, shall I say? If it were judicial, it would have been a Belgian officer," watching her carefully. "I am afraid that I am the bearer of bad news."

"What can that possibly be? It's about my husband? You were asking for him."

"I asked for him to see if, by a last faint chance, I might be mistaken." He gave her the photo to look at; it helped to have something in one's hands. "Is that your husband?"

She frowned. "It's certainly like him, but I'm not sure it is him. Will you please explain?"

"The man in that photograph, who carried your husband's papers, is dead."

She looked at him sharply. Carried Gerard's papers? Something queer there, something gone wrong. She stared across the room, puzzled.

"You're from Amsterdam, you said? This happened there? I don't understand. Carried papers? My husband certainly has not been home for a few weeks. But that's not unusual. I can't tell you exactly where he is, but what would he be doing in Amsterdam? This can't be him."

"I understand, Madame, that you can't accept this easily. Unfortunately, there's no longer any doubt. We've taken some trouble over this. This man, we feel quite sure, is Gerard de Winter."

She heard that with mixed feelings. A relief, and yet not a relief. "I recall saying that the photo looked like him. But it looks wrong."

"That could be because it is an official photograph, taken for identity purposes. After he was dead."

Her eyes jumped at him, then again at the picture lying on the black glass table. She seemed to unwind a fraction, then looked at him, very wary.

"There is some mistake. Or something that I do not understand." She wasn't going to be trapped. If Gerard had made a mess of things... "That's not my husband."

"Will you tell me what makes you so sure?" His voice was easy, friendly.

"There's something about these clothes. They don't look right. I've never seen them. I don't think they're his. And the ring. He's wearing his ring on the wrong hand. Directly I looked I knew it wasn't right, somehow." There was triumph in her voice; she hadn't been caught in any conspiracy.

He could have kicked himself. Of course, the Dutch wear their wedding rings on the right hand, but the French on their left. He took off his hat mentally to Mr. Stam, that thorough, careful man. A woman would never miss that detail, but he had. He made his voice gentler still.

"There is a rather odd explanation of that."

Her voice challenged him, edged and abrupt. "Is this some trick? What is the meaning of this?"

"It is certainly a trick. Not us, tricks aren't our line. But your husband was a man for tricks—you didn't know that?"

She suppressed her relief; she hadn't been caught. Gerard had. "We're not even on the same train."

"This trick had a tragic result. I've been wondering whether you could throw any light on it."

She closed her face. "I'm sorry if you've been wasting your time, but on the evidence you've shown me, I cannot accept that that is my husband."

Her face wanted to throw him out; she wants a fight, he thought.

"Oh, more evidence." He poured cassis into his wine. "There is more."

She regarded him steadily, refusing to accept, refusing to be shaken.

"That is a striped suit. My husband detested them, never wore them. Nor did he play games with his wedding ring." She twisted the diamond on her own hand.

He sipped his drink. "Let's accept your word for it, Madame. Good, this is not your husband and I am quite mistaken. Can you suggest a reason why another man, who looks so like him as to deceive anyone—even you only guessed from the clothes—who masquerades as him"—sarcasm in the voice, relish of the word—"who carries his papers, why this man would wear a striped suit and play games with his wedding ring?"

"No. I cannot."

"It doesn't strike you that the explanation is the other way round? Not that a man was masquerading as your husband, but that your husband was pretending to be another man?"

"I don't know why he should do that."

"Evidence...you know we wouldn't decide about something just on the basis of a photograph. Would you recognize your husband's personal possessions? His handwriting?"

"Of course I would. Yes...that is...certainly...his. Monsieur—what has happened?"

"And this?" Stam's little notebook, with the initials and the figures that were understandable now after being in Valkenswaard.

"I've never seen the book before, but the writing is the same."

She was pale and tense under her make-up. That could mean innocence as easily as guilt, no?

"Tell me, tell me, what has happened?"

"I am sorry, but it is as I have told you. Your husband has been found dead in a house in Amsterdam. I am inquiring into this death because it was caused intentionally, by a person or persons unknown, as the English say so scrupulously."

She clenched her hand on her empty glass; the stem broke with a dry little snap. She looked down at her hands, at him, round the room.

"We would like you to tell us anything you can that may help in explaining these matters."

"Yes...I understand." She laid the broken glass carefully in the ashtray. "I think, Inspector, that I will ask you to come to my private rooms. There are too many eavesdroppers in the public rooms of a hotel."

He nodded and stood. Her walk was good; she held herself straight.

Her living room was like her bedroom, which Van der Valk could imagine, looking about him. That elegant silkiness everywhere; he found it detestable. The Pekinese went from horrible growls to shrill barks and back again; the Alsatian bristled.

"No no, children, you must go in the bedroom and keep quiet."

He liked perfume, but here there was too much of it. The Empire furniture was at its grandest here. Like her, it could easily be genuine. That idea amused him. Here he was having a quiet chat with a woman who could be a murderess, and he was thinking about whether the Empire furniture was genuine. But it was not altogether silly. This woman was like the furniture. You might not like it, but it had style and worth.

Her hand made a movement inviting him to sit; the diamond ring caught his eye again, and he was reminded of another analogy that had, perhaps, helped him. This woman was also a diamond. She had contributed to the peculiar life of Gerard de Winter. She had cut some of his facets. He crossed his knees and fixed her with a glassy eye, waiting for her to speak. She had the ball; now let's see her carry it.

"I must take you into my confidence, I see. You will not be satisfied until you know about my relations with my husband.

Yes, smoke if you feel like it. Gauloises? Not for me, thanks, I can't abide them… Yes, I do smoke, but only filters. I don't know quite how to begin. At the beginning, you will say. Very well. I married Gerard when I was a young and inexperienced girl. I am from the country here. I am Ostendaise. My mother is still alive, my father died some few years ago. He had bronchial trouble. He was a hairdresser, the best in Ostend. My mother sold the business after his death; she now lives in a flat in Brussels.

"No, I am the only child left. I had a brother, but he got T.B. during the war. He died in Davos in 'forty-eight.

"Yes, it does look as though the women had the strength of the family. Does that mean anything? Isn't it often the case? You are in Belgium, Inspector. The women run many businesses here.

"Gerard, yes. He was a local figure. I won't say prominent, but known, certainly. I think that he has always lived here, yes, as far as I know. I don't know about wartime; he never spoke of it. But he had had the business since the war, and before that his father owned it. No, I have made the modernizations, but it has always had a good name and done good business.

"The marriage—oh, I will be frank, you will see—was not a success. No, never, right from the start. I don't know what kind of woman he wanted. He was always—withdrawn?—call it what you like. Say it was my fault if you please, I don't care. I am not a housewife, I admit it. Housekeeping bores me stiff. It may have disappointed him that I had no children…he never mentioned it and I never asked him… He has always made a habit of going away…I don't know where, I have not been curious.

"Yes, I suppose he does have other women. You don't believe me? I can't help that. It was our agreement and we both kept it. I would never query or comment on what he did. I haven't spied on him…I wasn't sufficiently interested, perhaps. I had plenty to occupy me…he made me a full equal partner in the hotel, and he left the running of it to me. He knew that was what I wanted. It's what always interested me.

"I'm not ashamed of being a businesswoman—why should I be? I am a good one.

"Certainly, I have doubled the value of this place, turnover, profit, everything. It was always a good building in a good position, yes. But it was terribly old-fashioned—kitchen in the basement, plumbing all over the place. Now every room has its private shower, and the kitchen is modern from one end to the other. Those details mean nothing to you, possibly, but I am a professional hotelier and proud of it. And known as such.

"Yes, he tended gradually to go away more often, and for longer. This last year, I've hardly seen him. But he would be fair; he would take my place when I wanted a break or even a holiday. I want to be fair too; he was not mean. I have no complaint against him, and we have never quarreled.

"Would you like tea?" she asked suddenly. "I've ordered some sent up."

"Was he secretive, though?" asked Van der Valk. "You didn't ask, but he hid—or did he?—what he did, where he went, who he saw?"

"That was his right. I do know, vaguely, that he spent a lot of time in Germany. I assumed, without his ever saying so, that he must have a woman somewhere. But as for what he did—I have no idea."

"I appreciate your being open. It helps us greatly."

"But I have nothing to hide. Though I don't think I'm bound to answer any questions about my private life."

"You aren't bound to answer anything at all. But if you didn't, and I wasn't satisfied, there might be a judicial inquiry set on foot. Police, mandates, the examining magistrate possibly, clerks taking everything down—you notice that I'm writing nothing. You would quite likely get the press as well. By answering everything freely now, you will probably avoid a process that might bring disagreeable publicity and even do your business harm."

"Do you think I haven't realized all that?" she said coolly. "I only act in my own interests."

"Yes," he said.

"You still have more questions?"

"A few. Inoffensive, but perhaps indiscreet."

"As you have seen, that is not one of the things that bother me greatly."

The tea tray was brought in and she served. She had made a good recovery. Was it, then, only the initial shock, the hearing of a sudden death, that had unnerved her? She was oddly impersonal about this dead man now. He might have been a total stranger to her. Her heart was completely armored, yes, but by egoism alone? Or, in addition, by the self-control and dramatic skill of the accomplished woman criminal? Could she really feel no loss at all? She was feeding the Pekinese cake out of her saucer. What would she do if one of the dogs—her children—got killed?

"When was it last, about, that you slept with your husband?"

"Three years. Four perhaps. I didn't write the date in my diary."

"During wartime, you lived in Ostend?"

"Yes. I was no more than a child, really."

"And he was here?"

"The hotel was, I think, requisitioned. I seem to remember hearing that he went into the maquis, or at least that he was involved with the local resistance."

"He took no further interest in the hotel after turning it over to you?"

"He never was greatly interested; he had no feeling for it ever. He knows the work, of course. He is able to check the books, all that goes on here."

"But if I have understood correctly, you make the major decisions as well as having the heavier responsibility?"

"Certainly. I planned every detail of the new buildings

with the architect, and arranged all the financing, everything. I saw the builder every day. He only had to sign a few papers."

"Doesn't it seem unfair that you have only half the profit?"

She smiled at the little pitfall. "It has. I have thought the same. But it was a reasonable price to pay for freedom."

"Freedom of action. Not freedom to live as you wished. You never wished for a divorce, for example?"

"No. I am at liberty to do as I please. Remarrying has no appeal for me."

"But the hotel remains his property?"

"Yes."

"And is yours now? What arrangement was made, in the event of his death?"

The clear aquamarine eyes were level and untroubled now. "I've been waiting for you to ask that. The financial interest in a death. Isn't that the policeman's obsession?"

"Money and sex are most people's obsessions," cheerfully. "Policemen are no exception."

"The truth is simple. I become sole owner. If you wish to conclude that I had something to gain by Gerard's death, I cannot prevent you."

"You said that he went away but that you never had the interest to find out more."

"I said it and I'll confirm it. I'm not ashamed of it."

"There is a difference between interest and curiosity. I ask these questions out of interest—I wouldn't do so out of curiosity. I admit that you had no interest; I might find it more difficult to believe that you never had any curiosity. Never, ever."

She considered the point, unflustered. "I suppose I felt curious, sometimes. I don't think I showed it. What good would it have done me?"

"I should think that you could have satisfied it without showing it."

"What do you mean? That I would follow him? That I

was jealous? Not at all." Contempt in her voice. For Gerard? For him, the stupid policeman? Or for other women, those who did feel jealous of their men, their husbands?

"Not necessarily. You have the figures of the business at your disposal?"

"I see what you're getting at. Did he take money?"

"For example."

"Certainly not more than he had a right to. The net profits can be calculated. The accountant does it. The two halves are banked separately. No question of his taking more."

"You have told me you were not jealous. The picture I get is of a man who was not jealous either. Is that correct?"

"Perfectly correct. We did not interfere in each other's lives."

"He showed no interest in your emotional life?"

"Why should he? He had his own, I imagine."

"He was normally sexed?"

"Is there any such thing?" coolly.

"No," grinning. "Lawyers like to pretend there is."

"I suppose he was."

"I can ask you the same question?"

"You're bound to show an interest." She had a remarkable calm. Too much calm. "You'd find out easily, I suppose. I prefer to answer rather than having you rummaging about among the staff."

"Exactly."

"Then I will tell you that yes, I do have lovers."

"Several?"

"I don't know what you call several, Inspector."

"I don't know either. What I meant was together? One at a time? Do they last long, or is there a high rate of mortality?" He was beginning to assume the unconscious, brutal joviality he sometimes showed in examining a person he suspected of a crime.

"I like the way you put things; it's charming."

"I'm not a moralist. Or a jurist. I merely assemble facts. If I

ask, for instance, whether they are local people or strangers or both,
I simply want to know. I haven't any morbid, obscene interest."

"The simplest answer, then, is to tell you that they are tem-
porary, casual meetings, mostly with guests in the hotel. There
is very little emotion involved."

"If you like a man, you sleep with him."

"I generally wait for him to ask me," almost gaily.

"And you don't particularly make a secret of it?"

"Chambermaids know everything," indifferently. "And for
that reason I do not care to get overintimate with the neighbors
or the local people. This is a village and they all gossip. I let
them gossip, but I don't cause local scandals."

"And your husband did not bother to listen to the gossip of
chambermaids?"

"I should have been most surprised if he had; it would be
most unlike him. He knew all about me." Very good answer, he
thought.

Really she was as efficient—and about as lovable—as a trench
mortar. He would try a last throw at penetrating this armor.

"You don't like emotional involvements, do you?"

"No."

"What does involve your emotions? Your dogs?" He had
not seen the bedroom but he made a guess. "Your own good
looks? Your possessions? The well-filled linen cupboard of Ostendaise tradition?"

His tone stung her. Blood showed in her face. She did not
answer; her hands went to the big silver table lighter and clicked it
irritably several times. She might have wished it were the action of
a gun, he thought, pleased, and pressed his little advantage.

"Are you so afraid, then, of emotions? They are quite normal things to have."

She refused to be discountenanced; she had herself again
under control. "I am exactly like many thousands of women, Inspector."

"I can't say I agree, you know. I'm not trying in the slightest to be rude, but I find you unusually efficient, and perhaps ruthless."

"I see that I have given you the impression of a very cold and calculating woman, Inspector. I seem to give most people that idea. I don't see it myself. What is so extraordinary about having common sense and being businesslike? But I was good friends with my husband. I am sorry, really sorry that he is dead. I want to ask how he came to die. I care. Can you understand that, or are you, too, so prejudiced?" Me too, he thought. This is a woman who has no friends, whom nobody trusts, whom nobody will ever love, and therefore a little tragic.

"I cannot answer that yet, Madame. You will still have to be patient a little while. Your husband died under circumstances that aren't yet explained. When they are, you will hear, I promise. Meanwhile I should like to ask you—I don't think you should find it too difficult—to go on living and acting exactly as when your husband was alive. Just common sense."

"Yes." She had to accept. Had she not boasted of her indifference, of her control? If necessary, thought Van der Valk, I could put so much pressure on this woman's nerves that she would snap like a dry stick. Bah, these females who have no emotions—they have not the suppleness of a normal woman. They have no reserves of love, of warmth, of courage. They have nothing but their lousy cold blood. To me, they are zero. He could not help disliking this woman. Believing her guilty of a crime was another matter.

He walked out of the hotel indifferently, as though he was perfectly satisfied. She could easily be a criminal, he thought. The cool ones—wasn't it often the cool ones, the well-organized ones, with their lives wound round and buckled like a belt, despising emotion, who one gay day saw their lives explode and emotion turn round and claw them?

He drove a little way to avoid the curious eyes that, by now,

Erneghem would have trained upon him, and stopped to look at his road map. It was quite interesting—here he was following the path that de Winter had driven, week after week, and then month after month. Which way did he go?

Sometimes, no doubt, he would have gone north, toward the border, to make his little arrangements. Which way did he drive? Along the coast? Hardly. It was a boring drive, and one had to skirt the Wester Scheldt and then along the border north of Antwerp. He doubted whether de Winter ever came that way. The roads are less good, and the country dismal to a man who loved the woods and waters of Limburg.

More likely, he went straight on, the way Van der Valk himself had come, along the fast motor road through Bruges and Ghent to Brussels. And when he went to Germany he could go along the Liege road out toward Aachen and Cologne. He thought about the black Peugeot, and started to drive in its track, meditating.

What had he found in Belgium, then—apart from a promising suspect? He would have to think about the widow de Winter. He had no idea still why Meinard Stam should have bought a white Mercedes or a house in Amsterdam. The widow presumed he had a woman somewhere, and he believed that. Because the widow's story was certainly true—as far as it went. The man who had married the smart, pretty hairdresser's assistant from Ostend had very soon realized that she was long on business sense but short on affection. He had waited to see if she became pregnant, a physical change and growth that might warm and ripen that arid character. When she did not, he had cut his losses. Where in the course of the history had he found, and slipped on as though it were an old overcoat, the personality of Meinard Stam? How had he stepped into the even more careful and exclusive company of the butter smugglers? In these surroundings he had found a personal life—could one say an emotional life?—that he had lacked. Had it been enough? Had it satisfied a

romantic spirit? A man like that, with a need for emotional outlet, had found something like happiness in the woods and fields
perhaps. But had that continued to satisfy? Might he not have
come to long to share, to confide, to give? Had not his life, too,
perhaps come to appear arid and pointless without a woman?
The romanticism of a Ruritanian shooting lodge might easily
become a thin cardboard affair, concluded Van der Valk.

De Winter had behaved sensibly. He had not misjudged
his wife a second time. The pact, for instance, that would have
seemed unthinkable to Arlette, say, had appeared reasonable and
natural to him because it was logical and sensible to Solange. He
would have lost confidence in women. It might have been a long
time before he could again bring himself to trust one, to yield to
the need for one. But if he had yielded, it would be with a bump.
The surrender would be total, an infatuation.

Van der Valk was nearing Brussels. He could get the civil
servants here to look up de Winter's family and origins, but it
was not, he guessed, really necessary. He was certainly what he
claimed to be—a man who had lived in a small place virtually
all his life. There would be people still alive who remembered
his father.

At some time, during the war presumably, he had become
acquainted with the border. Maquisard formation, doubtless. It
had laid a groundwork for later ideas. Not only useful knowledge and contacts when it came to smuggling butter, but the
idea of living in a hide-out in the woods, dear to this kind of
character. Somewhere during the war, de Winter, an ideal type,
probably, with his romantic ideals and his imaginative courage
for resistance work, had met a man called Stam. Something of
an age, with some—at least—physical resemblance, and perhaps
an affinity. The Dutch army officer and the Belgian hotelkeeper
had been friends. De Winter had learned enough of Stam's past.
Then Stam had perished, leaving no trace. Had been deported
to Germany, there to perish—with his family, perhaps—under

night and fog. Or had simply been killed in an affray. Either way there had been no witnesses, and de Winter had seen a chance to acquire false papers that might at any moment be very useful. He had kept them. It had occurred to him, two, three, four years later, to use them. When he had met the baron, and given the name of Stam, it must have been a shock to realize that here was someone who could pierce his alias, but the baron, already old, forgetful, and capricious, had not recalled the features of a man who had been a very young officer when he was already a colonel. And from a danger the baron had become the greatest asset, an invaluable reference to make the alias above all suspicion. Who would query the baron's word that this was an officer and a gentleman?

The system of fast motor roads approaching Brussels makes this city unusually easy of access. From the direction of Ostend, for instance, one hurtles into the suburb of Berchem, and the autostrade meets the Chaussée de Gand, the old highway, at the Avenue Charles Quint. The Chaussée de Gand itself goes straight to the heart of the old town, at the Porte de Flandre. Here there is a system of ring boulevards that turns around the town and brings one out to continue hurtling south toward Namur. Or from the Porte de Flandre one can enter the majestic town, up to the Place de la Bourse and all those monuments to bourgeois pride that had witnessed also the Joyous Entry of the Emperor Charles the Fifth.

The Emperor has also given his name to the boulevard that leaves the autostrade going east, skirting round the north edge of the old town. Here too it is very simple for the driver. If he turns left at the Porte d'Anvers, he will continue to hurtle out through Vilvorde on the main road to Antwerp. It was this road that Van der Valk intended to take, and it was this road, probably, that Gerard de Winter had taken, north through Mechelen to his haunts along the border. Every month at least, to keep track of his pickup and delivery services, to make his payments and keep all his personnel on their toes. To keep the machine oiled and smooth, the warning system sensitive.

The driver can go on, also, and turn right a little later, at the Porte de Schaerbeek. Without ever stopping hurtling, he finds himself headed out toward Louvain, on the main road to Liège and the German border.

There is no town in Europe through which one can drive with greater speed and ease. It is very handy for Europe's new technical bureaucrats.

Van der Valk's mind was far away, but just outside Brussels he glanced at his dashboard long enough to register that he was low on gasoline. Plenty of garages round here. Just ahead, surely, handily placed for the fork to the Chaussée de Gand, there was a big one. Yes, there it was. There was an outside bay with automatic pumps, for night work and people in a tearing hurry. He wanted the inside bay, with operated pumps and service. Oil, air, polish; maps, lavatories, paper cup of coffee; have it washed while you wait and we'll check the windshield wipers free. He didn't want washing while he waited, but he did want a chit for his thirty litres—it went on the expense account.

He stared heavily through the windshield while the girl filled his tank. He noticed butcher-blue overalls outlining a very pleasant bottom, but he was too distracted to take any interest. It was not till he had to pay her that he woke up, saw a tall blonde who looked familiar, and recognized Lucienne Englebert.

It cheered him an hour later, on the dreary stretch north to the border. It took his mind off his thoughts; they were beginning to go round and round and bore him. He had ended up a little—more than a little—disgusted with Solange de Winter, and nobody could have been more of a contrast than Lucienne. She had matured, obviously, but she had not changed. She still had her contempt for money and her hatred of trade, her pride and her lack of vanity. Yes, she had meant it then, that remark about earning her living as an oil-pump girl. What was more, she was still doing it, undiscouraged.

He had thought her remarks childish, but on forcing his mind back to their last meeting—yes, in the Vinicole on the Leidsestraat—they had had something more than only immaturity. What was the word? Quixotic? In any case, rather nineteenth century. Romantic, yes. Very romantic, a pleasant quality in this dreary world. She had always reminded him of his favorite nineteenth-century heroine, the dashing Mathilde de la Mole. Who was capable, remarked Stendhal, of loving a man "who has done more than give himself the trouble of being born." Lucienne had that. She had, too, something of the soul of another nineteenth-century figure, Danton. Who, the night before he died, remarked, "The verb to guillotine, you notice, cannot be conjugated in the past tense. One does not say 'I have been guillotined.'" That remark, ever since, had been Van der Valk's own passport to courage.

She had seemed quite glad to see him; they had spent three or four minutes on pleasantries. She looked well; open air suited her. Her face was less chubby, older, marked by fingers of experience. It added to her good looks.

"What are you doing here?" she had asked without curiosity.

"Oh, something that tied up with a job I'm doing," vaguely.

"How's Amsterdam? Built the Ij tunnel yet? No, of course."

"Don't you read the papers?"

"French papers, mister. We aren't Flemish here; what do we care about your farmers' affairs?"

He grinned at that. "But I notice that you all still eat our butter."

She had frowned. It seemed to irritate her. "Butter," she said sharply, "thanks very much, I use olive oil and I eat dry bread. Keep your stinking butter."

He had disregarded it. One never knew nowadays what would upset the Belgians. Well, she was like all people who went to live in foreign countries—they become more Roman than the

Romans, and will not hear a word in favor of their own land. Was she still sensitive, then, to the old wound, and still thinking that Holland was the enemy of liberty and promise? Of youth, and the right to say what you liked, and the pursuit of happiness? Well, sometimes it was. But so were all countries.

At home he found that Arlette had yielded to one of her recurrent compulsions and had changed all the furniture around. Recently he—and she—had wanted to seize the chance of exchanging their big, old-fashioned, tatty apartment for a new house, but when she saw how small the rooms were she had refused.

"We'd have to buy lots of new things and we can't afford to waste the money." She preferred to spend it on records, books, holidays in France. Well, so did he. They had stayed in the old apartment. To make the furniture look new, as she called it, she would change the position of everything. Sometimes these arrangements were a success. She was standing in the doorway when he came in, a hammer in her hand, looking critically at the big studio couch that would never have fitted in the little new house.

"The angle's right, but shouldn't it be a bit farther back?" He forgot, mercifully, all about Solange de Winter and Lucienne Englebert. At least he had a home and a woman of his own.

It took him some time to go to sleep; Arlette was snoring slightly and he pushed her behind with indignation. Arlette was often an annoying woman, but she had a talent for making money go a long way, for making a home pleasant, for imaginative housewifery. Her food, her clothes, her house were original; she had excellent taste, of a very pragmatic sort. One didn't mind her rages and her sulks, her forgetfulness and casualness, and her prejudice against the Dutch and cauliflowers. She was getting rather fat; she would have to stop overeating. But how nice to be married to this born homemaker, and not to a bitch like Solange de Winter. He dared say he would have run away too. It was better to be an inspector of police, and by no means rich, and have a home full of warmth and affection, of flowers and music and pieces of cheese long gone dry (that Arlette could never bear to throw away).

Sitting in his office over his report the next day, he wished there were some way of hammering that woman. But alas, there was no question of bringing her in and harassing her, not even of having her watched. Not much point in that anyway; the kind of surveillance he wanted would need to be inside her head. She could be picked up, even in Belgium, but only Samson could authorize that. As head of the department he was an officer of justice and could sign warrants and mandates—but the old man would do no such thing, he knew well. Still, he could not resist a pious hint in his report. Mr. Samson, of course, was disagreeable about the whole idea.

"No no, boy, picking her up would be impossible. Creates a scandal; have to ask the Belgians—out of the question without a moral certainty, and you're very far off that. You're probably right in saying she's capable of anything, but that's no earthly good. No harm in leaving her where she is; she won't run away. She doesn't know how much we know, or what we're doing about it, and as long as she doesn't know, she'll wait to see which way the cat jumps.

"Trouble is you've no evidence to prove she knew Stam. I've told you already, you're being pigheaded, boy. You're worrying about de Winter—I'd rather you concentrated on Stam. Who is, remember, an entirely different person. That's the difficulty if you like, here. It was Stam who was killed. Not de Winter."

"But when we are able to prove that Stam was de Winter…"

"Not the point. You have to prove she knew it first."

"Could squeeze her a bit, because it wouldn't surprise me that she did know it."

"Not on your life. Find some evidence that puts her in touch with Stam, on Dutch soil, and you can have all the mandates you please. However, it's opening up. Got someone in Valkenswaard looking into that end of it?"

"Yes. Every known or suspected contrabandist who might have had contact with Stam."

"That's where we'll find the answer,"

He didn't agree. He thought it was damn stupid. What leverage had one there? Nobody had ever seen Stam with a pound of butter. A moral certainty that Stam was a smuggler didn't help. And he certainly had no certainty, moral or otherwise, that Stam had been killed after a fight over loot. Who would have driven—in Stam's car—to Amsterdam, knifed him, and walked out, leaving the car in the middle of the road?

He didn't like any of the other theories either. He didn't see Stam as a blackmailer—one of the early notions. No, that was all wishful thinking. Just because the authorities liked the idea, and it would please the Belgians, and save money.

His own theory was not much good. He didn't really believe that the widow de Winter had killed her husband. Too weak. Possible, but Samson had pointed out the flaw. Could she have followed through the cutout in Düsseldorf, through to Venlo, thence to Amsterdam? Nothing explained the white car, just as nothing explained the house in the Apollolaan.

The hell with Stam. He had battered his head against those walls long enough. The car, the cigarettes, the picture, the champagne, the knife, the spare bed—if only he knew more, just a little more, about Gerard de Winter.

Now that the widow knew they suspected murder, what would she do? She could have killed him. She could have done everything. She might have left all sorts of things lying about as false trails, to point to other people. What other people?

He got the reports that morning of weary hours spent in Valkenswaard, and as he had expected, it was all sawdust. Weary hours of sawing had produced page after page of rubbish. Take this one, the scrap merchant, the suspected contrabandist, the man who had been photographed having a drink with Stam outside the café Marktzicht. The only halfway hopeful lead they'd had.

Query: You did business with Stam?
Answer: Didn't even know his name.
Q. I didn't ask whether you knew his name. I asked if you did business with him.
A. No, I didn't.
Q. How did you come to be drinking with him?
A. I'm a sociable man.
Q. It's your habit to drink with strangers?
A. It's my habit to drink with anyone who asks me.
Q. Why did he ask you?
A. Must have been feeling lonely.
Q. He approached you?
A. If you like.
Q. In what terms?
A. He said good day and chatted.
Q. Chatted about what?
A. Fishing, for instance.
Q. Are you such a great fisherman too?
A. I never miss a chance to meet new people. Might turn out business.
Q. And in this case it did, didn't it?
A. I'm a scrap merchant, not a fishmonger.
Q. You declare then that you never saw him before?
A. I may have seen him. I didn't give it any thought.
Q. Give it thought now.
A. I've told you; I may have seen him.
Q. You think that a safe answer—in case we have evidence of further meetings between you?
A. I don't care what you've got. Talking to strangers isn't against any law I know of.

Q. Been in Venlo recently?
A. Not for years.
Q. Let's come to the fourth of this month...

This sort of thing could go on for weeks—reading it, Van der Valk could almost believe it had. No, the truth lay in Brussels. Somewhere.

The telephone rang on his desk, and he grinned at hearing Charles van Deyssel's very beautiful, rather affected-sounding Dutch.

"That you, at last. Charles here. Oh my God, what a relief. I've had, I do believe, every policeman in Amsterdam on the line. I've been trying to reach you since yesterday. Listen, are you still interested in that Breitner picture you showed me?"

"Sure."

"Well, so am I. What's happened to it, or what will happen to it?"

"We've discovered no relations—that is to say, no really legal relations. Anyway the man was a criminal. A smuggler—that's defrauding the state, and all property is liable to confiscation."

"Who confiscates it?"

"When the inquiry is over, the ministry does."

"So the picture will be for sale?"

"I should think so. It's no good to them."

"Could you put me in touch with the officials of this ministry?"

"I can tell you how to go about it, at least. Probably be glad of an offer. Mostly these confiscated things end up going for auction."

"Well, I want it. And I deserve it. I've done a tremendous piece of detection for you."

"You have?"

"That picture was bought in Brussels."

"Ah." Long, satisfied breath.

"You don't sound sufficiently surprised."

"I'm never surprised; I'm a detective."

"Well, you should, occasionally, be astounded."

"So I am, but not now. It is logical, you see. You couldn't possibly have known that, Charles, so it's very clever of you. Now tell."

"In some extraordinary way the picture was never valued. It was the property of some lousy bourgeois—and don't ask me how that came about—who didn't think anything of it. Thought it a crude rubbishy thing and put it in the attic. The sort that prefers oleos of the Route de Middelharnis, wouldn't you know it, a huge one over the dining-room sideboard. God, how that picture bores me..."

"Now, Charles, stick to the point. No prejudices now."

"Oh yes. Well, after his widow finally burst from years of overeating, a whole huge houseful of hideous objects came up for the saleroom. The very worst—you know, massive marble and mahogany, and of course nobody bids for that, in fact nobody gave it all more than a passing glance; they're tearing their hair now. So it all went to the junkshops. Classic story, isn't it?" with relish.

"Why?"

"Ha. Well, one of the colossal excitements of picture dealing is that it is still possible for these dreadful people, who will take anything in settlement of a debt—they never, by any chance, buy anything, and they never can bear to throw anything away—to possess things of real value that, being themselves colossally ignorant and piglike peasants..."

"Charles, you're gibbering."

"They sometimes have lost Leonardos. I mean that one never really knows in what circumstances a lost or even completely unknown picture—even a real beauty—may appear. The fascinating thing is that there's a firm called Coremans, right there in Brussels, and not long ago a completely unknown Rembrandt self-portrait turned up. They specialize in authentications, and they've just certified it as real. It's been passed by Lugt in Paris and Rosenberg in America, and now it's been bought by the Municipal Museum in Stuttgart for three and a half million, and they were all congratulating themselves. Of course a Breitner isn't worth a quarter of that, but even so they missed it and I didn't, so I go ha ha ha."

"But how did you find all this out?"

"Aha, a man actually in the picture business saw this gorgeous thing in the junkshop; that's why they're kicking themselves. That's the great drawback of overspecialization; he doesn't know a damn thing outside the seventeenth century. Not his period, therefore he despises impressionists. Well, so do I often—all those horrible green Cézannes, so vulgar. But they're greatly sought after and worth vast sums—and therefore I make it my business to know something about them. If it had been some boring old Abraham Pijnacker, he'd have been jumping all over the street, but this he just sneered at. He's quite right in a way, because these impressionists are easy to fake, and very often they are faked. The number of false, smeary, vile Renoirs there are in the world you have no idea."

"Continue, Charles. You're the world's worst witness. By this time the judge would be picking his nose in an attack of nervous frenzy. Only Officers of Justice are allowed to be so emotional and to talk so much."

"Well, I called him names, asked where he'd seen it—he recognized it, you see, from the photo you'd given me. So I whizzed over to this fleamarket to find where they'd got it from. Very nasty, disagreeable people who smelled as they can only smell in Brussels. They said they couldn't remember who bought it. But I refused to be deterred; I even thought of a small mean bribe for these small mean bastards…"

"Listen, you're killing me. It was bought by a Belgian businessman, called de Winter, who, oddly enough, is identical with our dead friend, Mister Meinard Stam."

"Now fall in it," said Charles in horrid glee. "It was bought by a woman."

Electricity shot through Van der Valk.

"And can they describe this woman?"

"No, of course not, but I thought you'd be interested."

"I am. Oh, yes, I am."

At the border again, fitting his mind to being in Belgium again, thinking in French instead of in Dutch, he told himself that this was a technique, now he came to think of it, that de Winter had brought to a high pitch of perfection. It couldn't have been all that easy. In Belgium of course he had spoken French. Ostend is in West Flanders, and they are bilingual there, but French is the language that comes to them first. De Winter had thought and acted as a French-speaking Belgian. No strain—he was one.

But in Holland he had acted, and spoken, and made himself think as a Dutchman. Not an ordinary Dutchman, though. That was the heart of it. He probably could never have made the deception complete. A border Dutchman. Stam had been born on the border, in Maastricht, and there in Limburg or in South Brabant the Dutch is far from pure. The whole thing rested on the fact that the border between Belgium and Holland is a fantasy, a political invention. There is only one real border, between Belgium and Germany; that is the Maas. And between Belgium and Holland the real border is where the people cease to be Catholic and become Protestant. Neither the Maas nor even Arnhem is at all Dutch in character. Not Dutch as Utrecht, or Haarlem, or Zwolle, is Dutch. Stam—or de Winter—would have been a conspicuous foreigner in Alkmaar; in Venlo or Breda he was unnoticed.

Nevertheless he had engineered the transformation with great care. The French car changed for a German one, the typically Belgian clothes for others that at a glance were cut in Groningen, the cigarettes for cigars—Willem II, made in Valkenswaard, a very pretty touch.

His urban, Belgian hotelier's personality, which was not really natural to him, exchanged for one more congenial—the country gentleman, the retired officer devoted to field sports. Lastly, his wedding ring had gone on to the other hand—that was symbolic, the seal on the whole change. When that rested on his right hand, he no longer had to act as though he were Dutch—he was Dutch. He was Stam. He thought as Stam would think. And there was the crux of the affair.

Stam had been killed. Stam had bought the white Mercedes. Had instructed the cleaner to keep the spare bed made up.

Samson had been right and he had been wrong. It was not de Winter who had done these things, and therefore nothing would be known about them in Erneghem. If there was a woman, another woman, she had belonged to Stam. She would not be a Belgian woman; she would be Dutch.

Not necessarily. She might be neither. Where did she live?

The Breitner picture had been bought in Brussels. Did she live there? Not very likely that she could have met Stam in Brussels—Stam never went farther afield than Düsseldorf. Well, we shall see.

Outside the junkshop it said, in faded purple paint on an ordure-brown background: "Antiquarian and bookseller. Picture dealer and restorer." A legend that had been there since Louis-Philippe. Underneath, in the script of 1919, was added: "Contents of houses bought and valued." And two fly-specked, yellowed cards stood in the window. One said: "Gold and silver bought at keenest cash prices." The other, simply: "Wardrobes bought."

On the window glass were pasted witty mottoes, in cheap blunt print on pink and baby-blue postcards. One of these said: "If you're so clever, why the hell aren't you rich?" Another said: "Slow for a brunette, reverse for a blonde, brake hard for a redhead." Van der Valk thought that Charles van Deyssel would not really have known how to handle these people.

The inside of the shop was like all such shops. Stuffed lizards peered into bad copies of Dresden teapots; art-nouveau chairs from the roaring twenties found themselves, resigned and unastonished, jammed under the Biedermayer writing table they had found comic in their carefree youth. He was reminded of the admirable English phrase that expresses hatred, ridicule, and contempt: "I wouldn't be found dead in a ditch with you."

Now they were.

The windows were even worse. Pink Chinese dragons leered at dead pheasants; Ashanti masks, which should have been masculine and terrible, lay sad and castrated on a bad eighteen-sixty copy of a Regency escritoire. The yellow cheese dish apparently carved out of soap, distorted into resemblance of a dead and bloated cow; the sugar tongs with brass showing under the cheap tarnished electroplate; the verdigris-green soup tureen with handles made of a murdered child's arms; the hateful water jug, white and flabby, covered in blowsy, bleary roses—all were of an ugliness, a uselessness, a beastliness that would sour the strongest stomach.

They certainly sour mine, thought Van der Valk. I cannot even guess at the purpose of nine-tenths of these objects. Look at that—is it to keep peacock feathers in or to wash one's feet?

The owner of the junkshop was a thin dyspeptic man in a gray dustcoat. His face was folded in thin folds of the same gray, threadbare and dirty as a worn army blanket. His hair, his hands, his painful shoes, all had the same gray and dusty texture.

His wife was a contrast. She was a big, sloppy blonde with extraordinary white skin that had never known sun or wind or rain. Her flabby figure was crammed into a youthful green frock; her eyes were large, pale and protruding. She resembled some water creature, bleached and soaked to whiteness by years of submersion under deep salt water. One day, greatly to its surprise, it was dredged up, and dumped, still in its primeval silt, in the center of Brussels.

She could only exist, thought Van der Valk, in this dim aquarium of an atmosphere. Scarcely any light penetrated to the curtained, shadowed back of the shop, and less air, and there this couple sat. Endlessly drinking tea off a hideous round table of inlaid brass, which had come from Birmingham workshops at the time of the Indian Mutiny. Now it stood, absurdly, in Brussels instead of in Cheltenham.

The man, he decided, was totally ossified, the woman liquefied. Her face is that of a balloon, filled with stale soapy water, which has probably stood…no no. Remember what Colette said, *"Pas de littérature."*

He felt for Charles. The smell was of incense, dirt, and brass polish. If these people made a living, it could only be through petty crime and pettier vice.

The woman stared at him with her stupefied mouth, still wet with tea. The man's eyes were sharp, under brows like the bars on a workhouse window. Van der Valk entered with a jaunty look, and sank his voice to a nasty whisper.

"Any books?"

"Certainly."

"Good books—you know, a bit peppery."

The little eyes scrutinized him. "You're a copper."

Van der Valk smiled happily. "Right first guess."

"What you want?"

"I want to know all about the picture. Who bought it and exactly what she looked like."

"You're a funny copper. You ain't Bruxellois, neither. French, ain't you?"

"I'm André Renard," in a sudden bellow, "come for the contributions. Now stop fooling, or I'll throw that misbegotten iguana through the window and let in a little fresh air."

The voice began to squeak. "Nothing doing. It was bought and sold in honest trade. It wasn't stolen and it wasn't never signaled."

"You slipped up. It's worth money."

"Then it's worth money to know where it went, ain't it?"

"You tried that one on yesterday. It didn't wash. Don't get funny, little man. You could find your business closed. You could have a fire, and it could be the insurers wouldn't pay."

"Look, Officer, I told that Dutch chap with the fancy accent"—he cherished this description of Charles van Deyssel—"that I couldn't remember what she looked like, and that's the honest truth."

"How often have you been prosecuted?"

"Never, but the…"

"Any histories of flagellation in the house? Any snappy stories?"

"Mister—I—honest…"

"Do better than that."

"Fornicate and sodomite all coppers. Skins of cows."

"That's better. Memory's worth more than honesty, huh? You haven't that many customers and you remember them all well; there could be blackmail money in every single one. Now—young or old?"

"Far's I remember, young."

"Dark or blonde?"

"Don't know."

"Hat or scarf?"

"Some sort of beret."

"Then you saw her hair. You want trouble?"

"Blonde."

"Height?"

"Maybe five foot ten."

"You notice real good, when you want to. You're sure she was that tall?"

"Pretty near."

"Age?"

"Twenty-three, four."

"What language she speak? French?"

"Yeh. Near as good as you," spitefully.

"What she say?"

"Just pointed to that picture—it was in the window—and put the money on the counter."

"How d'you know she spoke French then?"

"Because the bitch took the picture, and going out she said, 'You didn't know it was a good one, did you?'" There was a ghost of parody of an educated woman in the vicious mouth; he was like some desiccated old rattlesnake. The memory of how he had missed easy money was so corrosive that he had not forgotten an intonation. Plainly it had been true—it had been a good picture. What was that dealer doing asking about it—and now this copper? He had not been fooled into telling any lies.

"What clothes did she wear?"

"Red raincoat. Didn't see no more. It was only a street in Bruges or somewhere. Didn't look antique. I've made good money on pictures; I know about them. This didn't look any good—only put it in the window because it was showy, sort of. It was only there two days."

Van der Valk had lit a cigar to act as a disinfectant; he blew a protective fan of smoke. He thought this wood louse was telling the truth now, but he would test the tale a bit.

"So I know, maybe, how you'd recognize this woman. Now, how would I recognize her?"

The eyebrows worked with effort, thinking how to get out of it.

"Come on, pithecanthropus," said Van der Valk, like Captain Haddock.

The eyebrows blinked, floored by the terrible word.

"No way, except from hearing her talk. Spoke French a bit fancy. Like I say, not like a Bruxelloise. More like you."

Van der Valk went to a café and drank brandy. He took an evening paper and glanced through it without enthusiasm. A sort of disgusted lassitude was possessing him. He was sick of real life; he sympathized with Stam.

Perhaps because of this, he found himself looking at movie advertisements. Tripe. Tripe. More tripe. A little one caught his eye. Well, he would be damned.

There he was, wanting peace, and beauty, and to remember his childhood. Wanting romance, like Stam. And there it all was waiting for him, the pure vintage of nineteen thirty-four. Charles Boyer and Greta Garbo in *Marie Walewska*. He slammed coins on his saucer. He had just time, if he hurried.

Better. Rested, cleansed. Happy—yes, happy. He belonged to the generation that would have cheerfully laid down their lives for Garbo. He went and ate *choucroute* in a brasserie, still possessed by the film. It was raining, not a greasy winter rain, but a soft, springlike rain that washed everything clean. Even the neon lights it made blurred, romantic, and beautiful. He was tired; he bought a paperback copy of *Gone With the Wind* at the station bookstall, and went to bed with it in a cheap hotel. It was a struggle to get the window open at all, but when he did, and let the night air blow on his face, there was a tiny edge of crescent moon, and a scud of low cloud, and he could hear the trains. He had an idea picking somewhere at the edges of his mind. But tomorrow, as Scarlett said, was another day.

He woke once, in the middle of the night. Somewhere, a radio was playing. He had no idea why he should suddenly have a memory of many years back. In the years just following the war, there had been another late-night radio program, on a transmitter for the occupation troops in the American zone, but strong enough to be heard on the medium wave all over Europe. It was a gramophone-record hour and had been called "Midnight in Munich." The comic-serious, chanting, youthful American voice used to say, every night, "Half past twelve—and it's time for 'Heartbreaker.' " A sentimental melody, catchy in a sugary way, like a pot of jam. Van der Valk, in Hamburg with British troops, had been in bed, contrary to several regulations, with a tall (five foot ten), blonde, intensely romantic girl called Erika. She had adored "Heartbreaker."

When he woke again it was seven as usual and he wondered for a second why he did not hear Arlette's coffee mill. Then he remembered where he was and what he had to do. He shaved carefully with a new blade, ate croissants with appetite, and read *Le Monde*. When he had finished that he had still not made up his mind; he smoked another cigarette, staring at the wall. He wasn't going to ring up Amsterdam and risk making a fool of himself. What he had here was a hell of a silly idea; he'd better keep very quiet about it. If it came off, it was nothing to do with being a good policeman. It had to do with the past, with Greta Garbo and Erika, Marie Walewska, and other tall, blonde women; that was all. Nothing evidential about it, nor would there be. No question of any elaborate, clever policeman's tricks. But he was bound to obey his instinct. Evidence was not necessary. He had, at last, what Mr. Samson called a moral certainty.

He drove down the Avenue Charles Quint and pulled in at the garage just where the autostrade hits the Chaussée de Gand.

"Hallo, Lucienne."

"You back again? What's happened—you fallen in love with me or what?"

"No, I need your help. Something happened here in Brussels for which I need your help. I thought of you because you know this sinful city. I thought I'd pick your brains; got a quarter of an hour?"

"Well, I could think of better ways of spending it, but I don't mind. I've got a coffee break coming up... Philippe...," she called in her clear voice, and made a gesture of lifting a cup to her mouth. A rather spotty youth, in overalls too small for him, made a gesture of acquiescence with the air hose he held.

They went and sat in the coffeeshop; she stuck a cigarette in her mouth in a gesture he remembered. Not a very pretty girl really, but attractive—like Marie Walewska.

"It'll sound damn stupid. If it hadn't been for knowing you, I would never have had the idea. Now that I have had it, it's an inescapable conclusion, sort of."

"What is?"

"That you know a man called Meinard Stam."

She did not react in any way he might have expected. She put her coffee cup down and gave no answer at all. For a horrid moment, he thought he had made the ludicrous mistake he had imagined.

"We found a man dead in the Apollolaan. Someone killed him, but there's no evidence to point to anyone at all. He was a smuggler, and the vague official theory is that there was some quarrel with an underworld character. There are a lot of strange things about this man, which I've been trying to piece together bit by bit. And just thinking about them, I don't know myself quite why, I thought of you. I thought that you would know something about this man."

She picked up her coffee cup again and drank the coffee in a breath. "Are you being quite honest? Who do you think really killed him?"

"I'm doing my best. I think you might have. I haven't anything to support that, at present; it needs a lot more work."

"And what are you proposing to do about it?"

"Ask you."

"I don't intend to answer any questions."

"Then I'd have to take you in. I have to know, you see."

"Arrest me?"

"I don't want to cause an outcry. Just ask you quietly to come with me."

"More timid, aren't you, than you would be in Holland?"

"If you like. What difference can it make?"

"Have you the right to arrest anyone in Belgium?"

"Oh, I could make a phone call. Have papers forwarded to the bureau here."

"But you've just come. Like that. To ask me what I know about some man who's dead?"

"Yes."

"You aren't in a very strong position, are you? No warrant, no evidence, no nothing. If I chose, I could have you thrown out of here."

"I daresay," equably. She could, but if she talked about it, she wouldn't.

"I could scream. I could say *'Sale Flamand!'* They know me here, they like me and respect me. If they thought you were annoying me, they'd lynch you. You're Dutch, and they're Belgian. I've only to lift my finger."

Van der Valk smiled. "If you want to prove to me that you're just a cheap little fake, go ahead and lift."

As he had intended, she got angry. "Am I supposed to be a sheep that just stands still to be pinched by a penny-halfpenny policeman? You've got nothing on me. And ask any of the people here, whom I work with, whether I'm cheap or a fake."

"Oh, go and hide behind your bunch of Communist mechanics if you've a mind; I won't stir to stop you." His voice was contemptuous. "La Pasionaria. Saint Dolores of the working class. Who spent the war safely in a hotel in Madrid."

"Better. I like you better so. Less stupid. Less officious."

"We've always been able to understand each other. That's why I'm here. That's why I'm now getting bored. How long do we have to sit here making pretty talk?"

She might easily have got up then and gone with him, as he had intended, as he had thought she would, once taunted with cowardice. But another factor came to interfere in his plan. A shadow fell across the table.

A big man, quite as big as Van der Valk and looking a lot harder. A tough Belgian. There is nothing tougher than a tough Belgian from the Borinage; they can be formidable. They come from a hungry, dirty land that produces miners, boxers, and political agitators. Coal and iron sit in their blood. To get a quick idea of them, study their sports. Long-distance bicycle races and fighting cocks.

A fighting cock from the districts round the French-Belgian border, if shut up in a room with a full-grown man, will kill that man. Van der Valk knew this.

"What're you doing, Lucienne? That boy Philippe's moaning that he's got too much work."

She got up without a word and walked through the door at the back that said "Staff." The big man turned a quiet eye on Van der Valk.

"Customer? Or just passing through?" The voice was gentle and polite.

"Just a passerby, but I came for a purpose. I'm from the police."

"Then it's better to talk to me than to my staff."

"You're the boss?"

"I am."

"Then yes, now I'll have to talk to you. I have to take that girl in. She knows it, and the reason. Ask her."

Pale gray eyes studied him, with neither approval nor hostility.

"You're a policeman from where? France? Let's see your card."

"Not here. Office."

The big man considered this. "Very well." He walked, light as a cat, through the door marked "Staff" and Van der Valk followed, frowning. He would have to handle this fellow too.

They were inside the garage, a concrete cavern stretching a long way back. Over to the side was a row of offices and stores. Ahead were the repair bays. Mechanics were busy there, working quietly. One of them straightened up a moment, cramped, and stared at Van der Valk incuriously, his lips forming a soundless whistle, his eyes very blue in his smudged face.

Over on the other side was another row of low buildings; the big man walked toward this and not the office. He followed. From outside, by the service bays and the pumps, a gray light filtered through and was lost in the dimness of the oil-splashed concrete apron, where a half-hundred cars stood patiently waiting for treatment, like outpatients, the diagnosis and prescription for the ailment of each tucked neatly under the windshield wipers.

It was a locker room, where the staff ate, changed, washed, smoked, and gossiped. It was warm and still; a gas radiator made a small hissing noise from a blocked jet. The room was untidy with old shoes and empty bottles. Someone had left greasy paper from his sandwiches; a large ashtray shaped to imitate a tire was heaped with stained and ragged butts. Lucienne stood by the window at the far side, her hands in her pockets. She blew the ash from her cigarette on the floor, the way the mechanics did.

The big man shut the door quietly and turned round, his hands tucked into his jacket pockets, like the English Prince Consort. Those were hands like mechanical grabs. His suit was expensive fawn flannel; he had a chestnut-brown silk tie and a cream shirt. It was not incongruous on the muscular body; it was even elegant.

The body had the unself-conscious swagger of a man who has made something out of nothing and is confident of his ability to handle life.

"You're some kind of police, then. And you're after her for something. What's she supposed to have done, huh?"

"Ask her."

He turned, slowly, to look at Lucienne. "What you done— anything? Anything he can prove?"

She made a face of contempt. "No."

The massive, supple body turned again to Van der Valk. "So you reckon on coming over and sort of quietly screwing it out of her? I know cops. There's two kinds, with two ways. Smacking everyone about, being very tough, or being clever,

filling a fellow with sweet talk till he don't know himself
whether he done something or not. You've got nothing definite, or you'd come in here with a big mouth. You come in
quiet, so you got nothing to go on. Let's see your medal."

"If I'm scaring anyone to death, I see no sign of it,"
remarked Van der Valk, showing his identity card. The man
studied it carefully, reading the unfamiliar Dutch slowly
with lips that made soundless sketches of a word's shape and
substance.

"Dutch. You haven't authority to blow your nose here in
Belgium."

"If I want authority to blow your big nose for you, I'll get it
with a phone call. Why don't you stop playing Crusaders now?"

The man looked at him impassively, without getting angry.
"Fellow, you're on my premises, and questioning my staff during working hours—that's my business. You tell me what this is
about or I chuck you out."

"Ask her. She knows why I'm here. And drop the drama.
If I'd wanted I could have been here with the riot squad in steel
helmets."

"Squash him, Ben," said Lucienne. "Drop him in the ashtray. He can't prove a thing."

"Stop sounding so scared, Joan of Arc."

She turned her head. *"Va te faire encular."*

The big man grinned. "Here's your card. I don't give a
burned match for it or you. You're out of this door and keeping
walking right now."

"You bore me," said Van der Valk. "Your mouth's even bigger than your nose. Come on, miss. I don't need any riot squad,
and I don't need any proof. If you've two sous' worth of courage,
you'll admit that."

Muscles tightened in the big man's face. His feet made the
sliding step of a boxer; his shoulder dropped and the big miner's
fist came with it. Van der Valk, without knowing why, made

little effort to avoid the punch. He could have. People had tried to hit him before.

He did nothing. Instinct tucked his stomach in protectively, but he dropped his hands and stood. His ribs took most of it, but the second one took him in the temple. The wall behind smacked into him from behind, numbing his shoulder; the floor rocked, and he sat on it. Ludicrous situation—he felt the comedy of it. Like a scene from Raymond Chandler—"bells rang, but not for dinner."

Feet walked across the room; Lucienne's moccasins, indifferent; the big man's expensive handmade size forty-fours, beautifully polished leather, hard pointed toes. His ribs winced, expecting a kick. There was a draft of cold air from the open door, a whistle. He got slowly on his feet and dusted tobacco ash off his clothes. Two mechanics were leaning against the wall by the door, with impersonal faces; one chewed gum.

"You got an auto?" said this one, taking the gum out of his mouth and examining it. Van der Valk nodded, feeling his temple; it hurt.

"We'll tuck you in," said the other. Each took an elbow, not roughly. They marched over to the Volkswagen without anyone even looking up. The chewing-gum one pointed northeast vaguely, with a hairy arm.

"On your way, Monsieur le Flamand." They strolled back to their work without even looking back. In their judgment, it had been smoothly done; not too much, no noise—just right. And if the police came afterward, he had been on private property and had been annoying a woman. Police identity card? Nobody would ever have heard of it.

He rubbed his forehead again, and made a face at his bruised ribs.

He started the motor of the Volkswagen and slid away from the forecourt. When there was a gap in the traffic he made a U-turn across the autostrade. Parking was forbidden here, of course; he was sufficiently noticeable. He cut the motor and stayed where he was, dead opposite the garage, the car's nose pointing toward Brussels. He lit a cigarette and summoned up patience. Time passed, reflectively.

The stream of fast traffic was soporific; he wished he had a beer. Lueienne did not reappear on the forecourt, but the broad-shouldered fawn suit stood for some time, immobile, by the pumps, near the door of the coffeeshop. After a while it shrugged, turned, and went back in. The street, the shoulders said, is public to all, even imbeciles from Holland.

A policeman came, and stopped to examine the Dutch number plate, then him, with leisurely curiosity. The yellow-caped figure came round to the driving window.

"Monsieur is Dutch? He realizes—it is surely evident—that one may not park here." His Flemish was awkward, but quite understandable. Van der Valk took out the police card and passed it over. A chubby, bucolic face studied it, held between not-very-clean hands. He compared the photograph carefully with the subject's charming features.

"Is it business? They know at headquarters?" Nod. "You need some sort of help—cooperation?" Headshake.

"I won't be here all that long," he said comfortably, in French. The face relaxed and smiled.

"Ah, you speak French, good. Sure I can't help? What is it, the garage?" with a jerk of the thumb. "The big Ben? What's he doing then, handling stolen cars? He's too rich. They're all a nest of Communists there."

"Nothing to do but wait. Little pressure on the nerves, sitting there wondering what I'm doing."

The policeman grinned, saluted vaguely with his glove, and strolled on.

Van der Valk was there an hour and seventeen minutes. He was not quite certain what he expected to happen, but it did not surprise him when it did. When the door opened he looked up and grinned. The fawn flannel suit filled the whole space available; the little car rocked on its springs. The big man did not know what to say; his hand tattooed on the dashboard, and he smoked nervously.

"What would you say to a quiet beer?" he got out at last.

"Been thinking of hardly anything else for an hour."

"Well...you know the way. Or if you'd rather not..."

Van der Valk was not so sensitive; he swung the car round.

"Try the first door. Kind of a private office." They went through, past a big desk and a paraphernalia of modern aids. It was businesslike, but friendly and disorderly. "Fellow gets snowed under with all those catalogues," said the big man. "Through here." A connecting door led to a small warm room, with tomato-red tweed, and a geranium. It was bright and cozy; there were two armchairs and a couch, and a little bar in the corner. There was a television set, and a radiogram; there wasn't room for anything else. It was simple, unpretentious, and pleasant.

"Special bay, for trying out the new models," opening two bottles of beer from a minuscule refrigerator. "Here's looking at you."

"Here's to the new models."

"Your head all right?"

"Sure. A little tender maybe."

"I hadn't ought to have hit you."

"Wasn't a great pleasure for me either."

"You take a good punch." High compliment; he was no longer a dirty Flamand. "I reckon maybe I ought to explain."

"To be honest, I'd rather you didn't."

But once set on his objective, the big man was not easily deterred. "You know, Lucienne, she won't let herself be touched ever, by a man I mean. I had her in here once, a year ago. She shoved a broken glass in my face," with affection.

"Hardly shows."

"No, but it counts. Maybe—I'm not saying it is so, but maybe some geezer made a pass, and she hit him like she hit me.

Maybe she hit him too hard. I don't know why you're here, but she let fall that someone got dead."

"There's a man dead. He's got nothing to say. Long as she hasn't either, I don't know what happened. I'm not quite sure it's as simple as all that."

"She doesn't talk much when she doesn't want to."

"What did she tell you?"

"Nothing much. She cried a bit. Then she threw a spanner at me. Said I was a fool. Well, maybe I am, and when that's so I like to know it, so I reckoned I'd better see if I could have a quiet word with you when I saw that you didn't go away."

"She over the border by now?" indifferently.

"I didn't ask. I told her she'd better stay away from borders, probably be signaled there. I told her she could hide up—I got a country place. I knew she wouldn't listen to that. So I gave her my little Porsche and told her to get the hell out of here. She did that, not that she wanted to, but I made a kind of a bargain with her that I'd tell you, that I'd talk to you."

"Why?"

"I don't know. I came out to you because I saw you didn't say nothing to that flic out there. I thought you must know what you were doing, better than what I did, seemed to me. Here, the hell with this beer. I got something better—I got friends in Bordeaux."

He had expected armagnac. The more of a surprise when the perfume of greengages filled the room.

The big man tasted his carefully.

"Good," he said with approval.

"*Vachement*," agreed Van der Valk gravely. He got a slow, serious look. The big hand dipped into the inside pocket and came up with a plastic folder, which he tossed on the table next to the bottle.

"I don't know myself exactly what's in there. Sixty, seventy thousand francs. Not withdrawn from any bank; I keep that

here—my mad money, you can say. Small notes. Never be queried—there's no proof it ever existed—it's been held back from
takings a hundred or so at a time. Take that, and let her go. If
she killed anyone, he deserved it. I may be real dim, but I don't
think you've signaled her. I don't think you really want to take
her neither. I think you could forget about this, if you wanted."

"You love her?"

"Yes," said the big man. He shrugged. "I'm mad to marry
her. My wife's dying of T.B. She could be dead by now. I've not
told Lucienne that."

Van der Valk had several times been offered small bribes.
He had sometimes wondered whether he would give in if he
were ever offered a big one. He had hoped it wouldn't ever happen because he was scared he would give in. Now he was quite
surprised to find himself indifferent. It was comic—a bit like
Henri the Fourth, who was a coward till the first time he saw
fire. He tossed the folder back across the table, and in revenge
poured himself another glass of mirabelle. The big man put the
money in his side pocket without looking at it. He despised it; it
hadn't done its job.

"I'll tell you something," said Van der Valk suddenly. "It
doesn't depend on money, on circumstances. It depends on her. I
acted this stupid way because I didn't know what else to do. She's
not a criminal; I can't arrest her. I told her the truth— that I
couldn't prove a damn thing—I'll tell you the same. Now it's up
to her. I don't know what she'll do. She has to realize herself and
do whatever she feels she has to. Why am I telling you this?"

"You're a hell of a queer cop, if I may say so without of-
fending you."

"Everybody is. You. She. If nobody was queer, nobody'd
get killed."

The big man said nothing. He broke a cigarette in half and
laid the corpse in the ashtray; with tender care, as though it were
a little bird.

"I'll see you get your Porsche back."

I'm by no means sure of that, he thought, either. Now that Lucienne had come to the last thread of the vise, he had no notion what she might not be capable of.

I can signal her. She would rely on me not to do that. This is between us; she'll trust me there. She had me beaten up because I allowed someone else to interfere in an affair that was between me and her. Now I have to decide what it is she has done. I have to follow her rules.

He drove away from Brussels with relief. He had felt small and contemptible there. He had felt that way before, often. But then he had had an office to run to and creep behind. He had been able to hide his faint heart behind a broad desk, to busy himself with papers and telephones. The shell of officialdom had protected him. There in the garage he had just been futile.

Helpless, snubbed, pushed into corners, thrust down into red tweed armchairs that were much too low. He had not been able to snap "Sit down," nor push the cigarettes across the table with that disdainful kindness. He sat, very small. She stood, and towered over him. He was her prisoner. He was a stranger to this sort of humiliation.

He'd bloody well better be right now. Otherwise he could just creep back to Amsterdam and send in a shamefaced report, that yes, the gentlemen had been right; it must have been a smuggler that had killed Stam.

If he arrested Lucienne what would happen to her? A few years in prison. No guillotine for a girl who was absolute for death, like her father. How would the judiciary sum her up? Three years? Six? Ten?

War, somebody had said, was too serious an affair to leave to the generals. Had he ever felt that a crime could be too serious an affair to leave to lawyers?

Lucienne had been in prison. However many years she got, it would be too much—and too little.

The weather was not encouraging; thick mist hung over Holland, and it was cold, colder than it had been this year. The mist was not thick enough to stop traffic altogether, but thick enough to discourage all but the most persistent. Thick enough to stop planes landing at Schiphol and London. The thermometer hovered just above freezing point; nobody who had to be outdoors that night was enjoying it. The border guards were cross and miserable; moisture formed on their sleeves and collars, their noses dripped, and large cold beads of water stood on the head-lamps of cars, the leather of polished boots, the barrels of carbines.

That evening and that night, three panzer autos loaded with butter crashed the barriers between Holland and Belgium. A customs officer was hit by one while signaling it to stop. He had a broken femur, a broken tibia, rib injuries, lacerations, and severe shock. He was taken by ambulance to Eindhoven. The brigadier at the post south of Valkenswaard stamped his feet viciously in the cramping boots. Anyone else who played games on the border that night would get a rough reception. He instructed all duty guards to carry their carbines ready for instant use and set to "rapid." Any person or auto that failed to obey one single categorical call to stop would get half a magazine in its tires and bodywork.

In the woods around Tienray it was dark and still, and not a mouse stirring. When Van der Valk saw the red Porsche parked in the clearing between the beech trees, relief flooded his lungs and took the cramp out of his bowels. Through the trees came a faint glimmer from the oil lamps.

She was just finishing the dusting. She had shaken the rugs out, and gone over the stone floor with a damp mop. How strange this is, in the circumstances—but how Dutch, he thought. And Lucienne is, after all, a Dutch woman. Come death or disaster, the dusting gets done.

She scarcely glanced at him when he came in; she had been

expecting him. He sat in a corner, quite prepared to be told to lift his feet while she swept under them. She spoke after a minute, in a calm, unhysterical tone.

"I'm nearly finished. Put the kettle on."

He obeyed. It was charming there, the two together in that house, to hear the most homely of all sounds, the rasping whirl of an old-fashioned hand coffeemill. She felt it too.

"It is pleasant, making coffee for a guest in my own house."

"You were going to live here?"

"Not permanently. I'm not a countrywoman. Rabbits and toadstools, and wash under the pump—I'd soon have enough of that. No, the house in Amsterdam was bought for me. But I have lived here. This is my house."

"I can understand."

"You knew where to find me."

"There wasn't anywhere else."

There was silence. No wind, no traffic; only the purr of the wood stove.

"Peace at last," he said appreciatively.

"How did you come there in Belgium?"

"Pure chance. The Breitner picture. If I hadn't gotten interested in that, I'd never have seen it."

"What would have happened, then?"

"It would just have been written off as one of the things for which there's no adequate explanation. It happens often."

She thought for a while, and then spoke suddenly, with decision.

"There isn't any explanation. But I will tell you the story. It is right that you should hear it." He said nothing. "But will you put it down, or make reports out of it?"

"No."

"Will it stay that way?"

"It'll stay between you and me. You have my word."

"I was very happy, you know. I should like someone to know about that. I don't think there is anyone but you I can possibly tell."

She told, what he already knew and what he did not know. The facts were simple—those he had, almost already guessed. But the other part was poetry. Only in her words did it remain poetry. When he tried, later, to put it into words, they were flat and pedestrian. He could never have made it into a report.

It did not take long. They finished the coffee, and went to the shed to get wine. The padlock was stiff and he had to help her. She noticed that there was a bottle missing; he told her that it had been he who had drunk it, sitting in the same chair. How could he have known then that the chair on the other side of the table was Lucienne's?

When it was over it had not helped him to know what he must do. How was he to get out of this situation? How could he do what officially was called his duty? He didn't know what his real duty was—his official duty, to do him credit, never entered his head.

The trouble was that he did not feel clever; he felt very stupid. And yet if he took refuge in his official mask the whole thing became simple. He came immediately out of his false position and could feel with absolute certainty that he was acting correctly. He had simply to write a report, brief and unemotional, arrest Lucienne, and see that the Officer of Justice got all the facts.

That gentleman was learned in the law. Her punishment and her "rehabilitation" were things for which he took full responsibility. He was a sincere, humane, kind man, who would in no sense be vindictive. Nobody expected Van der Valk to carry the slightest responsibility for Lucienne Englebert. In fact, by police regulations he was expressly forbidden to concern himself with these questions.

It was this course of action that did not enter his head.

Oh, he was furious that he had ever got dragged into this. Why did it have to be him on the road there, that time outside Utrecht? Why had be been so stupid as to let himself be attracted by Lucienne? Why had he answered the telephone call from the Beethovenstraat, and gone over to Brussels? Why hadn't that nosy Charles van Deyssel been able to mind his own business?

But he could do it all now in simple terms. He could write that he had questioned her, that she had admitted the killing. Wipe out what he had been told in this room. Go back to Brussels, ask like a good boy for a warrant to take her into custody and bring her back to Amsterdam like any conscientious postman. Tidy. His Highness would approve.

He wouldn't consider it for a second.

Why had three sober people behaved like idiots over this girl? A Belgian garage owner, a Dutch policeman, and a Belgian-Dutch smuggler.

Can't go letting the Officer of Justice ask questions like that, can we?

Come on, Van der Valk. Forget this—this idyll—and these ridiculous surroundings, in which he imagined he had understood Stam and Lucienne and their story. Forget this—he had almost said honeymoon.

Goodbye to all that.

PART III

LUCIENNE ENGLEBERT first came to Brussels at a good time—a time when imaginative ideas were becoming respectable. The Congo had been resolutely forgotten; the number of smooth gentlemen in the Avenue de la Joyeuse Entrée, who spoke so many languages, was increasing daily. The Belgian mercantile sense had been fertilized, so to speak, and a rather arid town was becoming exciting. Horizons were bursting open on all sides, the sky was the limit, and a career was open to talent as it had not been in Brussels since the year before Napoleon went to Russia. For Lucienne, it proved extremely simple. She walked, in her Castillo suit, into a carefully chosen large garage, asked who the boss was, and simply went up to him.

Bernard Toussaint was then thirty. He had come to Brussels from Marcinelle at twenty-two. A year later he was cruiser-weight champion, and married to Léonie Vaes. By the time he was twenty-eight, and well knowing that he was not world-championship class, he had learned a lot and was ready to retire before somebody licked him, while he still had a title and a name that brought money in. He was lucky too, because he succeeded in acquiring the garage at the autostrade junction. It was a wonderful site, but the buildings on it were sagging apart; leaking, rusty, and hopelessly small. His savings bought the site, but the hardest of all Bernard's fights was the one for capital, to put up the new buildings and still keep back enough to work with.

This fight renewed the hatred he had had as a boy and cemented it forever, a hatred for people who did not work with their hands, and who had money. As a hungry fighter he had been in their hands, and had hated it. To fight, to make himself into something, he had had to fatten and enrich these parasites, and now he had to do it again.

Never trust a man with soft hands and a soft voice. Never trust the men who measure everything—those Sinclair Lewis called the men of measured merriment.

But now that he was thirty he had won this fight too. After two years with the garage, he was on an even keel, which meant on good terms with his bank and rapidly paying his loan off. Any financier in Brussels would have been delighted to lend him money, but he would never again take it. Bernard liked being rich, but he did not live to become more and more rich. He lived for the day when he could tell them all to go to hell.

He had one great disappointment in his life. Léonie had always been too tame, too quiet, for the company he enjoyed. She hated racing cars, boxing matches, fighting cocks, and cycle races. Now she was too sad as well. It was depressing; he had truly loved, truly fought for her, truly done his utmost to make her happy.

She was a nice girl; faithful, kind, gentle. At twenty she had been amazingly pretty and he had been ferociously proud of her. Pale, clear skin, lovely ash-blond hair, wonderful sapphire eyes. Her shy, hesitant manner had been enormously attractive. But at twenty-eight she was totally faded, like a badly pressed alpine flower. She looked anemic; her body was too thin, her breasts too flat, her hands and feet too bony. She coughed all winter, and her two children wore her out. It was difficult to love her; she was born to be sat on. A congenital underdog, who had never had the vitality or the character to be anything else. She was frightened and repelled by Bernard's friends; she loathed night clubs and refused to dance with anyone but him; movies gave her a headache; she didn't care about clothes and hair styles, and no wonder: even the finest frock looked like a rag on her meager back.

Bernard was generous to her, patient with her, and remained fond of her, but she bored him. When they told him that she was far gone with T.B. and took her off to Davos, he was too nice a person to be happy, but he could not help being relieved. He slept with a long row of shopgirls and typists, who did not please him at all; he felt nothing but the familiar contempt and boredom. He was now a king; the garage was his kingdom, and he was looking for a queen; none of these trashy girls would do. Kitchenmaids they were and always would remain.

When Lucienne walked up to him, he thought her attractive but was not in the least interested. A lady; he feared and distrusted ladies. During his boxing days he had had an experience or two with rich women—horrible... A little embarrassed, he started talking too much.

"What can we do for you, mademoiselle? A sports car? I've a Facel Vega, a honey. Driving lesons free, first year's insurance free..."

Lucienne smiled, her wide, disdainful smile. "No, thank you. A job is what I've come to ask for."

He could hardly believe his ears.

"You are? Well, I employ a bookkeeper, a secretary, a telephonist—but why come to me?"

"No. A job on the pumps or the service bay."

"You're kidding." He thought—too late—that that was no way to talk to a lady, but he was taken out of his stride; it made him awkward.

"I haven't come just because I like the view. I'm serious."

"You mean it. You'd better come in here." He led the way into his office, curious. "Sit down, mademoiselle."

"I prefer standing."

"As you wish," he said awkwardly. He sat at his own desk; that restored his balance a little.

"If I may say so, you don't look quite the type."

"I dare say not, but mightn't that be good for business?"

He considered that. "It might, yes, but it's pretty hard work. Dirty, too."

"I don't like office work. I don't like paper, nor smiling over desks. I hate the stink in shops. I'm strong and healthy and I'm not stupid. And I won't put the boys off their work. No hips, and no eyelashes."

He liked that; he could feel more at home with a girl who talked like a daughter of the people, despite her educated Parisian French.

"You've a point there. Know anything about cars, Miss...?"

"Englebert."

"Like the tires?"

"Yes, but call me Lucienne. I don't know much. I can park without bumping, and get into the garage without scratching, and drive without breaking the gearbox."

"That's more than a lot of men ever learn. But no maintenance?"

"I can change a wheel or a plug, no more. But I think that a woman can learn to service a car as well as a man, and the customers like to see a girl behind a pump."

"That may all be true. But can she get along with the men working alongside?"

"Would you be prepared to try and see?"

"I might. I might. Just to see how it worked. All right. Come if you like tomorrow morning."

Next morning Bernard was inclined to regret his impulse. "I'm not sure this will work."

"Why?" calmly. She had overalls in her carrier bag. New, but washed out to get rid of the stiffness, and neatly pressed.

"Well," he began dubiously. "The boys change over there. I've three girls in the office building, but they don't change. There's a women's lavatory over there but..."

"I see. But do you mind if I change over here? If I work with them, I'll do whatever they do."

"I don't mind—if you don't."

"I don't."

Well—if she didn't. He stayed at the door, out of curiosity to see what she did. It was a warm spring day with sunshine; all the mechanics had left discarded sweaters and trousers in untidy, ragged bundles. Lucienne took off her sweater and skirt without as much as glancing at him; it was most disappointing—she wore woolly camiknickers about as startling as a competition swimsuit. She buttoned her overalls, put a beret over her hair, and said coolly, "Sorry, no sexy pants."

He had to laugh at himself, properly caught.

"You'll do," with appreciation. "Old Hervé will show you your job for a few days. He's a quiet old chap."

To old Hervé—to all the mechanics in turn—she held out her hand like a man. "*Bonjour*—Lucienne." Bernard watched her with amusement.

He went on watching for the first month without ceasing to be amused—gradually tinging it with respect. For her act— if it was an act—was consistent and successful. He had never thought it would be possible for a girl to work—really work— with a bunch of mechanics. An older woman, a married woman, yes, there were plenty everywhere, but a pretty girl of twenty-two was fair game for all. But she did, and there was simply no hanky-panky. She put them off unemotionally, without coquetry and without being disagreeable.

To Robert, the killer, when he kissed her hand, she said pleasantly, "I'd rather you didn't touch me, please; I don't much enjoy it and it's a waste of that charm." Robert had never been so squashed, and pleasure and admiration jumped into his face; from that day he was devoted. To Marcel, the storekeeper, she was sharper. When he stroked her breast absent-mindedly— he thought himself above mechanics, that one, with his clean hands—she seized his neat hair with one oily hand, poor white-collar Marcel, while she wiped the other oily hand all over his silly face.

"That gives you pleasure? No? Nor to me."

And when young Roger, the seventeen-year-old apprentice, whose nickname was Tiger, suddenly seized and kissed her— (put up to it, for a bet)—she did not think it funny. She went supple as though about to yield, and suddenly jabbed a hard knee into his crotch so sharply he yapped and fell away as though stung by a hornet; indeed, the effect was the same. The unhappy tiger could not sit straight on his motorbike for three days, and all the mechanics laughed at him.

"You asked me to kick you—I did you that small service," she said calmly. She was as direct as a country girl, though not coarse about it. Madonna, thought Bernard, the factory girls are not like that. She paid no attention to the boys' language and used it herself, but not grossly. Robert said, quite seriously, "Lucienne is a miracle worker. One can watch her undressing without thinking of offering to help."

She drank the same wine and ate the same sandwiches as they did. Bernard found out that she went to the public bath house every evening on her way home; he said nothing but had two showers installed. She kept herself as clean as a Balinese, but the cigarette ends on the changing-room floor she let lie. Once, someone suggested that, being a girl, she could clean up.

"I'm not anyone's housewife; clean it yourself."

With the customers, there was no doubt of her immediate success, reflected in her tips—she earned well. They liked the attitude: "You needn't think I'm going to try and sell you anything, but whatever you ask for you'll get done and done well." She was polite but not servile, and her tongue was quick enough to defend her against the frustrated ones. She did this in a loud clear voice that doubled the mechanics in laughter. The first time a hollow mockery of a button salesman said unctuously,

"What y'doing t'night, sis?" she replied in a serious, apologetic tone, "Sorry, but you see, I'm not homosexual." He drove away puzzled and only got furious after he had understood, which was two kilometers down the road. To butchers' boys she said "*Va crever, voyou*" like any fishgirl, but she knew that rich customers would complain to Bernard if they were insulted.

And to the fat men who whispered that their wives did not appreciate them—odd how many still do that—she would say with innocent sympathy, "Well, you'd better go home to Mum then, hadn't you?" which disconcerted the unfortunates.

Robert asked her seriously if she were lesbian. She laughed; no.

"*Je n'aime que les hommes doués.*"

"*Mais les couilles, j'en ai, moi.*"

"*Tu en as, mais de lapin.*" There was a loud laugh; the remark was repeated to Bernard, who laughed too, and then stopped laughing. To him it was no longer an amusement. He thought of Léonie, dying in Switzerland—and even then still faithful; T.B., he knew, made most women casual. And then he looked at Lucienne and chewed his lip.

Her presence nagged him like a broken fingernail. He was at work himself all day and needed no excuse to have her frequently under his eyes. He was everywhere in the garage, and spent as much time with the engineers—or the panelbeaters, who are traditionally lazy—as with the bookkeeper. As for the service bay, it was very important, though it did not make much money. He liked to get a car in good condition; he cursed the cheap peeling chrome on bent and rusted bumpers and the corner-cutting factories that did not underseal.

"I wish all cars were made of aluminum," he said, half seriously, "but if these trashy things were still good after six months, we'd never sell any new ones either."

Professionally, he approved of Lucienne, who never tried to paint over rust, not bother topping up batteries, or shirk getting under an auto on her back, on the cold concrete. He was only bothered by being physically overconscious of her. That solid female curve, from the back, when she was upside-down in a motor, with her shins braced against the wing; it persecuted him to be disturbed by that. And at the end of the day, when she was tired and sweaty, her hair straggling under her beret, he was thirsty for her, and ashamed of it.

But it was her character he found the real challenge. He would look at her in her overalls, pretending to be thinking of urgent and important things. Really he was remembering her in her Castillo suit. Half turned, perhaps, leaning back casually, arm along the bench, yes, like that—she was reversing a big Jaguar into the inspection pit. But it would be her own auto—or his. He was unaccustomed to imagination and had more than he thought, though it had made him a good boxer.

Was she not the blood he needed? Would she not give him a son?

Léonie had two daughters, both strongly resembling her, he feared. Poor bitch, she'd done her best.

Most of all, what held and drew him about Lucienne was her self-possession. She had deepened this; it was no longer a façade but a fact. One speaks of a person being self-possessed; one means, generally, that he is a levelheaded sort of person, reliable in a crisis. Lucienne understood more from the word. She wished to own herself. Nobody able to force one into anything. Nobody to bow down to. To be possessed by no one, unless one gave, freely; and then, but only then, one would give the lot.

She refused to join unions, societies, brotherhoods. When urged by the mechanics to join the Communist Party, she refused with contempt.

"I don't approve. They are all sold, your Communists. They're slaves. What do they say? 'We can't get in ourselves, so we'll vote in a few Socialists too. Vote Mollet, vote Moch.' Moch—who turned tanks on the strikers in Clermont-Ferrand.

Well, I'm not saying he wasn't dead right. But every coco vomits the name Moch, and still—discipline, boys—vote him in, you others. And Mollet—that coat-turner."

"But Lucienne—the Front Populaire."

"To hell with your Front Populaire. That let Adolf in on us in 'thirty-nine and was scared to let refugees over the Spanish border."

Argument waxed in the changing room.

"Lucienne wants to tear up her identity card; she's crackers."

"Now, look, Lucienne, what you say is impossible; it's a myth. One can't exist on one's own—it's a compromise, every minute. Dirty life if you like, but it's all we've got. You can't be rigid and—uh—doctrinaire. You are like the old boys, the old Jacobins. 'Property is theft' and all that. Old Hervé was like that, and look at him now, poor old bugger. You know how he got his gamy leg? Strikebreakers smashed it for him in 'nineteen, and they wouldn't let him in a hospital, so he's still working on the pumps. If you'd seen some of that, you'd know you were being childish."

"One must make friends with the mammon of iniquity," said Jean-Paul, the Catholic Socialist, pompously.

"Hark at our Bible puncher. But he's quite right, for all his precious cardinal."

"I don't care," said Lucienne. "I've been in jail, and I don't care, you hear. Not for laws or cards or the bloody benefit, none of it. And there are men just like me."

"No, Lucienne," said Robert seriously. "I admire you, but you're wrong. They've got us surrounded. Papers and passports—tax, social security card, children's allowance, stinking pension—all part of the scheme to hold one down. But it's impossible to live without it. If you haven't your papers, you're a *clochard*. No job, no money. Maybe you can make a revolution against tanks, but you can't make one against paper. They are clever, the bastards."

"You can't, maybe," said Lucienne seriously. "You're men; you've homes, families. You have to eat it, fill your mouths with it; I can see that. But I can. I'm a woman."

"Yes," said Robert, "the economic argument, we've heard that one. You become a whore; you sell your property and you still always keep it."

"Am I a whore?" angrily. "I am a virgin, and I intend to remain so. Until I find a man that's not a slave."

"My poor girl, you'll die a virgin," kindly. "Knights in shining armor don't exist any more."

Bernard thought she just needed taming. She would settle down; she was too young to have felt the iron hand of the system, and all that student-ideals talk would soon disappear if she had herself a home and a child. As a boy he had thought that way too. As a boy he had become a boxer thinking every punch was a blow for freedom. He had learned that every punch put money in someone's pocket, and always the wrong one's. And he was a capitalist himself now. What she needed was someone to fall in love with. He planned that it should be him.

How? Less easy. He could think of nothing better than the classic pitch one made for a girl. Not crude. This wasn't a girl to fall for two gins and a visit to the movies, or for being told exciting stories, illustrated. One had to wait patiently for a good opportunity of showing her that one was worth something after all.

His chance came with a public holiday, hot clear weather and fierce sunlight. The Communists didn't work—they all went to Knocke, riding in their own cars. But people still need gasoline, and still need their autos fixed—all the more. Everyone was on the road, all impatient, all willing to spend money just to get on and have a good time. So the capitalists had to run the garage.

The office was shut; the service and repair bays were dead, but the coffeeshop stayed open, and Lucienne would look after the pumps. Old Hervé was too old and slow to be alone now, and the boy Philippe too unreliable. Bernard himself ran the breakdown wagon, and delivered a big bitch of a Buick he had had his arm twisted into promising, and did emergency repairs. Between times he helped Lucienne with gasoline and roadmaps, cold Coca-Colas and sunglasses, giving traffic directions and lowering the pressure on tires. They could not stop, and did not stop, even to eat; they wolfed sandwiches standing, and swigged white wine out of cold bottles he had hidden in the refrigerator. When the flow slacked off a bit, and the evening service attendant came on as usual, they had worked twelve hours straight, with no break.

Every muscle aching, drowned in sweat, eyes stinging from dirt and fatigue and the salt sweat that dripped into them, he was bending backward and forward to get the kinks out of his back. She was sorting the notes in the cash register; she worked a rubber band round the thick dirty bundle and gave it to him.

"I've kept the float back, but Johnny hasn't checked it yet."

"He will, don't worry." He peeled off three or four hundred-franc notes and slapped them in her hand. "That's extra, kiddo; you've really worked today, so we slip it off before it's counted. Tax-free."

"Thanks." He could see she was pleased at the appreciation.

"We've earned a beer, I guess. Shower first, or drink first?"

"Shower. I feel disgusting."

"Okay. In the office when you're ready."

Letting the merciful hot water beat the grime and the fatigue out of him, conscious that four feet away in the other shower she was twisting her naked body contentedly out, stretching her jaded muscles under the water needles, he rehearsed carefully casual words.

She grinned happily coming through the door. Her wet

hair still stuck to her neck; she wore cotton trousers and a beach shirt. She yawned with splendid panther's teeth, and he poured the beer with longing.

"I'm accustomed to it—Christ, I ought to be—but I felt we'd taken a bashing today. These holidays, you need six pairs of hands."

"I'm all right now." She drank half the glass and wiggled her toes with enjoyment.

"You going to go home and cook?" topping the glasses up. She drank, went "Ah," and made a face of disgust at the idea.

"Cold meat and potato salad, when I can face it."

"What d'you do when you get home? Play the radio, or records?"

"Haven't a radio or records. Read, mostly."

"Potato salad's fine muck after a day like this. Doesn't sound much fun."

"I'll live."

"Oh, don't think I'm any better off. But I've got an idea. Let's not bother changing, but take the auto and go and look for a bit of fresh air ourselves for once. Why should they have all the fun? We could eat later, somewhere along the coast maybe."

She looked at him with a vague smile, more than half attracted. There were smudges of fatigue under her eyes.

"It's an idea; the fresh air would be lovely. Then what?" Her eyes rested on his face vaguely, on his eyes.

"Oh, I don't know. Can't gamble; casinos will be too full for comfort. I'll think of a place and twist their arm for a table. We can just follow our nose; get some ideas on the way maybe; I'm too tired to think right now."

There was a silence; her eyes still studied him, less vaguely.

"Bernard, you're cooked," she said suddenly.

"Huh?"

"Cooked. Your eyes have gone all soft. I can give you the program, because I know it. Eat shellfish along the coast, because that's the thing for a quick pickup. But shellfish make one thirsty, so plenty more of that nice white wine, which isn't really strong at all. Then a drive again, because the dark and the lights are pretty, and the air will stop us from getting very sleepy. Drive very fast, because a hundred and fifty an hour makes a girl all rubbery. And then a country hotel, where they know you and will put us up, because it's too late and too much trouble to get back to town."

How does she know, he thought; uncanny. He went on acting. "Why don't we just wait and see?"

"Your eyes are all soft," she said again. "Do you think I'd be good in bed?"

He didn't know what to say; he stood up, to cover his awkwardness and not let her see his eyes.

"More beer?"

She shook her head; she still had the empty glass in her hand, forgotten.

"I'm going to have one." He drank it; it fizzed in his head, and fermented; hunger and fatigue and the ache for her. He forgot how to rescue the campaign and go through with it. She had pierced the pretense; he might as well be honest. He stooped over her and put his hands on the arms of the chair, smiling fuzzily.

"You're a girl in a million, Luce."

Tac went the thin glass on the edge of the table; her hand jabbed upward and stung him. His reactions were too slow and hazy to get him out of the way. It stung, but he hardly felt that. It was the sensation of wet on his jaw that drew his hand, and what made him recoil was her face—her eyes looked at him along cold gun barrels. He wiped his hand along his jaw and looked stupidly; covered in blood.

"You've cut my face."

"Yes," still holding the glass dagger. "You wanted to eat me."

"But Jesus, woman, you might have had my eye."

"Yes. I'm sorry. If there'd been beer in it I'd only have thrown it; you forced me. You were like a stallion there, ready to strip me and fall on me." She started to cry suddenly, out of rage, remorse, bitterness, exhaustion. "I don't take it, I won't have it. Nobody just swallows me. Nobody, nobody plays with me." She made an effort, breathed in hard, caught it, and stopped both the yelling and the weeping. "I'm sorry I hurt you; I like you. I'm not angry with you, I lost my head."

"I did too." The bloodletting had cleared his head; he had recovered his balance. "It's a scratch, nothing at all." He found a bottle of cognac in the little bar cupboard; he poured some on his hand and wiped his jaw. On second thought he poured some into a glass too, and handed it to her. His hand shook slightly; the bottle clicked on the lip and slopped the beer glass half full. "You are quite right; I was an imbecile."

"You're married, Ben." She sipped, but shuddered so violently she put the glass back to stop spilling it.

"What a stupidity," he said, heavily. "What a stupidity." He picked up the glass and drank it off; nearly half a beer glass full, without noticing.

Lucienne had found out how to judge customers. Most of them looked first at her figure, which was very good in overalls. She always looked at their eyes. Some eyes were just cheap and greedy. Others had the weak, spaniel look she so detested, that Bernard had got that day, and to which she was unpleasantly sensitive. Others had naughty, insolent stares, thinking it outrageous that a garage girl should be healthier and prettier than their dumb-bunnies, condemning her for being "working class," for wearing trousers, for having dirty hands, for heaven knew what. Those were the hypocrites, her enemies; the holy sanctimonious ones that took such pains to hide their measly sins.

Others had the hard flat eyes that saw everything as merchandise, and pinned a price tag to her back as thoughtlessly as they did to rolls of cotton, a sack of coffeebeans or a box of oranges. And very many just looked, dully, without seeing anything at all, neither her nor around her nor beyond her. To them no sight was new, no sound was fresh; in their whole lives they had seen nothing but their own faces, heard nothing but their own voices. The great brigade of don't-knows, and don't-want-to-find-outs.

The best were the abstracted eyes that were occupied from within. They were thinking, worrying, counting, or writing poetry—what did it matter what they did, since they were doing something? They mostly did not notice her even if they fell over her; she was grateful for these. It was a rest from the constant sweep of greedy eyes all day long, which ended by making her skin sore and irritable, as though constantly stroked by a single hair.

Two or three she liked. Among the regulars, that is, those who dropped in every fortnight or so for their autos to get a shave and a haircut, or even only for gas, because it was handy on their route, and the sight reminded them to look at the fuel gauge. She liked the much-bumped, deeply-scratched green Opel belonging to a thin, nervous man, the type that wanders round parking lots wondering which car is his, since he never knew the number and has forgotten the color. He was hardly more than her age—was he an actor, or a musician? He was the world's worst driver, the sort who clutches the steering wheel despairingly and never sees the lights change. He stares blankly, in his world where lemons ripen and figs burst suddenly open.

Or the big rakish blue Fiat, whose driver was the other kind—so busy talking, waving at friends, turning round to look at nice buildings or pretty women, snapping at the filthy recalcitrant lighter, that they never have any hand on the wheel at all—the type that makes Paris traffic what it is. This one was a broad man, of about fifty. He would jump out of the car on springs, leaving it quivering like a race horse pulled suddenly in, and when he thanked her, his big Italianate eyes would vanish in wrinkles of amusement. Always he shook himself down like a boxer to flip the crease out of his superb suits. His body, big and firm in a short camel coat, was more supple and resolute than most boys' of twenty. He was a doctor, the bookkeeper told her; children's specialist.

There were others she liked, though never many, among them the rather boring black Peugeot. It came in most weeks for a refill and a quick wash; it was always dusty and muddy from long stretches of road. He was a neat, quiet man, like his car, with an outdoor skin and nice manners. When he tipped Lucienne he did so apologetically, as though aware that offered money is an insult. A pity there weren't more of those. Strange, people; she had never known that there were people who gave one five francs as though ashamed of being seen, others as though it were a private joke between you, others as though it were something that called for an apology.

What did she do with her free time during that first year? Her room was small, mean, and dreary, its advantage that it was simple to clean, easy to warm, handy for work, fairly quiet, and moderately cheap. She had an electric fire and a Buta stove; a tiny balcony where she kept her food and hung her washing; a bed, a table and a chair; there was little more. She had brought few things from Holland: a pretty crystal vase and a couple of ashtrays, a few pieces of china, a photograph of her father in a characteristic attitude, which she liked. She had sold everything else. She still possessed one picture that she had always been fond of—a landscape of the Ile de France: a cart loaded with turnips, two Percheron horses, and a tremendous horizon. In this room she spent little time. Hardly more than she did in the public library. For eating cold meat and salad or vegetables from the dairy, for washing and ironing, for sleeping, reading, stretching out and thinking.

She did not bother with concerts. Music, which she had lived with ever since she was a baby, was an irritation. Things never sounded quite the way one wanted them to sound, the way one knew they ought to sound. Pictures were better. She liked the silence and simplicity of a gallery; the comments of others who look; the ribald laughter and the esoteric, professional joke; the enthusiasm of knowledge and the naïve admiration of the stranger; the familiar pleasure and the sudden discovery. The contact with other visions, often inarticulate, struggling.

She liked, too, the theatre and the ballet, and sometimes the cinema. She enjoyed going to an expensive hairdresser; she was rather revolted by the preciosity, but enjoyed the unreality, the snobbery, the vulgar wealth and atrocious decor, the elaborate fiction that a notary's fat wife can be Helen of Troy if only she takes just that tiny scrap more trouble. She liked Monsieur Charlot, who tutted so over her hair, and she liked the desiccated Mademoiselle Adrienne, who mourned so over her hands; a faded soul, but kind and gentle. Poor Charlot, who treated her as a lady because of her easy manners, her educated voice, her expensive clothes. How horrified he was when she told him she worked in a garage.

She liked, too, on her free days, to be free of the tyranny of food. Working days it was all right to eat nothing but salad and sandwiches, but she had the idea—it was one of her father's notions, lodged in her mind since early childhood—that one day a week it was important to have "a good meal." So she would go and eat in a restaurant, alone with a book. It had to be a good restaurant, because bad ones were worse than salad. She found it pleasant to eat elaborate, expensive food after a week of sausage and raw carrots, mussels and fried potatoes. Here she would study the waiters with a professional eye, and judge from other customers' faces the tips they would leave.

On one of these days, eating *sole normande* and reading that year's Prix Femina in a crowded, gilded, perfumed restaurant to which she was attached, she glanced up idly. Who did that familiar face belong to? He was standing by the service door as though he had just come out of the kitchen, and was talking to the headwaiter in a confidential whisper. Brief phrases with an impassive face; slow nods of episcopal approval. Business, evidently; she lost interest. It was the man she liked with the black Peugeot and the courteous manners, but it was unimportant. It would mean nothing if he saw her; he probably would not recognize her and it mattered little if he did. Would he have good enough manners not to comment at all?

She went back to her fish and her book; the fish was good; the book she thought dull and faintly disagreeable. It did not bother her, though she felt she ought to find merit somewhere in a book that had won the Femina. She didn't have to like it; but she was puzzled at finding it so bad.

When she looked up it was at the gentle intrusion, delicate and punctilious as a hypodermic needle, of the headwaiter's silken voice. "Mademoiselle, would you permit a gentleman? I excuse myself; we are today a bit disorganized. He has no reservation, but we do not wish to disappoint him."

Lucienne nodded vaguely; she didn't mind. She put down the Femina and reached for her gloves, which she had left lying across the far corner. Only then did she see that it was the man with the black Peugeot. Clear blue eyes; polite, no hint of impudence. She hadn't seen him without a hat before; his head was a pleasant shape; he had short brown hair, looked young and tanned. He bowed with his usual good manners.

"I regret that I should disturb..." No hint of recognizing her.

"You don't disturb me at all, monsieur."

"Thank you, mademoiselle." The headwaiter bowed and slid a menu forward; he did not look at it. "Oysters, Monsieur Raphael, and an *entrecôte, bordelaise*—not too blue. Plenty of marrow, a green salad, a few plain boiled potatoes, and a bottle of Auxerre today—the Irancy." The waiter melted into obscurity; Lucienne, bored with her Femina, put it down with a slap and speared a last stray mushroom.

She did not know why she spoke—perhaps out of curiosity, to know whether he had recognized her.

"Auto running well?" He smiled; he had known her, then.

"Certainly. It is a good workhorse, and, of course, I get it well looked after; it seems content... The book does not interest you—or have I regrettably broken your concentration?"

"No, by no means. I'm just glad of an excuse to put it down a little."

"What is your opinion of it—or is it still too early to say?"

"I find it—a little silly and a little disgusting...even if it is a prizewinner."

He swallowed bread and an oyster, neatly. "I'm extremely pleased to hear you say so. I read it myself last week. It appears to be admired, but I thought exactly the same as you did."

The waiter drifted up and took away Lucienne's plate.

"A little cheese. And a filter."

"I found," deliberately, between oysters, "the girl a little difficult to swallow... Unlike oysters."

"I find her a fool, and unreal."

"That's interesting. You will be a better judge of her than I am."

"I don't think I'm a particularly good judge of other women. Not at all in fact; I don't know any."

"You can know yourself. But perhaps you only mean that you prefer the company of men to women?"

"That's true; I find that at work."

"I find that quite normal," eating the last oyster with regret. "I must admit that I like the French oysters better than I do the Zeelanders."

"I like them all," said Lucienne, surprising herself a little.

He grinned. "Well, so do I, to be honest. It was an affected remark, intended probably to impress you."

She responded at once to this scrap of honesty; as little as that and still rare enough. He could not have known that he had originally gained her confidence with a frivolous remark about oysters.

"I don't believe in women like that. And I certainly don't like them."

"But such things happen, all the same."

"Not to me they don't."

"You are subjective." He ate his steak; he had been rude, too personal. Her coffee dripped slowly; she looked to see how it was getting on, angry at having made a stupid, childish remark. He wished—what did he wish? Not to apologize; that would only make things worse. But to break the tiny crust of ice; to talk to her again. Would she snub him now?

"Have a glass of wine."

"Yes, please." She was afraid she had put him off for good by her clumsiness; her relief made her almost too eager.

He wiped her glass out solemnly with a clean napkin, waving away an officious waiter.

"I'm pleased to offer it to you, because it's really good. Tell me whether you like it."

"It's perfect. I'm no judge, I'm afraid."

"Then you can have the pleasure of learning. Why not, since it is important, after all, to learn about the things one enjoys? If only to learn how one may enjoy them more."

"Yes. I like eating, and drinking. I would like to learn. I'm just beginning to find out what is likely to be nice in restaurants."

He smiled at that. "And why—important too, in restaurants. Not much, as a rule, I'm afraid. It is a business I know something about. But this is one of the best in Brussels."

"My father was quite expert about wine. But when he told me about it, as about other things, I was childish, and stupid. I didn't pay attention, telling myself it wasn't important. It was so with a lot of things. I regret it now."

"You speak as though he cannot continue his lessons."

"No, he can't. Dead." The word *mort* fell damp and heavy; he covered it with his manners. "A misfortune. It robs him of the pleasure, among others, of teaching you things."

Lucienne thought this a nice remark. No stupid condolences. She did not regret having mentioned her father for longer than the instant it had taken him to answer her sudden confidence.

"I enjoy this very much."

"Yes, have some more. Auxerre is nice; they make very good wine around there. Not easy to get outside; this is one of the few places in Belgium where one sees it." Sounds very pedantic, he thought. I must learn to be less stiff in the company of this girl.

"I don't think I've ever been in Auxerre."

"It is a personal remark, and unforgivable, but your French is not learned in Brussels."

"No, you're quite right; I was brought up in Paris. Later, we came to Holland. I am Dutch, really."

I didn't need to blurt all that out, she told herself.

"I am Dutch too." Her regret did not last; nor did his really, though he reproached himself. Just the sort of tiny thing... "Is it a pleasant coincidence?"

"I think it is, really."

He pushed away his plate and refilled both glasses. Was it the Auxerre? Was it Lucienne? What led him at that moment to a further, considered, deliberate indiscretion? Was he just sick of never being reckless?

"Would you think me very impertinent if I asked you, occasionally, to be my guest? I am often in Brussels, but I have no friends here."

"I think that would be very nice," said Lucienne. This time, neither of them regretted it at all. She felt curious. He didn't look Dutch, nor behave at all in what she thought of as a Dutch way. But he had not been curious about her; the least she could do was to honor that. Anyway, she didn't sound Dutch herself. Didn't even look it, she hoped. Maybe he didn't care either to be so obviously labeled.

If he had a struggle at getting to know her, if he hesitated at lowering barriers, if he sometimes wondered whether it were not very foolish to abandon carefully constructed and camouflaged defenses, she was not conscious of it; she never noticed a thing. She was too busy lowering her own. And too happy to have made a sort of friend. For that was what they were becoming, friends. Her life had taken on another dimension. She did not mind, even if she noticed, the pompous stiffness of his manner at first. Perhaps it was a pleasant change from the overfamiliar, casual intercourse of her days. And if his remarks sounded didactic, they were more interesting than the unvaried, monotonous quibble of the garage, inflected only by oaths.

He took her out three times to dinner in Brussels at intervals of about a month. They drank a Tavel wine from near Avignon, a yellowish strong Jura wine, and the last time a very fine and expensive Clos de Tart. They had three bottles, and both got a bit drunk. They talked about whatever came into their heads; he did not share her taste for the theatre or movies, but he liked pictures, and he liked music. He was enchanted to find out who her father had been.

"But I am a terrible ignoramus; I know nothing about music, and the music itself only from records."

He passed toward the end into a long silence, staring at his glass. It may have been only Burgundy that melted the strictest of his barriers; perhaps it was also the feeling of togetherness, of sympathy. A beginning of love? He had loved other women;

perhaps he was out of practice. Was one always impelled to indiscretions? What did it matter?

"Lucienne, I would be happy if you came and stayed for a weekend, as my guest. But I live alone. You would mind that?"

"No. I live alone myself."

"And you wouldn't mind that it is an odd house? A cottage, very isolated; no electric light, even."

She didn't care at all.

"How do you run your gramophone?"

He was glad that was all that worried her. "Oh, I am most ingenious; I have an arrangement with car batteries."

"It's a deal.""Sure, you can have Sunday and Monday," said Bernard. She had expected a fuss; she didn't know why. She waited with pleasure till she saw the black Peugeot. Tuesdays, mostly.

"I have the weekend free."

"Good," was all he said. She was slightly chilled—she could not know that he had regretted that vinous enthusiasm, and more than once. He had come meaning to put her off. When he saw her face he had neither the will nor the courage. "I'll pick you up, then, at Venlo station. Just wear country clothes."

She was already happy when she crossed the frontier at Roosendaal. She had not been in Holland for over a year; even a frontier railway junction was charming and sympathetic. It was cloudy, but still and warm; Dutch June weather. In Venlo she found him hard to recognize; she had never seen him except in business suits. In gay spirits, she went out with him to the car.

"You've bought a new auto?"

He laughed. "No, I have two. The Peugeot is in to be serviced in Germany. I move around a lot, and rely on the auto—simpler in the end to have two."

The back seat was full of parcels.

"Are you fond of Kassler rib?"

"I love it."

"Good. Red wine and cabbage, then. But you don't know yet that I am a good cook. It'll be nice."

Anything would have seemed nice to her just then. She exclaimed with pleasure at the shooting lodge.

"You really live here? But it's wonderful."

He was pleased with her enthusiasm—he had in fact taken pains to make it look nice and to have everything very clean—not that she suspected that sheets had been put on the bed just for her.

"But it's your bedroom. Where will you sleep?"

"On the settle—oh, I often do." He liked her directness. "You won't have to worry that you might be invaded—I had a lock put on that door." She gave him a smile for that, amused and pleased. She took to everything with enthusiasm; getting water from the well charmed her.

"I've never done it myself, and now I have. What a good taste, after horrible Brussels water."

"But don't drink too much of it; I've a cellarful of wine and we're going to drink a lot."

"Lovely to be among trees. Not very like Holland—we may even walk on the grass."

"I know just what you mean. But why do you think I choose to live here?"

"Oh, the lovely copper pot!"

"Nuisance to keep clean, rather."

"I'll clean it. And your books, wonderful. Conrad too, fantastic."

"Yes, I read a lot here. Here I don't think about business; I just enjoy life."

She was impressed. A man who made, obviously, a lot of money—after all, a Peugeot and a Mercedes—who preferred to get his water from his own well, and read Conrad by oil light, surrounded by beech trees. She could understand that; she was suddenly intensely glad she had come and was going to get to know this man.

"You are king of all this."

"Not quite king. One never is, you know. Perhaps skipper next to God."

"Like Captain Lingard."

"Yes, the brig *Flash*. This is my effort at that."

He made grilled *entrecôtes* on the top of the stove, a smoky charred smell that went well with the tarragon and the sneeze-sharp boiling vinegar of the béarnaise. There was bread, and watercress, and big lumpy streaky local tomatoes; good. Not many dishes; she washed them while he lit the lamps and chased a noisy June bug out; it was beginning to get dusk.

"One can't walk easily at night in the woods, otherwise we might have gone out."

"I'm wonderfully content. Couldn't we make some music?" She was looking at his records. "*Figaro* and Kleiber—wonderful."

"I'll get a few more things to drink."

"Why do you have the motorbike?" admiring the bottles in the shed. "You have lots of transport."

"Yes, I like lots of transport. I use it to get away on, and for work it's handy often. We'll go for rides on it; more fun than the auto."

It was, perhaps, the happiest weekend she had spent since her childhood—why not, since it was her childhood she rediscovered? She was not required to have any worries or responsibilities—one of the nicest aspects of the desert-island feeling. He did not make the slightest move to touch her—she had not supposed for a moment he would, and was pleased; it was, to her, a question of loyalty. Anyway, sex is such a bore. Nothing interfered with her unself-conscious enjoyment, and the hours moved with a quiet, liquid rhythm like the slow movement of Beethoven's Sixth Symphony.

What did they do, the whole weekend? What the brook did.

Lucienne would remember the smells: woodsmoke and the smoke of the lamps, grass and moss covered in dew, the very clear clean air of beechwood, and the ancient complicated smell of indoors—a rich musty smell of earth and wood and flagstones, very welcoming.

She remembered his tact. The mornings and the evenings were chilly, June or no June, and she crawled out of bed on Sunday morning—her own loyalty had forbade her to lock any doors—and found the living room humming with warmth, a big bucket of hot water, and a note. "Gone for a walk till 8:15. Have a bath if you like."

When he came back she had made coffee, and they dipped bread and butter into the bowls, while she put Mozart violin concertos on the gramophone. "The bishop of Salzburg listened to them during dinner, so why shouldn't we listen to them during breakfast?" Afterward they went out, deep in the woods; she got wet to the knees, and she got her first lesson in natural history. She was such a towngirl—she listened open-mouthed. Why field mushrooms do not grow under trees but toadstools do, why rowan branches are a good protection against witches, why thyme is good for a cold and sage for the circulation of the blood, and how, in the winter, woodcock will explode suddenly out of the dead leaves, frightening one to death.

The sun was high and warm in a bright sky when they got back, though it would cloud over again that afternoon, and they dragged chairs outside, and sat drenched in content with a bottle of white wine.

"If it's fine tomorrow," lazily, "we could go swimming. Take the car over the border, up to France if we liked, up the Maas. Down here the water's not clean—Meuse is better."

"Where does the Meuse go to?" sleepily.

"Liège. Namur. After that it's nice. Down into the Argonne—Sedan, Verdun. Very historic."

"I would like it. I like history."

"Yes. History's so much more interesting than we are."

She opened an eye and studied him. Odd how different he was, how completely different from the formal, wary man of Brussels. Did men always look different, then, at home? A mask had been peeled off and allowed to fall on the uneven grass of the clearing. Normal, she supposed. All week they had to be big, tough businessmen; they had to be able to look vulnerable sometimes. Had her father always looked the same? She thought so, even in his evening-dress "working clothes," but she had been a child; she had not noticed. And what other experience had she of men? You couldn't count the boys she had known in Holland: they too were children. Franco, say; nicest boy imaginable, but tiresomely simple. As a child she had prized that openness, that rapidity and gaiety, but adult men were deeper, darker water. Secrets; pools and currents one could not guess at. Two years ago she would have feared and hated that; now she was beginning to prize it.

Stam, his eyes closed against the dappled sunlight, was reflecting without rue that he was in danger of loving this girl. It bothered him only that loving threatened his existence. He didn't care; bringing her here had made him so happy that he was astonished. But his Belgian identity was compromised—he would go no more to that garage. She must not be allowed to know about Gerard de Winter, or about Solange—now that was a worry to him; he would have to consider seriously what should be done about Solange. Here, it would not matter. The *veldwachter*, the woodwatchers—though it might be better if they did not see her.

He had been indiscreet, but he refused to care; this girl was true to the imaginary woman he carried in his mind. His private life had satisfied him for years now; it had been his refuge from that lousy hotel, that terrible woman. There his life had become a poison. His passion to be free—that romantic nature that had

had outlet enough in wartime but so little since—had gone into his secret life. Skillfully he had built it up step by step. But was it true that all this life had just been a substitute, a sedative, until he met this girl? Was he right in jeopardizing it for her?

She could hardly be worth it. He had long ago decided sensibly that a woman worth all that could not exist. Was he not now deceiving himself? Were not the results of that self-deception likely to be fatal—to his enterprise, which he had built up so carefully from his wartime knowledge? The business was important. It had made him rich. Now he could get away from the hotel altogether, cut completely loose from Solange. But he could not neglect the business, or even take a holiday from it. In a way he was as much the prisoner of smuggling as he had been of the hotel.

How easy it had been, really. Then it had been respectable to diddle the occupying authorities and learn the precautions against being betrayed. To him it made no difference whether the authorities were German, Dutch, or Belgian. Butter was easier to get across a border than many other things had been.

Is there something after all very sober and bourgeois in my blood? he thought. Damn this woman for filling me with dangerous longings. But I won't allow myself to be seduced.

Alas for the good intentions; at that second Lucienne spoke.

"What I like so much about your house is its independence."

"That's why I took it. Nobody else wanted a cottage in the woods. People don't want independence—especially not when you have to do without the things one pays taxes for—posts and roads and streetlamps and sewers and the company's gas and water."

"And if there was an earthquake, it would hardly bother you, whereas the suburbs would be running in circles. No tradesmen, no neighbors—you can't think how I envy you."

"Ah my dear, there is always trade, money, business. Think

of the word 'busy.' To me business means busybody. Whatever one does there is always someone trying to organize it and make money out of it—it's very disagreeable. Still, I'm as free as Captain Lingard ever was. Taken me years, and always very precarious."

"But you are skipper of the *Flash* for all that." She liked the notion.

"Yes. Always on the lookout for Dutch gunboats."

She laughed. He could make a joke of it, he thought. Lucky she would not realize that it was true. The gunboats...and the sneaking competitors for trade, who crept after him, spying. Like the *Flash*, he could outsail them.

"My father had a similar idea. He had a fearful wife, and he hated all the political seesaw of impresarios. He wanted to buy a boat and sail round the world."

"Why didn't he?"

"He didn't have the nerve. He knew nothing about sailing anyway—couldn't tell a mast from a knitting needle. It had to be small enough to sail with just the two of us, but big enough to hold a piano. A romantic notion, you see, quite ridiculous. But I always treasured the ideal. I used to envy Captain Lingard."

"In the end he got into a fearful tangle."

"He behaved stupidly over a very annoying woman."

"Yes. She isn't a very real woman. None of Conrad's women are."

"No. They all seemed very stupid to me; I never really understood them."

On the Monday they went up the Maas, bypassing Liège, over to the valley of the upper Meuse. He told her that this was the battlefield of France, the sore that only Germany could heal. She was fascinated, as he had always been fascinated. Condé and Turenne, Louis Napoleon and MacMahon, Petain, Gamelin.

"Think of it: three terrible defeats on the same spot, in one lifetime."

"But Verdun was a victory."

"Think again. Six hundred thousand dead, just for a name, for pride, to try and wipe away the shame."

"They did. *Ils ne passaient pas.*"

"Not for twenty-four years. Then they did. I was here in nineteen-forty."

"What did you do?"

"What could one do? Threw the uniform away. Stayed quiet till they'd all passed. Once they stopped fighting and started administering, we could start to hit them. But we couldn't fight them. When one did that they took hostages and shot them. We corrupted them."

"I was a child. Scarcely born. I am very much younger than you are."

"Does that matter?"

"I don't think so."

"Have you enjoyed yourself?" he asked her on Monday evening.

"More than I can remember ever doing."

It sealed, so to speak, his fate. He didn't know whether to he glad or sorry. He had thrown his dice, and it had come up five queens.

"Haven't you been bored?" she asked.

He smiled at that. "You are, if I may say so, incapable of boring me."

She is very undeveloped, he thought. Childish still. Very sensitive and touchy, full of immature fancies. She wants to fight the whole world, without ever cheating. I could tell her something about that. Without cheating, not possible. One can renounce the world, I suppose. Turn the back, disregard it. But fight it...all that honesty and courage—she will be very hurt, unless she is lucky.

For a month he was resolute, and never went near her, trying to force himself to stop loving her. Put her out of his mind; watch the business. Keep the walls and roof in good repair; keep a lookout for mice nibbling at the thatch. Sharpen the wits. He could never have kept the wits sharp, all these years, if it had not been for the cottage, where one could forget the tension, the fear, the excitement.

The work on the border he didn't mind; it gave him pleasure. What he hated was the aftermath: the mean bargaining in Belgium the next week; the forging of papers, the grasping of filthy paper money; the watchful eyes and the avaricious eyes. If only he could get rid of that. He had sometimes thought of getting Solange to do it—admirable businesswoman that she was—and she would enjoy it. But it would only tie him further to her; it would not really set him free. How he loathed Belgium. He wished he could kill Gerard de Winter.

He must take very great care that Lucienne did not find out about that gentleman, whom he was thoroughly ashamed of. What had possessed him to take her to dinner in Brussels, where every headwaiter knew his name and too many knew what he did? They were discreet, luckily. But he could bring her to the cottage. There was no reason why Meinard Stam, retired army officer, sportsman and nature lover, should not become interested in a young woman. Come to that, there was no reason why he should not marry her.

Lucienne had pleasant memories to enliven her days with. She had no struggle to get away from them; she treasured them in the evenings. In her work she was deeply absorbed; there she had no time or taste for daydreams. But when cooking or eating, darning a sweater or polishing the linoleum, before getting up and before slipping into sleep, she would renew a smell, a taste. The warmth of the sunlight on the wooden table; the lovely drowned coldness of the white wine that had been put down the well; the pearls of dew on long, curved grassblades; the pattern of a faded Persian carpet on flagstones.

When a fortnight passed without her seeing the black Peugeot, she put out her courage, and detached herself from hope of repeating that weekend. She was not going to count on being invited to Venlo again.

She did not deserve to be invited, she decided; she had been poor company. Shallow, crude, uneducated. And rather a fool. Her fault. She had never paid attention at school, and after leaving she had taken pains to forget what she had learned. It had seemed inconsistent with what she thought and believed in to be a well-educated young lady.

She wasn't a lady; she was a garage attendant, and the hell with them all. Too rough and stupid for a man like that. She had better forget those pretentious tricks, too, like eating in restaurants—ridiculously expensive anyway, when a meal cost a day's earnings.

Still, it had been fun; she had learned a lot. There were after all people who thought the way she did; she was not alone in the world. But she just did not know how to make a man feel at home with her; she was obviously too awkward. And too rough; her table manners had probably been bad. Or she used too much argot in talking; with the boys one simply forgot how to talk proper French. When she was called one afternoon to the telephone, she was astonished, and happy.

"It's you...I thought I had put you off for good... This weekend? Hold the line, I'll ask the boss...Bernard, can I have the weekend? Saturday and Sunday? Thanks, sport. Not Monday, but Saturday; is that all right?"

Stam's voice, very quiet and controlled, said softly, "Friday evening then, but I may be kept a little on business. Would you mind very much waiting in the station, in case I am delayed? I'll certainly see that you're not kept long."

"No strain; I'll just sit in the buffet." She ran out sparkling.

"You got a lover, Luce?" asked Bernard, grinning.

"Perhaps," grinning back.

"You sleeping with him?"

"Imagine. What a question. Certainly not, but does that concern you?"

"No."

"Well, then, keep your curiosity at home."

"*Merde*," said Bernard. "I'm just happy to see you happy."

She was happy, extremely so. It was nice that he hadn't after all wiped her off the map. It had discouraged her, this last month. She hadn't wanted to admit it, but she had been dreadfully disappointed, and disappointment, she had read, is the sorrow of the young.

In Venlo there was nobody waiting for her, but she had been warned. She went to the buffet as she had said and ordered a cup of coffee and lit a cigarette happily. It was raining outside, but she did not care. When Stam paused outside the window to see if she was there, he stopped to look at her, to satisfy himself that he had not misjudged. If he had made a fatal mistake, there was time to change his mind, to disappear. Nobody would be the wiser.

She had an elbow on the table and was staring at the wall, quite unconscious of anyone. A small smile on her face, as though she knew a good joke and was enjoying it quietly. He stayed still a second, clearing his mind, preparing it, like a fencer before the start of a fresh bout. Deliberately, he committed himself to the idea that he loved her. Irrevocably, like committing this our departed brother to the deep; salute. It was a dangerous decision, but there, it was some time since he had made a dangerous decision. He pushed the door open.

She turned her head and stared at him blankly, not recognizing him. He smiled; it was effective, then, his disguise. He had never tried it out so thoroughly. When he smiled she recognized him and lifted her eyebrows with some surprise. He was wearing waterproof trousers and a leather jacket, and a high crash helmet with goggles; his mouth and chin were masked with a silk scarf, such as many motorcyclist use, who dislike windscreens and yet want protection against dust and insects.

She jumped up eagerly and waved at the waiter to draw attention to the money lying on her table.

"You're on the bike?"

"Yes, business. I must excuse myself for it, as well as for keeping you waiting, but I have only just finished. Fridays are my busy days. We'll forget all that now. Tomorrow I am free and so are you, and Sunday as well; that is superb. We are going to enjoy ourselves very much."

"We are going to the cottage?"

"Certainly, where else?"

"I don't know; I just hoped we were."

"Pigsty, I'm afraid; still, your room is clean and tidy. We may have to do some shopping, but that can be easily done tomorrow. Now, here is the bike. I hope you won't be cold, in that skirt and a light raincoat; the bike can be windy. However, I won't go fast and you can shelter behind me; you shouldn't feel it much then."

She swung herself sideways on to the back seat, tucked her feet carefully together, and gripped him firmly round the waist. The big BMW simmered and throbbed quietly like a boiling kettle; she could feel his back muscles under her hands as he swung the bike out and sailed round the first corner with a rush of effortless pace and power. Lovely; much nicer than a car.

When they drew up in the woods her face was fresh and tingling; in front of her scarf her hair was flattened and dewed with moisture; her pleasure as sharp as a seagull's wing. Being on a powerful motorbike behind a man one loves is a fine feeling for a girl. She had had no idea of it, but now she knew she loved him. His back muscles had told her hands.

She shook herself out happily; there was a damp triangle on the knee of her skirt, where her raincoat fell open. The smell of rain on earth and wood was intoxicating; she claimed it with a delight so keen it hurt and she shivered.

"Netherlands July," said Stam, dripping, opening the door. "You're cold, my child. Change your skirt quick and we'll have some Burgundy. I've a Vosne Romanée; just the trick."

"I'm not cold, or wet. Just happy."

"Your happiness has a very nice face."

"Wine's marvelous."

"Was a very good year."

"Wonderful-sounding name. Romanée, Vougeot, Montrachet..."

"There is a legend, which may easily not be true, that when the Grand Army was on its way to Spain, the regiments saluted as they passed the Vougeot vineyards."

"How lovely. I hope it's true. But why do you have to fly about on the bike on Fridays?...I'm sorry, I had no right to ask."

He took a drink, meditatively.

"My fault. I have no right to make you curious. I shouldn't have—but I was not able to resist the pleasure of seeing you."

"Is it such a pleasure? For me it is, but for you?"

"A most unbiddable pleasure. To answer your question, you will approve of my work. I am a smuggler."

"Oh, but that's wonderful."

"No, it's not wonderful. It's most prosaic and not wonderful at all. I don't even do it myself; I pay others to do it for me. And it's not even anything interesting. Butter to Belgium, where the official price is double what it is here. It is not only illegal; it is mercenary, cynical, and quite deplorable. Still, life generally is all these things. I would myself greatly prefer diamonds; unfortunately I have no acquaintances in the business."

"And is that why you are good friends with headwaiters?" Light was dawning upon Lucienne.

"Among a lot of other characters I don't greatly care for—yes."

She gave a great gust of laughter.

"But I think that's magnificent. And that is why you use the bike—to cover the frontier? And on Fridays you make your dispositions."

"Exactly," he agreed gravely.

"I understand. And the helmet, the goggles—I didn't recognize you, but I wasn't altogether meant to."

"You are acute." Ghost of a smile round his mouth. "I think it sensible that there should be no resemblance between the gentleman on the motorbike and that very respectable businessman in the black Peugeot. By no means impenetrable, but it helps. Politic, shall we say?'

"Please," said Lucienne anxiously, "please, mayn't I go with you some time?"

"But I have told you I do nothing myself. I am merely a middleman. I do nothing exciting."

"But to see."

He thought. "To see would not be too difficult. That could be done. It means lying very still for some time and not coughing."

"Will there be anything brought across tonight?"

"Certainly. Good night. Cloud and rain help. Otherwise it's best to wait for the dark quarter of the moon. Plenty of cloud—and rain—in Holland, luckily."

"Captain Lingard, you're a deep man."

He shrugged. "So is everybody, once you come to study them."

"That is a very important secret and you trust me with that."

"If you gave it away, my dear Lucienne, I should lose everything I possess."

"I will not give you away. I think you know that, or you would not have told me. But you could have put me off. You could have told me to come tomorrow. Why did you tell it to me, the secret?"

He had got up to fetch a match. He lit a cigar carefully,

turning it so that it would burn evenly. He blew the match out with a slim plume of smoke, gazed at the cigar as though it would yield him an important secret, and put it between his teeth with sudden decision.

"Because I love you," he said, walking away with the empty wine bottle. "It's one of the things men do when they love women. They trust them with secrets."

When he came back she was gazing into space, with the ash on her cigarette so long it fell when she lifted her head. She had a worried look.

"I am happy that you love me. I love you. But I am ashamed of myself for being such a cow."

"I love you exactly the way you are. And now we're going to bed. We must be up early in the morning, and we will make plans to have a good day."

❊ ❊ ❊

It was raining again in the morning, rattling faintly but persistently. Lucienne, in trousers and a sweater, lit the stove and put water on for coffee. He lay watching her with pleasure. She made a face at the weather.

"Yes. A pity; I had hoped it would be fine."

"I don't mind a bit. I like to be here, and I like to be with you. I have no need of other places or people."

"We will think of indoor pursuits. I'll go into Venlo and do a bit of shopping."

"And I'll do the housekeeping."

He came back with half a chicken, a smoked eel, and some shrimps; and a set of chessmen.

"Spanish risotto?"

"Oh, what a good idea."

"I thought you'd prefer that to going out to a restaurant."

"And shall we also drink a great deal?"

"Of course."

Late in the afternoon, as happens in Holland, the rain stopped abruptly. A busy sun came out, mopping up the water like a good Dutch housewife.

"You'd like to go out? On the bike maybe? Or car?"

"Bike, please. If it's not too much of a risk."

"No. Nobody looks at a man on a motorbike, and nobody guesses how old or how fat he is under those clothes. We must find you something to wear. Luckily you're almost as big as me; I've got a jacket that'll fit you."

"Can we go to the sea?"

"Even swim in the sea if you like. We can go to Ierseke and eat oysters. We can go right out to West Kapolle and watch ships. We can do anything you like. The bike's faster than an auto on the road. Autostrade all the way to Middelburg. You'll have to sit like a jockey if we go fast."

"I want to go fast."

"You're a bit drunk. Fresh air will do you good."

Lucienne had never gone fast on a motorbike, or eaten oysters in Tholen, or gone to the farthest point of land on a sea-coast, with binoculars to watch the train of ships heading for the Nieuwe Waterweg and Rotterdam, for Antwerp and Hamburg, Surabaya and San Francisco. She had never seen the great dikes that protect Zeeland from the sea.

"I am the girl from the Piraeus." She was staring out to sea.

"Yes. But the world's got very small. Everything under one roof, as those boring supermarkets say. Easier for Captain Lingard."

"What is there that we can still do?"

The last of the evening light silvered an oily summer sea, gun-gray as a tunny's back. It was very still. In front, the North Sea stretched out limitlessly. A lighthouse started to blink and buoys blinked back; flarepaths into Antwerp and the Waterweg. Behind them, the polder stretched like the sea; wind teased at their hair—there is always wind on Walcheren. To their right, the apparently small and insignificant works of the Deltaplan threw down Holland's defiance of the sea. Stam shivered; he was suddenly chilled. What was there they could still do? Lucienne gazed at the view with the vigor and enthusiasm of twenty-two years. Stam did not want to look at it any longer; he yearned for other horizons, less limitless and less *triste*. The rocks and tamarisks and sea-poppies of the Atlantic coasts; the cork oaks and umbrella pines and mimosa of the south. He wished that he were Captain Lingard, smelling the nutmeg scent of a landfall off Java in the 'eighties. Old and tired he felt, like the handful of arthritic civil servants retired from the Indies, who would never shake off their nostalgia for the Indies and that smell. They must almost all be dead now, but perhaps there were still a few who looked out on streets in Voorburg and Wassenaar and wished that they were twenty-two years old.

"We'll go to the border. Be dark by the time we're there."

"Isn't it dangerous? Mightn't we be seen?"

He smiled; she wanted it to be dangerous. "No. You see, when the border guards see a man and a woman on a motorbike, going for a walk in fields on a summer night, they don't think of smuggling. We've the best camouflage there is."

"But it's not a camouflage," she said.

He stopped on a deserted roadway and pushed the bike in among bushes.

"Like the last of the Mohicans."

"Wouldn't it be awful if we couldn't find it again?"

"Ah, but we will. Not the first time I've played Indians round here."

He took her arm and struck into fields. It was almost dark, and low twigs switched them across the face; brambles hooked their trousers. Hobble-bobble, the ground was uneven; it was by no means easy to walk. He pressed her forearm strongly; they crouched, knelt, lay flat, in wet bracken that dripped water down their necks. There was a sudden tramp of boots about twenty meters off, on a sandy path; they stayed very still. "Border guard," said a grasshopper in her ear. "Don't move even if it tickles." She did not stir; he could feel her breathing slowly through her mouth. The boots crunched into the distance.

"There is a friend who may be flitting about, who has certainly seen both the guard and us," said the grasshopper. "But we won't see him."

Lucienne's heart was making the horrible bumping ache in the throat that steals the breath; she lay with her face pressed into the bracken, looking up at the sky, listening to the sounds of the night. A rustling ticking purr of things growing and of small animals moving nervously. An owl whirred a few meters away; there were strange sinister steps in the bracken. She was frightened; everywhere about her there were stealthy creepings and cautious quick scutterings. Whatever was abroad, it was fierce. Hunting, prowling beasts; cats, stoats, foxes. A bat flickered very close above her, a witch or a spook against the pale darkness; she choked her start out on the breast of his jacket.

She turned cautiously and eased her cramped hip; she reached out and slid her arms round him, begging silently for protection. He held her comfortably; the tiresome bracken left her face alone. It was suddenly warm and safe. He kissed her hair gently; her mouth was an inch from his ear.

"What do the others do?"

"Which others?"

"The ones on motorbikes?"

"They make love in the fields."

"Then make love to me."

It was comic; they had to be slow, very slow, and very very still. It was infuriating the amount of clothes she had on; it seemed to take her an hour to get her hand up her back and unclip her bra—that casual, everyday woman's movement. His hands were cold and wet from the accursed bracken; when at last she could lay them on her breasts it was ice on fire; her body seemed alarmingly dry and burning, as though she had a fever. She clenched her teeth to try and control the shivering, and the sissing of her breath, which sounded to her like an old asthmatic German steam engine.

"I'm terribly sorry, I won't make any more noise."

"You're not making any noise."

"Aren't I? I thought I was making a din they'd hear in Tilburg. *O bella signorina putana madonna*; forgive me, I'm trying to stop shaking. *Ciel*, aren't they hard? Like two guns pointing at you." A soundless, nervous giggle. "I get the feeling that any second my breasts will light up like two electric bulbs." She gave a slow harsh sigh and deliberately collapsed all her straining muscles. "I'm afraid you'll have a wicked job getting my trousers off. Oh Cambronne, why does it take so long? Here, let me do my pants; I know the trick of them.

"I have to be destroyed. *Anéantie. Je veux succomber.* I have to give and give and give and give. *Donne, va.*

"*Ciel*, you hurt me, but I don't care. If I make a noise put your hand over my mouth.

"It's all lies about the earth turning. Earth doesn't turn at all, it's me. *Je sème à tout vent*, like Larousse.

"Let me rest quietly a second. *J'ai le vertige.* No, I'm all right; just leave me a second.

"*Vache*, how ridiculous I look, with everything either under my chin or tripping me up. It pricks like a lunatic, that filthy bracken. And I'm certain there are ants. I don't care. Beautiful.

"Moon madness—magnificent. I am happy like a queen. I fear no death."

"Lucienne…Lucienne…I'm going to dress you; you'll get soaking wet and very cold. But don't stand; you'd show against the skyline. If you crawl as far as the path, you'll be in the shadow. No, it doesn't matter if someone does come; he'd see nothing he hasn't seen before. No, they don't patrol at intervals, that would be too easy. Sometimes they come back unexpectedly. It won't matter."

"Wonderful. Do you really know where to find the bike? Where now? Home; please."

A little down the road—they were cruising gently and almost noiselessly—a jeep was parked. A torch flicked on, and off again directly; a hand waved them on casually. He cruised on till they turned onto the main road, where he swept out with a boom of the big motor and accelerated up the autostrade.

"Miss Clavel flew fast and even faster. To the scene of the disaster," Lucienne told herself, jockeying at a hundred and sixty kilometers an hour.

"I'm stiff, my God, I'm stiff. Is that from the bike?"

"Both perhaps. I'll rub you, and make you supple again. First food. Starving?"

"Like a wolf."

"Good. Brandy with lemon and sugar and hot water?"

"Oh yes, yes. Warm in here, marvelous. I glow. But I must wash before you rub me."

"Water on the stove. I'll go and cut bread."

When he came back she was wound in an old camel dressing gown of his; she ate three big pieces of bread.

"Do you like me to wear perfume?"

"At moments like this, very much."

"I've never worn any, but I'll get some. What should I buy?"

"Leave that to me. I'm going to give myself the luxury of buying you things. Here's your cognac."

"Give me a cigarette then, too. *Vache*, still boiling."

"Then let it cool, you impatient woman."

"I don't want to, but I have to. Oh, I'm stiff. You were going to rub me."

"So I will. What are you wearing under that?"

"Nothing at all, so I'm expecting you to take this off."

"Mademoiselle, you are learning fast."

"I have to. Oh, the insides of my thighs. *Sacrée fougère. Sacrée moto.*

"*Sacrée* fornication," he said happily. "You are a woman made for love. I thought so, and I am not mistaken."

"I am made, at least, to love you. I was not mistaken."

"Perhaps we are being very foolish. But one does not resist the thunder stroke."

"Nor does one want to try."

"As long as you don't think that I go about despoiling virgins?"

"You were more than welcome to this one. There's one more thing I would like to believe—that I shall never be your bad-luck bird."

He kissed her back with tenderness. But now, he thought, I shall have to do something about Solange.

The meetings of adulterers, furtive and filled with precautions, become tedious, but at the outset they are part of an exciting and fascinating game. Stam and Lucienne were not adulterers except in a technical sense, but because of "discretion" they behaved as though they were. She entered into this game with zest. She never saw him in Brussels; his occasional notes were delivered at her lodgings. In Holland they met at continually differing places; they did not show themselves in public, and even in the cottage they lay low. They went out at night on the motorbike, going to obscure places at odd hours, where they would see nobody but other smugglers, lovers, and poets. Because of the anonymity of cities, they got into the habit of Amsterdam, and spent much time there.

"I was born in this town," he said abruptly. "I've never lived here, but I should like to. This is the only town in Holland with any aristocracy and any underground. Other towns have only bourgeois—here there is a *noblesse*, and a *canaille.*"

"I have lived here."

"Would you like to again?"

"With you I would."

"Do you know that I wish to marry you? That I wish to be respectable?"

"It's quite respectable enough for me the way we are."

He did not raise the subject again. But it returned to his mind. A whole series of new ideas were taking vague shape. Buying a house in Amsterdam. Getting rid of Solange. Vaporizing Gerard de Winter, who had become otiose.

To get some detachment and calm into his decision he went south for a week.

That was a symptom of his unease, for one could not leave one's affairs—he had always watched every step, as a conductor does his orchestra, listening with a sensitive ear for the least note of discord, a dragging harmony, an unequal tempo. This close attention had made him successful and rich; now for the first time he was tending to be slipshod—that wouldn't do. He must take just as much care as ever—more.

Nevertheless, he went south, and pottered from Toulon toward San Remo, a coast he was fond of. Unemotional lot they were there—not at all romantic. The legend of romance along this coast is a ridiculous myth, he thought; they should come north for romance; we've got the climate for it.

Gerard de Winter, he considered, had no longer any reason for existence. Born in Amsterdam, Belgian father and Dutch mother. Lived with the mother till he was four, when the father offered to bring him up openly as his son. Mother agreed—don't know why; don't much want to know. Never saw her again. No ill will—she probably acted sincerely for the best. No ill will toward Father either. He might never have done it had his wife lived—or had he had legitimate children. Not going to be ungrateful, though. Got brought up, got sent to best school in Brussels, got left the hotel and everything else when he died. Let us not inquire why he did it—he did it. Owe him thanks, and respect.

"But do I still owe anything to Gerard de Winter? I played him obediently for years; I did my best for him, with him. Had it not been for the war, I should still, no doubt, be a known and respected figure around Ostend. I did my best, and when I married Solange I thought I was doing a good thing, of which my father would approve. Local girl, smart, pretty, clever, who would be a shining light. And I was quite right—she is a shining light.

"I do not intend to think about my life with Solange. But I do not owe anything more to Gerard de Winter. I have always felt more of an Amsterdammer than a Bruxellois. I do not even know the name of the street where I lived as a child, yet I have always felt love for the town—a sense of belonging. I've never had that in Brussels, or Ostend.

"As for Stam—I certainly owe much to him. More than I can easily find words for. He was not a particularly attractive person, perhaps, but I felt a kinship with him. He was adrift, too, without family or roots—he had tried to make the army into his life. I wonder whether there is still anybody who knew Stam personally. Must be, in Maastricht or thereabouts. There might even be people who would know I was not Stam.

"He died like a brave man, and alone. His death was never official, and the witnesses are buried in the same grave as he. All except that one—that soldier with the Swabian accent. Perhaps on some potato field between Stuttgart and Pforzheim there is a man still who knows that Stam is dead. I would like to buy that fellow a drink, and tell him that years ago he had shot me.

"Being Stam—tentatively, temporarily, in emergencies, then more and more, at last finally, permanently—has that changed, or altered me? Has it made me into a different person? Yes, because now when I play a part, it is the part of Gerard de Winter, hotelier. Had I not been Stam would I have become a countryman, nature lover? It is genuine in me. Stam was the first who told me to look at trees, at flowers, but it is in my blood all the same. I wonder who my grandfathers were. My mother's father may have been an Amsterdam dock rat, and my father—he never told me much that I recall about his father, but it seems more likely that he would have liked shooting, and flowers. Do I perhaps owe my career after all to my Belgian, de Winter blood? That would be amusing.

"Whereabouts is that hotel where the baron lives now? Somewhere round here. Wasn't it Menton, or one of those gloomy huge villas on Cap Saint Martin? Let's go and look the old boy up. Must be gaga by now, but he's a valuable person. Was Stam's commanding officer, and even in his good days never suspected me for a second. Through him I was able to bring the whole thing to life, to surround it with papers and make it official, to be sure I would never have difficulty with a driving license or a passport. Minor civil servants are still impressed by the idea of a baron, thank heaven."

It was a coincidence, if you like, that the baron should have been pleased to find a tenant for his house—a reliable tenant, sympathetic. His old acquaintance Captain Stam was a good chap; just the chap to look after things. Lucky that he should be looking just now for a little house in Amsterdam; lucky he should have happened to mention it. Well, he would write a fine letter of introduction to that fool of a notary. A gentleman's agreement. No need to make it too definite.

The baron knew in his heart that never again would he leave the lemon-scented air of Menton for the raw damp of Holland, but he pretended, still, that one day he would go back. No, a simple yearly tenancy. Stam was quite content with this.

He knew that the only contact the baron would again have with Holland was the black-bordered paragraph in the *Rotterdamse Courant*, with all his initials and titles. Order of Oranje-Nassau. Order of the Netherlands Lion. Légion d'Honneur.

But the old boy wasn't going to give up without a fight. He still dipped himself in the sea every day; it did his tubes no end of good. And that clever French doctor made him eat rye bread, and lots of sage and garlic; it agreed with him. He wasn't going to die yet, oh no. But a house unlived in halved its value in a year; it was certainly a good idea that Stam should go and keep things warm and dry in the Apollolaan.

Stam walked quietly around his new house, filled with longing, with this strange craze for virtue, for permanency, for a bourgeois life, that had been growing on him recently, and that he sought to satisfy by walking round furniture shops and occasionally even buying things.

If he could abolish de Winter, there would never be any question again of having to act Stam. He would be Stam for good. He felt sure that Solange would approve; it would leave her in complete and undisputed ownership of the hotel, and free to do as she liked. She did that now, but who knew? Maybe she too might wish to marry again. It was only fair—the marriage hadn't exactly been a success for her either.

Yes, a plan would have to be made. Regretted and unexpected death of Gerard de Winter, abroad perhaps. A road accident? Difficult. Solange could come and identify. Difficult, but not altogether impossible, with the good relations he had. Meantime he would see what he could do to make this house pleasant, habitable, warm. Say nothing to Lucienne yet for a while. It would have to be unassailable. Once de Winter was dead, he could marry Lucienne. He could, as Stam, marry her now. But somehow he hesitated to do that. Too like cheating.

He could not face any more cheating now.Lucienne, too, was thinking about getting married. She was not a great believer in it. Her experience of marriages was discouraging. Just look at Father, with those terrible perfumed hangers-on of his. She knew nobody who had made a success of getting married, and anyway the idea was against most of the cherished principles she had not yet completely discarded at twenty-two. Marriages were too often a fake. Hypocrisy, sentimental self-deception. It came to no good, and crippled one. How could one march through life as one should, like that? Marriage was too often no better than being a whore. Holy deadlock. Legalized prostitution. She knew all the phrases.

Why did her beloved, her captain, her King Tom, wish to kowtow to convention? It could do a smuggler no good to he married; it was even a danger. Poem—so-called—somewhere, she'd learned at school. "What hands cling to the bridle-rein/ Slipping the spur from the booted heel." Blush-making language, but sound. It was a weakness.

A man like that wasn't supposed to get married. Stam married to her was as unthinkable as Peter Abelard married. And she, like Héloise, was more than content to be his mistress. She could ruin him by marrying him. She had better refuse. Put a stop to it. It was a romantic impulse on his part. He was a very romantic person. She liked that, but it was dangerous. She would have to be very careful that her influence upon him was not bad.

Married, with a heap of brats—it was as bad as could be. Before one knew what one was about one was surrounded by a horde of civil servants wanting to tax one, to pay one's children's allowances, to fix one up with a radio license and a seat in the church; to make one vote and take an interest in the community and be a good boy. That wouldn't do. Directly they appeared in the town-hall files, they were lost.

What would she do if she got pregnant? She might at any moment. She didn't care; she would carry her child in love and truth and honesty. It was exactly like the Sixth Symphony. Careless happiness and joy in the first movement, complete peace and purity in the second, alcoholic gaiety in the third. And then the storm. And now the joy and fulfillment and love of the finale. She had almost finished her Sixth; she was ready for the thrill and attack and splendor of the Seventh, best of all.

She was happy. Happy in her body, used and at peace. Happy in her mind, confident at last that she had found someone as uncompromising as herself in honesty and loyalty. When he had given her his word, that was as irrevocable as hers. Truth corrupted; daylight and champagne. He had never married because he had never met his match. Now she intended to make it worth his while.

Lucienne lay on the long wooden settle, a cushion under her neck, a cigarette in her mouth, reading *The Rescue*. Stam stood by the window immobile, one hand in his pocket, the other holding a cigar, which he was smoking slowly and staring at between puffs, as though it helped him to think. It was a still, overcast evening, neither warm nor cold, with a sort of tolerant neutrality—very Dutch. He stared out the window, but turned now and then to study her. She lay lithe and comfortable, one knee up supporting the book, her hair nearly in her mouth, the lines of her jaw and lips strong and heavy. Her eyes glanced up at him with a sort of loving anxiety, as though to make sure he was still there. They caught his looking at her; she smiled and put the book down on her stomach.

"Lingard was an awful fool, to my mind."

"He wasn't very sophisticated."

"To be so stupid like that. I mean, you are an idealist too, hut he's so wet. You're not like that."

Aren't I, he thought. I wonder. Aloud he said, "You mustn't make the mistake of judging him by today's standards. Child of the Victorian era. And English. The English aren't like us;

they have a different conception of romance. But the world has changed; even the English aren't so like that any more. If, indeed, they ever were," he added reflectively.

"Do you love me, really? You like me, you enjoy me, but do you love me?"

"I do. I dislike saying it, because saying it seems to rob it of force. But I'll say it for all that. I approve of it."

"What is it? There must be something in me you think worth loving."

He looked at the cigar as though it would give him the answer.

"You're a woman of action, made for action. Most women sit spinning webs of intrigue, full of introspection and conspiracy, never doing anything, waiting for their men to do it all for them. You aren't like that; it is rare enough. You would not sit behind a desk, handing out smiles and bits of paper to men like slugs. Women like you tend to be fanatical."

"Oh yes, very."

"Like what's-his-name in the book, the Norwegian, blowing up the ship. I can see you doing that. Only northern Europeans do these things. I haven't the guts, myself."

"You are quite right. I approve of Jorgenson; I would have blown the boat up too. But it is not very interesting or pleasant, a woman like that."

"Yes it is. They are interesting women. But they have to be careful that they do not become very unhappy. I do not intend to let you be unhappy. I have been thinking of how to make you happy. And to tame that dangerous streak in you. I want to marry you. I know your objections, but you romanticize me, you know," with a grin. "Really I am very sober and proper. Otherwise my business would not be as well run as it is. I should like to stop flitting about, stop going to Belgium, live a life of calm in Amsterdam, where no one will ever suspect me of being a smuggler. I will invest my capital in very good safe shares— turn one piracy to the advantage of another. Companies are all pirates, you know; the only merit—and that only in their eyes— is that they're about fifty percent legal. You would think them monsters of hypocrisy. We will run away here for weekends—buy a yacht, maybe."

She smiled at him. "Are you going to be one of those cunning bastards, always able to talk me into things?"

"Probably."

"Are you so rich? Not that I care a damn."

"I've been making vast profits for years and never spending any of it."

"Wonderful. Well, maybe I will marry you; I don't suppose I want to grow old working in a garage. And I promised you all of me; if that means marrying you I will. But I insist on the yacht."

"Would you like me to start this tremendous program of bribery with a new auto for you? A ferocious one, that would suit you."

"Auto? For me? Not at all—you're daft."

"Why? I'm thinking of turning in the Mercedes anyway; it's getting to be a bit of a granny. But if we're bribing you I must admit a secret. I have had a house in Amsterdam for some time now. It has to be made ready for you; I've no more than camped in it. We'll live there. And outside, you can leave the car. Insolently. Leave it to me; we'll see about getting you a nice feminine one. Not too small, good and fast, and, like you, beautiful. I will give it thought."

"What a rogue you are not to have told me."

"Do you wish me to be a man totally without secrets? To tell you everything immediately? To make no move without asking you first?"

"Good God, no. It would be like a shop window, very dull. But I find you no longer like Lingard."

"But I am not really like Lingard. You must lose your illusions about me."

"Let me lose them gently. I will enjoy seeing the house, though."

"You know what I want? A house that reminds me of you. I want to live where there are clothes that carry your form, a bed with your imprint. Glasses that reflect you."

❃ ❃ ❃

When she arrived next time, she handed him a parcel with enjoyment.

"I've bought something for you. Nothing big. I hope it will give you pleasure, though."

"But what can it be? It looks like a picture. It is a picture."

"I even think it's a good one. I was taught something about pictures at home, and I've learned something since. And I got it cheap—I think I've made you a good investment."

"It's breath-taking," transfixed by the little Breitner snowscape. "I'm completely captivated by it."

"I wanted you to have it for your house, because you said you wanted something I'd chosen. I'm happy you like it."

"Like it? But it's magnificent. Takes the gilt sadly off what I bought."

"What is that?"

"A surprise which is now deflated. Look out at the back, by the shed."

It was not at all a deflated surprise for Lucienne when she saw the white Mercedes coupé and could try the angle of the steering and the feel of the pedals under her feet and sniff the soft blond leather and gloat with professional mechanical rapture over the motor.

"I think it will do a hundred and eighty on the autostrade," with joy.

"I always thought so, darling; one only needs a big enough bribe to give in like a lamb. I will marry you."

"I have to do some fairly tedious chores in Belgium, arranging the business. And then you can come to Amsterdam to do some shopping. Plenty to do; I've bought only a few essentials."

"I don't want to come till everything's settled. But I'm beginning to look forward to it like mad."

"I'm pleased to see you," said Solange agreeably. "It really is high time that you gave us a bit of your company. Not that I intend to stay and enjoy it for long, because I do need a holiday badly. You can arrange to stay a fortnight?"

"I should think so. Moon's in the bright quarter and the weather seems settled. Shipments will be scarce the next couple of weeks. You take your holiday; I'll see nothing runs away."

"That new waiter, the Italian boy, will do with a bit of pulling up; he'll try to take advantage of my being away."

"Excellent. Before you go, I should like a little serious conversation."

"Hm. I'd a feeling there was something in the wind."

"Now, then?"

"No time like the present."

"Good. I have the honor of informing you that you will shortly become a widow, Madame de Winter."

Solange threw her head back and laughed; she was not pretty when she laughed, but he was pleased to see it.

"I thought you'd come to something like that in the end. You're an original, Gerard. I've always appreciated that. How will it affect things though, as you see them?"

"You will have the pleasure of inheriting this property. It needs care; I haven't quite decided how it can best be done.

We need a respectable witness to this unfortunate death. You, of course, but another, since you benefit. Someone might think you'd knocked me off," grinning.

"I think that probably, some fine day fairly soon, you will get a policeman, all sympathy and embarrassment, on the doorstep. There will have been an unfortunate accident. Be very prudent, watch your words, and don't identify me until you're quite sure. Rather tend to say you're sure it can't be true, perhaps; must be someone else.

"What it amounts to is that you become sole owner of the hotel, which thanks to you will have reached a considerable figure at valuation, and which, moreover, you will be free to dispose of should you so wish. There is also a personal advantage; it will be more flexible being a widow than having a tiresome husband. I will continue, of course, to see that Gilbert has as much butter as he needs. And should you meet me in the street in Hamburg, let us say"—he smiled—"a discreet lack of recognition, hm? Are you satisfied with my plan?"

"I think so. I know you well enough to know you are perhaps the only person whose word I can trust, so I won't ask you to put it in writing."

It was his turn to laugh. "No, perhaps that would not be very prudent. We could have a fine time—each scared to begin blackmailing the other. We must be accomplices in this delicate affair."

"When I hear of your death, I shall be most remorseful, though I shall not attempt to conceal the fact that we have lived estranged. We've always got on well—nothing like telling the truth."

"I think that will be a most suitable note to hit. Well, my dear, have a pleasant holiday. Sorry we can't spend my last days together."

"Isn't it rather a sudden decision?"

"Business, my dear. I think the Dutch are getting curious—I intend to fade a bit more into the background. But you appreciate my being a man of my word—I appreciate your never asking questions. It's been an unfortunate marriage for us, but a good partnership."

"You may rely upon me," said Solange, smiling. "My dear Gerard, you are a most considerate husband."

"Mutual advantage, my dear. Always been our aim to both get something good out of it."

What a disgusting scene, he thought, drinking soup, served with care by the Italian waiter. That, now, was a piece of hypocrisy Lucienne would kill me for, she'd be so revolted. Oh, well, never again.

One should never say things like that without thinking carefully of what exactly they might mean.

❀ ❀ ❀

"Ben, can I come in the office, and can I perhaps have a drink?"

"Both, without regret. What do you want? I got some good whisky from those Englishmen."

"Yes, whisky. It's a celebration."

"I've been waiting for it. You've looked that happy, these last weeks."

"I'm thinking of getting married."

"Well, here's to you. I suppose I might have known it. I was afraid of it, don't mind telling you. You know what I feel about you."

"You aren't mad at me?"

"Mad? Never. I'm bloody angry, but not with you. Lucky bastard. Let me see him—I'll slosh him."

She laughed. "Ben, please—don't be vicious."

"Old or young?'

"Quite old—double my age."

He shook his head sorrowfully over the glass. "Lucienne... and you could have anybody."

"Thanks, I'm quite content with what I've got."

"So you'll be going then, I suppose?"

"I'm sorrier myself than I thought I'd be."

"Not as sorry as me. There's plenty I'd rather see go. When?"

"Not sure myself. Another month, maybe."

"Well, now the season's over we're all going to take a day off anyway, one of these days. Like last year, remember? We had a good time. Let them buy their gasoline some other place for one day. Works picnic."

"But of course I'll come. Buy a drink for everyone, what's more."

"Say, Luce…"

"Well?"

"If anything ever happens…I mean one never knows…always a place here for you, you know… And of course a job whenever you want one…and anything to do with an auto, you've only to say."

"Thank you, Ben. I won't forget you said that. I say, did I tell you I was given an auto, a sort of early wedding present?"

"You did? What? Why'n't the bugger buy it from me?"

"SE 220 coupé. White."

"Wow. I reckon I'd better take back some of what I said. Must be more to him than I thought."

"Did you think I'd accept anything else?"

"What does he do?"

"Sorry. Can't say anything about that."

"Must be in the black market," said Bernard cheerfully, "giving away cars like that one."

A day or so later she was in the Brouckère, buying cigarettes. A tall man turned from the counter as she waited, a cigar in his mouth. He paused to hold it to the little gas jet, and his eye caught hers. The face was vaguely familiar; hers was too, apparently, for he gave a half smile and raised his hat.

"Good morning, mademoiselle."

"Good morning," wondering who the hell he was.

"We haven't seen you in some time. Or Monsieur de Winter. We miss him."

"Monsieur de Winter?" And who the hell was that? Lines crossed somewhere. He saw he had made a mistake; his face set at once to a polite blank.

"*Mes excuses*, mademoiselle; I see I took you for someone else." He went out hurriedly, ready to kick himself for being stupid.

Hours after, she recalled who he was. She had only seen him in evening dress. The headwaiter, to be sure, of that restaurant where she had often eaten. Where she had first met Stam, and where they had eaten together a couple of times later. Proud of his eye, obviously. What had he said? De Winter? Fairly common name. Must be some alias of Stam's; she grinned.

Out of curiosity she looked in the phone book next time she was searching for a number. Just for fun. Not so common after all. Plenty of Winters. De Winters…de la Mare, de la Mothe, de la Motte…only two de Winters, one a gynecologist in Laeken, one a timber merchant in Ixelles; she would kid him a bit about that. Or might it be better to keep her mouth shut? He didn't much like anything said about the business. Quite right too; less she knew about it the better. She didn't even want to know.

There was a good deal of discussion in the garage about the "picnic." Everyone enjoyed the idea. Not that it was a treat in itself – they all had cars and could go to the coast any time they wanted. But this time it was a working day, which was pleasant; it was without their wives and children—doubly pleasant—and they would all go in a coach together. Gay, and a nice excuse for a big booze-up. Everybody knew it was no use making up to Lucienne, even if she wasn't getting married in another fortnight or so anyway—but there were various designs upon the virtue of the new telephone girl, who wasn't a bad bit of crumpet.

There were two schools of thought. One was for a longish trip, into the Argonne, or Germany. The coast was boring; they'd been there so often. The other school maintained that the coast might be dull, but it was near; there would be more time to gamble, to drink, and to sit and be gentlemen, and who the hell wanted to sit for half a fine day in a lousy coach anyway, with nothing to do but drink lukewarm beer looking out of the goddam window?

This school had the majority. It was decided to go to Ostend and stop anywhere and everywhere that looked nice, for drinks. And if the weather was not good for the essential lordly strolling along the sea front, well, we can always go over the frontier, Boulogne or somewhere. Hell, go to Touquet if we feel like it. Gambling's the thing; if the weather is bad make a dash for the bloody casino, boys.

Lucienne looked with amusement round her. Faces familiar in overalls, now well scrubbed and in smart suits; Robert had a gangster hat and looked fit to seduce every or any woman he passed. The bus was humming along the main road.

"Here; I know this place; there's a good café here. There it is—drive-er! Halt!" Everybody piled out for the first drink—the best drink—in Erneghem.

Lucienne, with Robert and two others, sat at a table in the window bay. They were still quiet so early in the morning—hadn't warmed up yet. Talk was not yet loud, or general. She looked about with contented curiosity.

To her left, and a little behind her, sat three youngish boys, playing cards and drinking beer. They wore fancy sweaters and elaborate ties, but all three had rather sluttish evening trousers. Assistant waiters, off duty after breakfast—she knew that breed. How many hotels had she not stayed in with her father on tour? And how many times, later, had she not sat in other cafés, on other terraces, with the Italian boys? They reminded her of her youth; she thought back to gay days in Amsterdam with Franco and Dario. And little Nino, who had gone to jail for pulling a knife in the Leidseplein. With slight nostalgia, she listened to the loud, carrying Italian voices. Just the same. Still showing off, still using naughty words because they thought nobody ever understood. Still full of the careless vitality that had made her enjoy them more than the stiff Dutch boys.

"...sent me back three times for more butter, the *scarabocchio*, with her hair in her plate. I had a wish to pour coffee over her."

"*L'enfant prodige* asked for English porridge. Porridge, *dio merda*."

"*Belote*."

"*Rebelote*."

"How many spades you got there then, pirla?"

"No trump left."

"*Sans atout, porco dio*."

She grinned. Nothing changed. But the next words made her listen with a strained attention.

"You saw the new lover of *la mère* de Winter?"

"*Della vecchia?* I served them. Made me change two saucers, *la vacca*."

"Leave her alone," Robert was saying. "She's miles away; hasn't woken up yet. Hey, Luce."

"Shut up," she said. "I'm interested in something."

"...do the same, if the husband was away all the time, so handy."

"*Putana vecchia*, it was quiet last month when she was away. *Il vecchio* did not make me change the saucers all the time."

"Hearts again, *dio cane*; always when Enzo deals."

"*Furna—Toscana*."

"All the same, I would not refuse it, a night with *la donna* de Winter. I will say to her, 'Signora, I will sacrifice. My heart is near...'"

"Watch the beer then, *pastore.*"

"'...and your husband is far. *Lontano degli occhi...*'"

"Come on, Luce, wake up."

"No, you go on. I've got to do something; I've just remembered. I'll catch you up easy. See you in the Casino."

She finished her drink with a gulp and hesitated a moment, then turned to the table of the Italian boys. They blushed and jumped to their feet. They were no older than she, but she felt a century older.

"Sorry to interrupt you."

"*Non non non,* Madame, at your service."

She almost wanted to laugh; these boys. They stood admiring her with bold, gallant eyes.

"The hotel where you work—is that far from here?"

"Well no, Madame, just down the road. Can we carry Madame's luggage?"

"I have no luggage; I just stopped here for a coffee. By chance I heard you speaking of Madame de Winter." She had to smile this time; they looked so hangdog.

"Madame understands Italian?"

"Some."

"Thousand pardons, Madame," with polished courtesy, "for the bad words."

"And this Madame de Winter—I do not know her, but I have heard her spoken of—she is the owner?"

"*La padrona, si,* but the owner, that is Monsieur. But he is always away; we do not often see him."

"Except like last month," put in the other. "She was away, and then Monsieur took charge."

"I wonder if it is the same one I have met. Middle-aged, brown hair, about your build?"

"Yes yes."

"And blue eyes? Very quiet, and a serious expression?"

"I see that Madame knows him."

"That is it, yes; it must be the same."

"Madame permits that we offer something to drink?"

"No. Thank you, but I must be going."

"A tiny glass Martini, to express our apologies to Madame?"

Ridiculous how like Dario that boy was. Plainly the leader; the others were hangers-on.

"And Madame? You find her beautiful, even if not sympathetic?"

The boy grinned, with sly amusement. "Not sympathetic. Certainly good to look at, but a character…" He shook his fingers loosely up and down, the classic gesture of "Ow." "Monsieur does not find her sympathetic either," he added impudently.

"He doesn't?" with what she hoped was indifference.

"Oh no, madame, it is well known. He amuses himself elsewhere. He is always away, nobody knows where; in Germany perhaps. He comes for a day every three weeks or so—just to see, perhaps, that she has not run away with all his money."

"So," uninterested. "I have met him in Brussels, I think. I had no idea he lived near here. He drives a black Peugeot?" casual.

"Quite right, Madame."

"Well, thank you very much. My friends have gone without me; I must get a taxi. You know where I could find one?"

"I will telephone for Madame."

Poor Lucienne; she was spared at least the sight of the boys grinning at each other after she went, the air of worldly wisdom, and the knowing winks.

She did not tell the taxi driver to go to Ostend but to Bruges, where she took the train back to Brussels. She had to see Stam; she had to find out whether this was true. A little tick of common sense at the back of her mind told her she must not decide immediately; she knew well enough that the gossip of a pair of Italian waiters was not reliable evidence. They loved tiny scandals as much as any old woman; to make themselves important, and for the sake of getting a pretty woman to listen to them for five minutes, they would invent any fantasy. Then they could preen themselves, and pretend that they had made a new conquest. She knew that perfectly well; unfortunately it was not altogether a fantasy. Just circumstantial enough, non?

These silly children. Would it not be rather ironic, an acid joke, if now for the second time they were to have an effect upon her life?

In the Midi station the Brussels–Amsterdam express was standing waiting. She could be in Amsterdam in two hours. But it was a Thursday. Wasn't he more likely to be at the cottage? She would go first to Venlo.

It was a fine autumn day; surprisingly warm—the sun still had a cheerful strength. A bus dropped her in Tienray; quite a distance to walk, but she had time, huh? It felt strange being here in town clothes; one or two farmers gave her open-mouthed stares. For the trip to Ostend she had put on a silk two-piece suit; she had a wide coat with elbow-length sleeves, and long gloves, and high-heeled shoes; on these country lanes a ridiculous get-up. Luckily the ground was dry; her shoes would not be ruined, she hoped; they were nearly new.

Wasn't it absurd to give any thought to ruining her shoes?

The cottage was still and shut; everything tidy and neat as usual. He had been here recently, perhaps this morning. He would be back by tomorrow; Friday—a business day, when he would be flitting about on the bike. Had he gone somewhere today? No, the bike stood in the shed, ready to roll, to attack the bypaths between here and Breda. And behind the shed, still shiny new and beautiful, stood the white Mercedes.

She thought of the day a few weeks before, the only time as yet that she had taken it out. They had driven north, up through Nijmegen and past Arnhem, winding round the countryside into the Veluwe. He had sat beside her while she drove; it was vivid in her mind. She could recall every second of that night drive, of her happiness with the lovely, singing car, her happiness with him, her heart singing too with the happiness. They had made love in the car, backed into a narrow gateway between overgrown bushes, heaven knew where. With a sour satisfaction she noticed that Stam had cleaned the car carefully—to keep it looking new.

Lucienne felt in her bag for the keys. Her hand met the cold heaviness of her knife—what was that doing here? She got into the car and headed it over toward Eindhoven, not knowing what she wanted. Perhaps the feel of it, the smell of it, the supple movement of it—would that reduce her fever? *Va*, let me go to Amsterdam. She had never been in the famous house, but she knew the number.

She knew there was a crumpled packet of Gauloises in her bag somewhere, and felt in it as she drove. There was the knife again. As handy a mechanic as anyone in the garage, and proud of it, she always carried a knife, to cut a frayed edge of perished cable, to scrape congealed dust and oil off a screw head, to lift paint and rust off tatty metal and see what it looked like underneath. It lived in her overalls pocket, but she recalled now that she had used it to knock a tiny crust of mud off the heel of her shoe. She must have dropped it back in her bag without thinking; it accompanied her now, as naturally as a lipstick.

The cold hardness of it comforted her hot dry hand through the thin glove; it gave her a sort of childish consolation, like sucking her thumb. She held it a second, and then dropped it impatiently in her pocket; she really needed both hands to steer. The car was heavy, and she was not yet fully accustomed to it.

It was a real workman's knife, that; it had a spring so that she could open it one-handed without looking, and when open it locked; no danger of it shutting under pressure on one's fingers. She had got it her second day at work, after she had tried, rather clumsily, to clear a sticking catch with a screwdriver. That had scratched a centimeter of good paint, bruised her knuckle, and given her a nasty little cut along a fingernail. She had never thereafter been without her knife. That particular type was illegal; one was not supposed to carry them. With just such a one the little Nino—hysterical little boy—had stabbed a corner boy on the Leidseplein, two years ago—three years ago and more.

But all the mechanics used them; they were the handiest for work. Robert had bought it for her, identical with his own.

Utrechtseweg, Rivierenlaan. Left turn, round the Europaplein. Past the exhibition hall, and into the Apollolaan. She was on top of the house before she had realized; she skidded the car to a stop and sprang out, suddenly shaky, very frightened, horribly lost. She rang the bell with her head swimming, with no idea what to say, how to say it. She was possessed by the same demons that haunt the high mountains, that make even experienced climbers lose their heads when they are surrounded by sudden terrifying mists, and hear the mocking voices of wind and snow and sun and ice.

There was a delay before the door opened; she had her hands clenched in her pockets, trying to stop herself from shaking. It did not strike her that Stam would wonder who his visitor might be. He would have taken a quiet, cautious look from an upstairs window and satisfied himself before opening any doors. When the door did open, she was in such a fluster that she just walked inside. He stepped back to let her pass. His self-control, his manners, his dislike of personal remarks—he did not allow himself to show surprise or resentment at her odd look, her abrupt, silent entrance.

"Come straight in; pleasant surprise. I had no idea you were free."

"We're all free." It was for the sake of saying something, of knowing that her mouth still shaped words. "We have a works party. The others went to Ostend, but I decided to come here."

"My poor child, you're frozen; it isn't at all warm once the sun goes down. And you're shaking; you've had a long drive. Very well, don't take your coat off until you feel warmer. Look,

I have a wood fire; the hearth was here already, and I thought it too good to waste. That will make you feel you're at home at once. Sit by it and unwind." His voice was as calm as his face, but his eye searched her. What could be wrong with the girl? He had never seen her like this.

"Nice you look; that coat suits you. Do you know, I've never seen you yet in city shoes. It is going to be a peculiar pleasure to discover these things about you—how you look in high-heeled shoes, in hats, in town suits, in evening dresses."

She was sitting by the hearth, huddled in her coat, staring. Her face was like a scraped bone. Very well, he would go on talking; words would gradually quiet her and loosen her. It was not a good moment to touch her or kiss her.

"You'll notice that I've hung the Breitner. But there is nothing done in this house. You must tell me now how things should go. What do I know about furnishing or arranging a house? One needs a woman for that."

"Yes." There was a long pause. "Yes," she said again.

"You're overtired. Luckily I've always kept a bed for you here, in case you took it into your head to come. Perhaps I am superstitious. But it seemed to me that the house would remain a dead empty shell until there was a place for you in it."

At least she wasn't staring any more; she was looking at him, and there was life in her eyes, but there was something wrong with her expression that disquieted him.

"Have you perhaps picked up a chill? You look on the verge of a fever. And I haven't anything in the house. Still, I may have something that would help—a moment."

One of the odd purchases he had made, wandering around thinking of things that would start making the house a home— a dozen bottles of champagne. He had drunk one; not bad at all. That would do her good. It was cold enough, but to make it look more cheerful, more like a touch of gaiety, he put it in an ice bucket and took both trays of cubes out of the refrigerator. Hm, he hadn't much to eat; after drinking champagne she would suddenly discover she was hungry. Probably hadn't had anything to eat all day, silly child. He had some bread, and a tin of pâté; that would do till tomorrow. He wouldn't let her go back to work if she were ill—he could always ring that garage and explain if it came to the worst.

"By the look of you you've the blues. This is the thing for that." He gave the bottle a turn to settle it into the ice and peeled the foil off. Busy untwisting the wire, using his thumb to ease the stiff cork out gently, he did not look at her. If he had, he might have realized what was the matter with her. But he had little experience with a girl of Lucienne's age. He ought to have thought of Captain Jorgenson. He knew that she thought of him as the center of confidence, wisdom, peace, and honor. But he was concentrating on getting the cork out.

"Two or three glasses of this, and then I think probably bed—that will settle you." He handed her the glass; she took it automatically. Really, his cheerfulness was beginning to sound very hollow; he drank his own glass quickly.

"Drink it, then." She drank it. She was wearing no lipstick—was it that which made her so pale? She must be ill, the child. To give himself time to think he peeled the cellophane off a cigar. He had better try and find out, very quietly. There, she was staring again. She was not ill; there was something very wrong, somewhere.

"Lucienne, what is the matter?" She looked up slowly, her face very haggard.

"I didn't come here to drink champagne. Nor to go to bed. Who else is it for, that bed?"

Good God, she was jealous.

"My dear, what ideas have you in your head?"

"We went today to Ostend. All of us from the garage. We went in a coach—to be together, you understand, to have a gay time. We would stop anywhere we felt like it, to have a drink and move about a few minutes. We stopped like that on our way. In a dorp called Erneghem."

It was a disagreeable shock, now that he suddenly realized. Naturally it had upset her. He would gladly have spared her that. But it was not the end of the world; she would understand when he explained.

He drew quietly on his cigar. There was no point in saying anything yet. First she must be allowed to spit it all out, and get rid of it. She would work herself up, no doubt, but afterward she would feel better. After all, it wasn't that bad.

"Go on. What next?"

"We went into a pub for a drink. Sitting near me were three boys. Waiters. Italian boys. They always have loud voices; they show off, and they think nobody understands them."

Of course—that tiresome one Solange had said needed watching. She'd been right, too.

"And what did they say, these boys? Was it really much worth listening to?"

"A few years ago, before I came to Brussels—when I was a silly girl—I used to be friends with boys like that. I talk a bit of Italian. I know the sort of way they behave. You will understand that I had a momentary interest. 'Momentary' is a good word, isn't it?"

"I can understand that. But why should it be more than momentary? Wasn't it just gossip?"

"Just silly, idle, half-malicious gossip, yes."

"Then why let it get a hold on you? Something discreditable about me—there are such moments in my past."

She leaned forward and put the glass down on the coffee table. That was better. Talking, and the champagne, were having some effect. Her face was less pale, her eyes less queer; she looked more natural altogether.

"I think I should like a little more. I feel very tired."

"Of course you must have some more. I understand now.

You need a bit of perspective, and this will come back into balance. I was beginning to worry; I thought you were ill."

"I am not ill. Frostbitten."

"Not really. You think so for the moment. It is without importance."

"That is not a phrase I understand." She picked up her glass and drank it slowly. "No, no more, it would make me dizzy."

"I suppose then that you have seen Solange?"

"Ah. Solange. That is her name, is it?"

"That is her name. She has good qualities; I do not want to be unfair."

"You married her."

"I did. It was meaningless from the first day. It became at once what it has always been, a business partnership—no more."

"But you married her. And you're still married to her."

How to explain now that Solange was married to Gerard de Winter, whereas she—Lucienne—had been asked to marry Stam? That de Winter was dead in all but name, having now no reason to live? That he—Stam—had gone to Erneghem last month to arrange for de Winter's formal demise? How was he to explain that? He had concealed it precisely because it was difficult, no?

"Listen to me, my dearest, if you will. I will try and explain. I was deliberately not going to tell you till after we were married, but now I must of course. You see I—as you know me—am not married to Solange. It must sound funny—ridiculous rather— but it is so."

"Ah. As you say, funny. But I dislike explanations. My father always had explanations for his various women. I made up my mind then to avoid them. No explanations, no complaints." Despite his control, Stam paced nervously.

"Who rides upon a tiger cannot get down. I must. But it must hurt you. I had hoped to avoid hurting you."

She had stood too, her hands clenched nervously in her pockets.

"You must try to understand, Lucienne. I was de Winter. I am no longer."

"You are no longer. But two weeks ago you were there, with her. It is a long story, I can see. Spare me. I can make explanations too. I am my father's daughter, and you—you are your wife's husband. Many thanks, but I do not want what belongs to another. Neither houses, nor autos, nor men. I made up my mind to that as a child; I do not share men. I must go."

"No no, Lucienne. To flounce out in a tantrum—you are more grown up than that. I cannot allow you to continue believing a story of which you know only half. Take a breath; allow, just for a moment, your head to rule your heart, and you will gain a hold on yourself."

"I wish to go."

Had he taken his own advice he would have been silent; he would have let her go. One must wait for the temperature to drop; a time for explanations comes later. But he felt he must not allow her to go on suffering. Her face, ripped up with pain, blinded him. He thought that with calm and a show of firmness he could tame her. There would be a crisis, and then pouring tears, and then calm, and he could use that calm to tell her why she was wrong.

"Leave me," she said.

"Impossible."

He had his hands on either side of her face; he wished to make her look at him. She would see that he was not lying. One thought possessed him. That he loved her truly, that he could never let her go, that she meant, by now, more than any of his lives.

Did he hear the click of the knife blade? He wished to draw her head to his chest, to hold her, to cover and heal the burning injury. He felt the fierce thrust of her hands, freeing herself, but he did not know that she had killed him. It was a pain, the pain in his heart, that she should thrust him away.

Doubled up, blind, he tried—a second perhaps—to stay on his feet. He lost them, and fell across and over the chair behind him.

Lucienne walked straight out the door. She did not hesitate; her only wish had been to leave the house. She had not even taken off her coat; her bag still hung on her left arm. She closed the door behind her, and walked without thinking down the street. She did not give the white car a glance.

Did she even realize that she had killed him? Not then, not for some time. She had cut loose, that was all. The knife had cut the cords that bound her, to an existence she found unbearable. She had had no thought of killing him.

The evening was cold and bleak. There was little wind, but now that it was night one felt that winter had come. Lucienne walked with rapid, nervous steps into the town. She did not wish to ride on the tram; she had no hunger, no thirst. She did not need to think of the way; she knew every corner and crossing. In the Roelof Hartplein she did not even raise her head to a building where she had lived eight years. She would never see any of this again. She felt no sentiment, or pain; quite the contrary, she felt free and light-hearted. At last, she felt, I am finished with my childhood.

Moments flicked quickly through her memory. Half a dozen pretty, charming women who had been kind to her—was she not her father's pride and joy? Dario's pale, handsome face; Franco's serious eyes. Italian boys in highly colored sweaters and evening trousers, their long legs stretched negligently out along café terraces. Erich Kleiber's back, dominating the Concertgebouw, and the Seventh Symphony of Beethoven.

She threw her right glove into a litter basket; it was covered with blood. Her sleeve was smeared, but did not show badly.

She had reached the Spiegelgracht before realizing that she looked silly carrying one glove, and threw the other away too.

The walking did her good. A noose of that old life had caught her by the foot; she had cut it through. On the Koningsplein, at the Singel crossing, she was nearly run over. In the Central Station she came to the conclusion that she still had her return half of a Brussels–Amsterdam ticket. It was not late. She could be home and in bed by midnight. Today had been a holiday, but tomorrow she had to be at work; that at least was a reality.

It was warm in the train; she took her coat off and hung it so that the stained sleeve did not show. She thought vaguely about the future.

At the garage she could say she had changed her mind—they would not find that extraordinary. But she did not want to stay there much longer. Belgium was too small henceforward. Well, she could go anywhere, do anything. She had plenty of money. Why not France, or Germany? She spoke both languages. No, not Italy, thank you.

"Lucienne, what a disappointment. Would have been more fun if you'd been with us."

"What happened—you felt ill? Ah, you were quite right to go home. We understood; we weren't worried about you. Our Lucienne; *merde.* That one can defend herself; no need to worry about her."

"Lucienne, there's a black DS somewhere outside, with a smashed rear light. When you get a second bring it in for us."

"Seen Ben, Luce? Someone asking for him in the office."

"Robert, lend me your knife, will you? Like an imbecile, I've lost mine."

"Keep it. Be a triumph for me if I can get you to accept something of mine."

"How sentimental you have become, my poor boy."

She was unwilling to go. She was happy here, and free.

Sooner or later, she would have to make up her mind to it. But for the present, it healed her to be where she was accepted, respected, loved. Heaven, if she were to want to get married she could do so tomorrow. Bernard, for example. He was a good man. His poor Léonie—for all she knew Léonie was dead by now, though Bernard had said nothing. His children adored her, too. She had no feelings for children, but she could learn.

If she were to tell Bernard what had happened—not that she would dream of it—she knew he would understand.

She wondered whether Stam were dead. And if he were? His wife would be the richer by a new Mercedes car, presumably. There would be someone else only too glad to look after the butter business.

She could not have told herself why she never bothered taking the cottage keys off the ring. What earthly use could she have for them?

"And now you have turned me inside out again," said Lucienne, tired.

"You had to come and worry it all out, and show me that he was right, and I was wrong. To come and make me pay. I have nothing left to pay with. In killing him I killed myself."

"You couldn't have known," said Van der Valk. "You can only see now, after I've told you what I know, and what I'd pieced together—the rest was inevitable, after we'd joined the two stories together. He was trapped by his past, just as you were. You ran away to Brussels. In a mechanic's overalls nobody would recognize the daughter of Monsieur Englebert. And here in Holland nobody would recognize Gerard de Winter. You were both ashamed of your pasts, and both caught up with you. You were wrong, because he was ready to give you a new life; you should have been ready to give him his."

"I was ready. I would have. Why did I have to hear those three boys talking?"

"I have those questions too. Why did I stop for gas on the way back from Erneghem? Why was it me who found that white auto? Me, who knew you, who hauled you out of your father's car. I only know these things happen."

"What's the result?"

"I sit here, wondering why I don't arrest you. I wish I hadn't heard your story. Or maybe that I hadn't understood it."

"I won't stop you arresting me."

His smile was a little sour. "You had your chance at stopping me."

"Yes. I saw. You let Bernard hit you."

He suddenly changed tack.

"You know where the money is buried here?"

"Yes. He told me. He trusted me with everything. I could not understand why he did not trust me with the story of his wife."

"You understand now?"

"Yes… In a direct line from the well, due south, you'll find a rowari tree. Under there. I think that there is a great deal."

There was a long silence; he heaved himself slowly to his feet.

"You see, I'm not taking you to Amsterdam. Town you've said goodbye to. But I have to bring something back. Luckily, the money will do nicely. That's what they care about. They don't care who killed Stam; they just didn't want to forgive him for pinching their money."

"You mean you're not arresting me?"

"What good would that do anyone? You're not a criminal. Go anywhere. You'll never see me again. Go back to Bernard; tell him you're sorry for being such a bloody fool.

"Nobody's seen you here. Nobody knows anything about you. Stam's death is an enigma. Everybody's happy for it to stay that way. Including me. I might say, especially me.

"Now listen to me attentively. One thing you must not do."

"And what is that? I know, keep my mouth shut."

"That's just what I do mean. You're always tempted by the big heroics. Just like the time in the Sarphatistraat. The grand scene, the big sacrifice. Don't let's have any of that, my girl."

"Any of what?"

"Just don't get any fancy ideas about killing yourself. You aren't a criminal, or I'd arrest you. But that would make you one all right. Now go. Pick up your little Porsche, go back to Brussels, and see that Bernard understands that I want to hear nothing more about this.

"You understand?" he roared, suddenly savage. "No more. Your Stam was a gangster and a hypocrite, who put one lie on top of another till it caught up with him, and in the last turn of the vise he hadn't the guts to be honest. Now out, you stupid mare. I'm sick of all this romance—this story out of a magazine for old women and adolescents. I'm a policeman. I only like stories out of real life. This whole thing has only existed in your mind."

He took a deep breath, and abruptly lowered his voice.

"And don't drive fast over the border. They're cold and wet, thoroughly fed up and probably all trigger-happy, so be careful. Now leave me in peace. And stop worrying about your lousy virginity—plenty of better girls than you have lost theirs in worse ways. No self-pity now. You've learned something about love at last.

"One last thing. Your Ben offered me every penny he could raise to let you go. Pity I didn't take it. And his Léonie's dead, by the way, but he didn't tell you; thought it wouldn't be fair. You'd better be a good wife to him, my girl."

When he had heard the little Porsche go, with a tearing sound along the curtain of mist, he turned to the last little job of all. It took him some trouble to find south without stars, and the digging was no pleasant job either in the wet clinging cold, but at last he found what he had known must he there somewhere—ever since he found the safe-deposit-box key on Stam's body. Hm, they would have an agreeable surprise. Van der Valk finds no criminal, the stupid, but comes up with something better for once. Well well, he should have taken Bernard's bribe. It was a big enough sack of loot to keep the whole Amsterdam police force from asking what he had been doing, fiddling around in Brussels.

Along the border it was still, cold, wet, and thoroughly disagreeable. Few travelers were abroad in such weather, or so late. The guard on the barrier was dreaming of a roaring hot stove, of sucking boiling coffee into his perished withered system, of Marijke, who had let him undo her bra last time they had been together, of arresting a whole carful of smugglers.

It was uncannily silent; the mist blanketed noise. One couldn't make out whether it was thicker or not. Sometimes he thought yes, sometimes no. Visibility wasn't really all that bad—fifty meters or so round here. Enough to let a car drive at a good lick.

Suddenly, quite close, appallingly loud in the stillness, he heard the roar of a motor at high revs. That was a driver going fast—and it sounded like a powerful motor. He stepped forward, pointing like a gun dog, his carbine in the crook of his elbow and his left hand up already calling for a halt. Please let it be one of those bastards—and if the sod doesn't halt, I'll give him the whole goddam magazine right in his bodywork.

The unseen driver charged down with a snarl and the car was on top of him. No, not one of the big panzer wagons anyway. Porsche Carrera, but—it wasn't stopping. His left hand came down like a knife, he jumped his right foot back for stability and threw the carbine into his shoulder viciously as it slashed past him, but even as he looked for the little car along his sights the brakes screamed on the slippery roadway. He ran, his boots pounding, gun nicely balanced and ready. Who was that maniac anyway?

"Don't you know you have to stop at a border post?" he bellowed furiously. "This is the frontier. Don't you read the notices?—'Drive slow.' 'Halt at barrier.'" The last of the bellow tailed off a little—the driver was a girl. And not bad, either. What eyes, what a mouth to kiss. Marijke would have to look out for her virtue, next time. Looked like good bodywork there, tucked behind that wheel. He stooped to the low window, already much softened.

"Jesus, miss, you take some awful chances. I could have shot at you—damn near did." Funny expression she had—almost mockery, one might have thought. Impossible. Might she be a bit drunk?

"The mist makes the notices hard to read," she said. Her voice was serious, but she was grinning. Goddam, one would almost say she wouldn't have cared if he had shot at her.

"You were driving very fast, miss," severely.

"Didn't know I was so near the frontier." The barrier was hardly three feet in front of the hood.

"You sure cut it fine. Papers, please." He hardly looked at them; Christ, he'd been within a second of firing.

"All right, miss; I'll raise the barrier for you. But you'd better drive easier. You don't want to risk a smash in that auto."

The customs man had appeared now, reluctant to turn out of the warm hut. He clapped his hands jovially against the cold, and rubbed them in a businesslike way together.

"No contraband? Hardly room, is there, ha ha. All right, miss, pleasant journey." He scampered back to the warmth.

"Did you take me for a smuggler?" she asked the guard.

Again that curious tone struck him. Must be drunk, he thought. Still, he wasn't a traffic cop.

"Well, miss, people who drive fast along here might be up to mischief, so we're a bit sharpish on anyone who might not stop where it says stop."

"Yes," she said, more quietly. "I can understand. I'll go more carefully."

Van der Valk was piloting the Volkswagen back toward Amsterdam. Visibility was patchy; it was late before he got home. Arlette was asleep but woke up when he stupidly dropped a shoe.

"What you been doing?" sleepily.

"Believe it or not, digging up treasure. I'm all finished. Home tomorrow for dinner, please God. What you got?"

"*Morue à la crème*," she said, muffled.